Wherever you go

MW00936715

LIPS
CLOSE
TO MINE

Wherever You Go Series

LIPS
CLOSE
TO MINE

Wherever You Go Series

ROBIN BIELMAN

Entangled Publishing, LLC
2614 South Timberline Road
Suite 109
Fort Collins, CO 80525
Visit our website at www.entangledpublishing.com.

Embrace is an imprint of Entangled Publishing, LLC.

Edited by Stacy Abrams
Cover design by Mayhem Cover Creations
Cover art from Shutterstock

Manufactured in the United States of America

First Edition November 2017

embrace

For Harry.

Chapter One

HARPER

Swimming and sex.

My two favorite "S" words. In that order. Unless you count that time with...

Nope. I'm not going to think about *him*.

Too late, you just did.

God, I wish I could wipe Levi Pierce from my memory.

We weren't supposed to see each other ever again, and then surprise! My best friend is dating his best friend, and he's in my airspace way more than I'm comfortable with. Pants Charming—that's what I call him because he could seriously charm the pants off me with only his stupid smile— is a problem I have to learn to deal with.

Ducking under the water, I push thoughts of Levi out of my head and swim another two laps across the swimming pool. I butterfly stroke this time. It's the most fun and most exhausting, and I'm good at it. It's not my fastest stroke, that would be freestyle, but I'm skilled at all of them. I trained in Olympic-size facilities. Raced against the best until my sixteenth birthday.

There's never a time I'm in the water that I don't think back on that night seven years ago when everything changed for me. I hide it, of course. I don't want anyone's pity or sympathy. It's private, something I keep buried deep but that, ironically, is never far from the surface.

I lift out of the water and once again check my phone because that will make it ring, right? I've tried for the past few days to tell myself this isn't a big deal. That if it doesn't work out, it's not the end of the world. I'll survive just fine and find another opportunity to raise awareness for swim safety. But the way my stomach is knotting tells me I'll be devastated if I don't get this.

I'm not used to caring so much about a job.

Unless you count camp counselor. Best first job ever, right there. No one rocks Crazy Hair Day like I do.

I palm the edge of the pool and push myself up into a sitting position, leaving my feet to dangle in the water. I've always worked, but giving swim lessons and lifeguarding isn't a "job" to me. It's my normal. My heart. My passion. And the morning hours I put in at the coffee shop are for fun and an extra way to fill my time. Although, ever since my best friend, Teague, quit serving lattes with me, it hasn't been as enjoyable.

The August sun is almost done drying the droplets of water on my shoulders and back when my phone finally rings. I take a deep breath, note the caller ID, and pick it up.

"Hi, Mr. Halloran." Shit. Do I sound like I've been sitting here waiting for his phone call?

"Hi, Harper. Please. Call me Brad."

"Right. Hi, Brad." It's a little weird calling one of my swim coaches from when I was a teenager by his first name, but I am an adult now, and he's not more than ten years older than me, so I need to make more of an effort.

"I've got some semi-good news," Brad says matter-of-factly.

"Okay," I reply, calm as a cactus, when I'm really anything but.

"The board agrees you're an excellent ambassador candidate for the foundation and our No Swimmer Left Behind campaign, but we're not quite ready to fully extend you the job offer. I know that's not what you were hoping to hear."

I swallow the bulging lump in my throat. It's not what I wanted, no, but it sounds like I haven't lost the job yet, either. "What are you offering?"

"As I mentioned when we met, we want to shoot a series of PSAs to kick off the campaign, and we'd like to use you, if you're up for it. Afterward, we'll talk about the future. Sound fair enough?"

"It does." I want this job. I *need* this job. If I kick ass with the public service announcements, hopefully the board will give me the full-time honor. Sometimes it takes baby steps to reach your destination.

"Can you come in next week to go over logistics and meet the team?"

"Absolutely."

"Great. I'll see you soon."

"Thank you so much. I'm excited." Excited to prove to everyone I should be the face of the Make A Splash Foundation.

"We are, too."

I disconnect the call, place my phone back on the towel, and jump to my feet to shake off the nerves pinching behind my knees and inside my elbows. When Brad started MASF, I immediately donated my time and money. The charity is still growing, but I'm passionate about teaching swimming so no one ever drowns again. If I can make my mission official through MASF, I know it will bring me the satisfaction that has been missing from my life *and* get my dad off my back.

My father is adamant I come work for him, but he's *graciously* given me time to "figure my life out" before I come to my senses and join him and my brothers in his bajillion-dollar media conglomerate. It's the very last thing I want to do. I'm a swimsuit, not a business suit, kind of girl. I need fresh air, sunshine, and chlorine to breathe. *He* thinks I need him, which is the complete opposite of true, yet he's losing patience with me. I love my dad, but if we were to have a professional relationship, I'd end up hating him.

It's bad enough that whenever he gets the opportunity, he hovers over me like I don't have a mind of my own. Last week alone he came into the coffee shop and proceeded to walk me through making his latte, step by step. I've worked there for seven months! I damn well know how to make his drink.

His controlling interest in my life is driving me nuts, leaving me super motivated to land this job with MASF.

The water glistens in the afternoon light, calling to me, so I run over to the deep end and jump in, hugging my knees to my chest. "Cannonball!" I shout even though no one is around to hear me. Underwater somersaults, handstands, and floating on my back follow until my lesson shows up a couple of minutes before one o'clock.

"Hey, Spider-Man!" I say to Josh. He has a thing for the superhero; his swim trunks, T-shirt, sandals, and towel always decorated with the popular Avenger.

"Hi, Hawper," he says in the cutest four-year-old voice ever. I love this kid.

For the next five hours, I give back-to-back swim lessons. The time flies by. I'm toweling off when Teague comes bounding around the corner. "Tell me, tell me, tell me," she says, full of her sweet, bubbly enthusiasm.

"I didn't get the job. *Yet*." I tell her what Brad told me.

"Harp!" She wraps me in a hug, not caring that my bathing suit is still wet. "You will so kick some PSA butt, and they will hire you officially, and you'll help make a huge difference. Congratulations!"

"Thanks. Fingers and toes crossed, right?" Teague's delight and optimism are hard to ignore, and I smile.

"Right!" she says, grinning back. "And one day soon you're going to be the best ambassador ever. Come on. I'm making you dinner to celebrate."

I hang my towel over a lounge chair, and we walk toward the guesthouse we rent from my aunt and uncle. They live in the massive Beverly Hills house a few hundred feet away, and as far as landlords go, they're the coolest.

"Are your special grilled cheese sandwiches what's for dinner?" I ask. I make Teague my exceptional mac and cheese. She makes me her outstanding grilled cheese. We're total opposites, but our love of cheese formed the first bonds of best-friendship during our freshman year at the University of Oregon.

"Of course," she says cheerfully.

"Are you sure you have time? When is Mateo picking you up?"

Teague opens our front door and heads straight into the kitchen. Her shoulders do a little wiggle, one that tells me the mere mention of her hot-as-fuck boyfriend turns her on. They're ridiculously in love, and I couldn't be happier for her.

"He'll be here at eight," she says in a breathy tone that further confirms her love sickness.

That's right. Love is a sickness, and I have no intention of catching it.

I pick up the T-shirt I left draped over the back of the couch and slip it on. Our place has an open floor plan with a bright polka-dot–accented kitchen, an office nook, and a comfortable but stylish living room. A hallway leads to our bedrooms on the right and a guest bathroom on the left.

"And I always have time for you," she adds.

Lately, that hasn't been the case, but I don't mention it. It's stupid and selfish that I feel lonely. Teague's new career as a honeymoon planner is taking off. Mateo's new travel job for NPR is, too, and together they're planning trips all over the world. When they're home, they're inseparable. I know my best friend, and while she and Mateo have only been officially together for a few weeks, he's it for her, the guy she wants to marry. And knowing guys like I do, he's equally taken with her. A good thing, because if he wasn't, I'd kick his ass. She's the best.

Speaking of getting married… "Guess who's pregnant?" I say as I take a seat at the kitchen table and push the sudden and unwanted thoughts of Mateo's roommate out of my head. Damn Levi Pierce and his connection to my best friend. Lately, keeping him at arm's length is proving harder than I'd like. Despite my animosity toward him, he smiles in response to my scowl, or he keeps a door open for me. I hate that he makes me feel things I don't want to. Things I've been able to keep at bay until now.

Teague doesn't miss a grilled cheese-making beat, plopping a square of butter onto the frying pan. "Who?"

"Colleen."

"Your cousin is pregnant?" Teague asks with surprise, turning away from the stove to look at me.

"Knocked up and due in March."

"Her wedding is in March."

"Not anymore. It's moved to next month. She wants to be married before she's a mom—and fit into the wedding dress she's already bought—so everything is going at warp speed now." I'd like to propel myself out of bridesmaid duty, not because I don't love my cousin but because with the new time frame, I'm worried about my commitment to MASF, too. I have to start off on the best foot with them, which means they get my time whenever they need it.

And then there's my mother.

She wants to know when *I'm* getting married. Or at the very least acquiring a boyfriend.

Never.

The frying pan sizzles, drawing Teague's attention. She starts cooking our sandwiches. "Holy cow, how is your aunt planning to pull this off so fast?"

"The wedding is going to be here in the backyard. You should probably book a work trip during that week so you can avoid the insanity. Aunt Betsy walked me around this morning to share the details."

"I'm afraid to ask."

"She's covering my pool."

Teague shoots me a sympathetic, yet unapologetic frown.

"Okay, she's covering *her* pool. But I have to cancel two days' worth of lessons while everything is set up, on top of my Saturday ones. I hate doing that to my students."

"Change of subject," Teague says, sliding our sandwiches onto plates. She pulls each gooey, cheesy one apart and adds ranch dressing, sprouts, and already-cooked bacon inside before closing them up. Best. Sandwich. Ever. "Did I tell you my best friend is one step closer to being an ambassador, and I'm really proud of her?"

"Your best friend is a badass?" I misconstrue, because "ambassador" sounds so grown-up and weird and it's not official yet.

"She's that, too." Teague gives me a soft look as she puts our food on the table. "I'm sorry I'm leaving town tonight, but *when* you get the job, we're going out to celebrate properly."

"Make it not so proper, and it's a date."

Teague rolls her eyes. She's the good and proper one. Me?

Not so much. I mean, I don't do anything illegal or hurtful, but I follow my own rules.

"Have anything fun planned this weekend?" she asks.

Ugh. This weekend. I have to go bridesmaid dress shopping. I'll definitely need some fun after that. I take a bite of my grilled cheese. "Just wedding stuff with Colleen. This is terrible by the way," I tease with my mouth full. "Thank you."

"You're welcome. I'm really happy and excited for you, Harp."

I'm really grateful for the girl sitting across from me enjoying her sandwich like it's the best one ever. She's been through thick and thin with me. She's my person, and we're more than best friends. We're sisters.

• • •

In my head, I recite word for word what my mother is going to say to me when I walk into the bridal store on Wilshire Boulevard ten minutes late.

"Harper, sweetie, how many times do I have to tell you to wash off the chlorine smell before you leave the house?"

Oops. I forgot the "sweetie." "Hi, Mom. How are you?" I kiss her cheek before turning to face my aunt, cousin, and three other bridesmaids. The five of them are standing in a line, eyes trained on me like I swam here from Hawaii, which makes no fucking sense, since then I'd smell like saltwater. "Sorry I'm late," I say.

So I didn't have time to shower before I rushed over here. What's the big deal? I'm clean. I'm dressed appropriately in a sundress that falls to the tops of my knees and covers my entire chest. My long, dark hair is mostly dry.

Colleen steps forward and gives me a hug. "Thanks for coming on such short notice." My cousin is two years older than me, and since we grew up the only girls in the family, we loved *and* hated each other, depending on the day. Mostly loved, though.

"Of course," I say. That's going to be my standard answer for the next month. If I plan on it, then I won't accidentally say something to disrupt the happy wedding vibe. Like the time I *had* to speak up when Colleen's college boyfriend came home with her for Thanksgiving weekend, and at brunch he asked my aunt to "please pass the milf" instead of "milk."

Aunt Betsy *is* hot for her age.

Colleen had glared at me the entire day, and the boyfriend didn't make it back for any more family gatherings.

"I've got the dress already picked out," Colleen says now. "Come see."

I follow her and the other bridesmaids to the dressing area with a silent prayer the dress is anything but green and ruffled.

My wish dies painfully when Colleen presents me with a strapless, full-length dress with a sweetheart neckline, shirred bust, empire waist, and front-and-center ruffle from rib cage to floor. In emerald green. The dress is pretty. It doesn't look anything like my sweet-sixteen dress, but the color and frill are enough to remind me.

"What do you think?" Colleen asks. "Isn't it gorgeous?" No one but me remembers what I wore the night of my party.

"It is," I say, forcing a smile. "I can't wait to try it on." *Liar, liar, pants on fire.*

I will not rain on Colleen's enthusiasm. This is her special time, and if I have to suck up my discomfort, then that's what I'll do. Better that than draw unwanted attention to *my* feelings. I know the dress is a small detail in the grand scheme of things, but sometimes it's the little things we remember most.

As I step behind the fancy champagne-colored curtain to

change out of my sundress, I obliterate my runaway thoughts about that horrible night by thinking about puppies. English bulldog puppies. Their wrinkly, tubby cuteness is a shot of happy endorphins straight to my brain.

I'm the smallest bridesmaid, and when the seamstress pins the ribbing at my back for sizing, the dress pushes up my boobs in a really nice way. Two of George's—that's Colleen's fiancé—groomsmen are single, so I'm happy to give them something to stare at. One, in particular, I may let do more than stare.

Who am I kidding? I absolutely will get naked with him.

My cousin's smile reflects back at me in the full-length mirror. "You look stunning."

"Thanks." I gather my hair and tie it in a knot on top of my head. "Up-do?"

"Definitely," Colleen says.

Maggie McKinney, mom of three, Serious McSnooper, and all-around good person even when annoyingly in my business, crosses a hand over her heart and says, "I'm going to cry. You look so beautiful."

I turn so I can speak to her and not her reflection in the mirror. "Please don't cry, Mom. If you cry, then Aunt Betsy will cry and then Colleen will cry and then I might cry, and I do not cry." Crying is contagious, like yawning, or something like that. And seriously? Isn't she only supposed to cry when looking at the bride?

"Fine." She straightens her back. "I'll stay composed."

"Thank you."

Once the fittings are done, we leave the tulle and chiffon behind and step into the California sunshine to walk to the Beverly Wilshire Hotel for lunch.

"I almost forgot to tell you congratulations," my mom says, linking our arms as we follow the rest of the group. "Your dad told me about the offer from Make A Splash Foundation.

I'm so happy you're a step closer to getting something you really want."

She says this with love and sincerity, but there's a hint of disappointment in her voice, too. This is because I've yet to give my mom what *she* really wants—me in a relationship. As her only daughter, I'm constantly being set up on dates with anyone who has a penis and a pulse, and she's always reminding me that all work and no love isn't the way to live. (Um, hello? I'm only twenty-three.) It's a bone of contention between her and my dad, who, despite setting me up with a trust fund, insists I focus on a career while in my twenties. (Thank you, Dad.)

This work mentality goes back years. My brothers and I busted our asses off around the house to get our allowance when we were young. I've earned everything I've gotten.

"Thanks, Mom."

"Oh! And I also forgot to tell you I had lunch with Marin the other day, and Chad is back in town. He asked her about you."

Marin is my mom's best friend, and for the past few years the two of them have schemed to get their children together. But Chad Buckley has zero chance of scoring with me. He's selfish, too serious, and in seventh grade, when I asked him to rank his favorite dog breeds, bulldogs weren't even on the list.

"That's nice," I say to keep the peace.

"He's single."

"Uh-uh."

"You're single."

I wrinkle my nose. Just because my mom met my dad when she was twenty and fell madly in love does not make it hereditary. "I—"

"He'd be the perfect wedding date, don't you think?"

It's moments like these that I need a teleporter. Or laryngitis. Or a flight to Paris I'm running late for. There is no way in hell I'm taking a date to my cousin's wedding. I think this. I know this. But somehow my mouth doesn't get the memo, because I say, "I already have a date."

I'm not proud of my lie, but bringing someone to a family wedding is a top-level serious date, and my mom will start planning Chad's and my wedding this instant. If I fake bringing someone she doesn't know, she'll have to chill.

Or not. Because her entire body shakes with excitement, and her megawatt smile is blinding. She steeples her hands like all her prayers have been answered. "Is it serious?"

Fuck. Those five words I vomited, and which left a nauseating taste in my mouth, have ruined me for the next month. Here's the thing, though. I *could* have a real date. He—whoever he is—just doesn't know it yet.

"It's—" I'm saved from having to come up with an answer when my phone rings. I quickly grab it from the outside pocket of my purse. "It's Dad," I say. More like I sing it, I'm so grateful for the interruption. Or I am until he talks on and on about the reason for his call. Then I wish I hadn't answered.

"It's the perfect job for you," my dad continues. "Gets you on my payroll, but not in my building. Yet."

I wave off my mom with the rest of the group, mouthing *I'll be a minute* as I tug at my earlobe. Dad knows how I feel about us working together, and while it may seem like the perfect offer, it's not. I want the job with MASF. "Dad, I don't think—"

"Don't give me an answer now. Let me know in the next couple of weeks."

"I have no idea if I'll know about the ambassador job that fast."

"I've got a sure thing for you, honey. Think about that."

His sure thing is some blockbuster movie where they need a swim consultant. My dad has invested in films before, but this one is the most commercial. It's *Jaws* meets *Pretty*

Woman.

"I know you've got your hopes pinned on MASF, but I've got mine pinned on you. Think of all the different projects you can work on with me, okay?"

His voice is considerate yet firm, and I hate the thought of letting him down. Again. It took some negotiating to get him off my back immediately after I graduated with my bachelor degree in business. "Okay," I say.

"I love you and only want what's best for you. You know that, right?"

"I know. Love you, too."

"Enjoy lunch. Have the lamb burger. It's the best thing on the menu." I roll my eyes. "And don't let your mother order anything with cheese. She's—"

"Bye, Dad." I disconnect and drag my feet toward lunch. He's got my head filled with what-ifs and worries about disappointing him—but worse, myself.

My dad has no idea what's best for me. How could he, when I don't have a clue?

Chapter Two

Attraction comes in all different shapes, sizes, and forms. I'm cool with that. I've got a mom and four older sisters and they've taught me to look beyond the surface. Let's be honest, though, when a guy hasn't been laid in a while, he's not going to think much beyond his first impression of a woman.

Take right now, for example. I'm sitting at the indoor-outdoor bar at Tenants of the Trees with one of my roommates, Elliot, and two smoking hot models visiting from New York who are also attentive and smart, despite laughing at Elliot's god-awful jokes. The brunette, in particular, has my notice with her killer smile and appreciation of filmmaking. I'm a cameraman. When I tell her this, she puts her hand on my arm, looks me right in the eyes, and asks if I've ever made a sex tape.

Smart and adventurous. I like it. The late-night landscape is looking full of possibilities. When her friend moves her attention from Elliot to me and says the idea of being filmed turns her on, I'll be honest. I immediately picture her lying on a bed with soft lighting, one hand cupping her tit, the other hand stroking between her legs, her mouth slightly open. My dick stirs. Both these girls are ridiculously good-looking, and I'm game for either one.

Threesomes aren't my thing, though. I'm a one-woman guy, always. Elliot, however, is about to fall off his stool. And, if I'm not mistaken, I think he's drooling. Maybe I'll give him an early birthday present and set up my camera on a tripod so the three of them can go to naked town.

I'll have no trouble rubbing one out on my own later tonight. All I have to do is think about Harper McKinney, and I go off like a porn star.

Elliot flags down the bartender and orders a second round of drinks. I take a minute to look around the popular, sophisticated venue. We're here tonight because I heard Leo Gaines likes to frequent the place. Leo is killing it as a film director, and all I want is to work with him on a movie. Or ten. He's the newer guy on the scene, but insanely talented, and in this town, when it comes to Hollywood jobs, it's all about who you know. If I can get in with him, my career will be set.

When my gaze tracks to the other side of the glass wall and onto the patio, I'm dumbstruck. It's not Leo, but the girl I just admitted I like to stroke myself to, standing right there with a small group of people.

"Hey, isn't that Harper?" Elliot asks, noting where my focus has strayed.

"It is." And she looks amazing. Legs for miles, toned arms, long, delicate neck. Her little black dress—simple, clingy, and maybe a little Playmate-of-the-Year-y—doesn't leave a whole lot to the imagination. But then, I don't need my imagination. I've seen every inch of her. Tonight, her dark hair is in a high ponytail, and shiny gloss coats her full, pink lips. She has a spectacular pillowy mouth. And the things she does with those lips have fueled my fantasies ever since our night together a couple of months ago.

"You should go say hello," Elliot says with hilarity in his voice before he turns back to our model friends. If there's even a one percent chance he can have both these girls tonight, he'll stick with them.

I, on the other hand, am now completely distracted by a sexy, interesting girl who hates my guts.

And I have no idea why. Which is damn frustrating. It makes me want to poke and poke until I find out what her problem with me is. Her dislike makes absolutely no sense. We had a fantastic night together. We met at a bar over a mutual appreciation for the Dodgers kicking the Giants' asses on the flat screen TV. I couldn't put my finger on it, but there was something familiar about her. We started talking, and when we realized we'd known each other as kids, we clicked even further. Before I knew it, we were on our way to her place. I made her come three times. I worshipped her body but was equally interested in her mind. We didn't just fuck. We talked. But when I asked for her number, she said she only does one night.

Then to my surprise and total gladness, she shows up on my doorstep two weeks later. It turns out her best friend is Teague, my other roommate Mateo's girl. Harper takes one look at me when I open the door and almost immediately goes cold and distant, like I ran over her dog or something.

So what did I do? I dished it right back to her. I was pissed. She damn well could be cordial to the guy who had been inside her. Worse, the memory of my ex and how she'd run hot and cold had slammed me in the chest, putting me on edge.

But as hard as I try, I can't forget the girl I spent the night with. We've seen each other a few times—a casualty of our best friends dating—and Harper's a good person. She's got a great sense of humor. She's approachable. To everyone but me, that is. The friction isn't all hostile, though. There's an underlining current of sexual tension, which makes this weird relationship we have even more frustrating. I'm not looking for a commitment from her, just some fun. Something sorely lacking from my life lately.

"Dude," Elliot says under his breath. "If you're going to keep staring at her, go say hello already."

The thing is, against my better judgment, I do want to go say hello, if for no other reason than to get under her skin. She sure as hell is under mine. *It's a bad idea, man. She wants nothing to do with you. Respect it, even if you don't understand it.*

I glance at my roommate to gage his interest in Harper. They're friends. I think for a time he wanted more than that, but Harper quickly set him straight on that score. Still. That he's indifferent to her presence is solely because of the models holding his attention.

"Better yet," Elliot says, like the best idea in the world just struck him. "I bet you can't get her to go home with you."

"*What?*" I heard him, but I can't believe what he's suggesting.

"A hundred bucks says you can't get her to sleep with you."

Yep, Elliot definitely wants our current company to himself. But more than that, I get the feeling his pride is rearing its head. Harper shot him down, and he's betting she'll do the same to me. He doesn't know I've already been with her.

I glance back in her direction, my body tightening at the memory of how good we were together. She might be all cold-shoulder now, but that night she was hot, willing female.

"Tonight?" I ask. The hundred bucks isn't really what's at stake. This is about the friendly competition that's existed between Elliot and me for the past ten years. Both of us hate to lose. Last weekend at Boardners, I bet him he couldn't get the bartender's phone number. He struck out in spectacular fashion and hated handing over a Benjamin. He wants a little revenge.

"I'll give you a month," he tosses out, like he has no doubt I'll fail. Given what he's observed between Harper and me, I'm not sure he's wrong.

"Deal," I answer anyway. I can definitely make a repeat happen in the next thirty days. Probably. Maybe. I rub the side of my neck. The bet doesn't exactly sit well with me, but it is the incentive I need to get to the bottom of her issues with me.

Here's the thing. It's clear she doesn't want a relationship. And after the shitstorm my ex, Kayla, put me through, I'm in absolutely no hurry for one, either. Honestly, I'm not sure I'll ever trust a woman again. But as I walk toward Harper, my heart is doing something weird in my chest. Rather than stay shut down, the sturdy fucker is…pitter-pattering. What the fuck? Obviously, it's also on board for more sex with the beautiful but aloof Harper McKinney, so this makes my motives at least partially respectable. Right?

When I'm halfway to her, she turns her head and our eyes meet. I can't explain what happens every time we see each other for the first time, but it's like we're starving for a taste of something we know is bad for us. Tonight, multiply that by a hundred.

I *am* wearing my lucky Calvin Klein T-shirt. Won a thousand bucks in Vegas wearing this threadbare tee *and* got out of two speeding tickets while in this fine cotton blend. Yes, it may have helped that the officer was a woman both times, but my smile only goes so far when we're talking about the law. Ergo, luck.

Exactly what I need right now, given the death-glare

Harper's giving me.

My eyes dip to those luscious lips of hers. I forgot to eat dinner, and devouring that mouth sounds like a good plan. Maybe I should walk up and kiss the hell out of her? That ought to thaw the chill she likes to sling my way.

Unfortunately, I get lip-blocked when she extends her arm straight out, flattens her palm on my chest, and says, "What are you doing here?"

"Hello to you, too."

"Levi?" says a girl next to Harper. I hadn't noticed her, too preoccupied with the hot-tempered, sexy-mouthed girl with her hand on me.

I look away from Harper. "Trixie?"

"Oh my God!" Trixie effectively knocks Harper's hand away and presses her body against mine, her arms looping around my neck. "It's so good to see you!"

"You, too." I wrap my arms around her waist. Trix and I have known each other since high school. "It's been a while."

She rubs a hand over the stubble on my face as she pulls back. "This is new."

I stroke my jawline. My sisters call it my eight o'clock shadow because it grows for a few days and then stops. It's weird. I couldn't grow a beard if I tried.

"It makes you look even sexier," she adds.

For as long as I've known Trixie, she's also *liked* me. She's an awesome girl, but she's friends with Kayla, which means it's never gonna happen.

Harper clears her throat, easily pulling my attention back to her.

"How do you two know each other?" Trixie asks.

"We don't. Not really," Harper says, but her gorgeous hazel eyes say something else entirely. They tell me she's thinking about the night we spent together with my cock, fingers, and tongue inside her. I don't know where the uninhibited, unselfish, unbuttoned girl from that night went, but she's still in there, somewhere. "We have mutual friends is all."

That's not even close to all, but I don't bring up my sex life with people. My best friends don't even know I've slept with Harper.

"What about you two?" I ask.

"I work as a nanny," Trixie says, "and Harper gives swim lessons to the little girl I take care of."

Harper's bare shoulders relax. While lying in bed the night we spent together, she'd told me about her lessons and that she'd been a competitive swimmer as a teenager, but gave it up at sixteen. Then she'd straddled me, and we stopped talking.

Trixie goes on to talk about her life and ask me about mine. I only hear half of what she says because I can't stop thinking about Harper and looking at her in my periphery. She's pretending to be interested in my conversation with Trixie, but her eyes keep moving around the bar. When one of the guys standing close by starts talking to her, she turns toward him. The two of them flirt, and the guy is definitely into her. I hear him say he's headed to the small, VIP-only, private space at the front of the building where a DJ is playing, and would she like to join him?

"Love to," she says.

Let her go, man, half my brain says. The other half says, *Don't let her walk away.*

So it's entirely my fault when she spills the drink in her hand down the front of her dress.

"What the—"

"Sorry," I say and mean it. I'm sorry I didn't make a move with a little better finesse.

She glares at me. Getting a reaction from her keeps me motivated.

"I'm going to go clean up. Be right back," she says to the

guy.

"Elliot's waiting for me at the bar," I tell Trixie. "I should go." We say a quick good-bye, and instead of the bar, I walk to the restrooms in search of Harper. I find her standing in line in the hallway.

Once again, she scowls at me.

"Hey. You okay? Sorry again about the spill."

"Clearly my leave-me-alone look needs some work," she says in lieu of answering my question.

"Is that what that is? I thought maybe your feet were hurting or something." I take a slow glance down her body to her silver heels that are surely the Mt. Everest of shoes.

"You find me dripping in vodka amusing?"

I take a step closer so there's little space between us. "Not at all. I like you wet."

"That's what they all say." The slight blush in her cheeks belies the promiscuous retort. I know Harper's no angel, but I'd bet my career she's more selective than she lets on.

"How about I buy you a new drink?"

"How about you leave me alone?" she says. Yet the two people waiting in line ahead of her have moved on, and she's still standing here.

"I'm finding that hard to do," I admit.

She leans against the wall, not in defeat, but in concession, maybe. She starts to say something, when her stomach growls. Looks like I'm not the only one who missed dinner. *Thank you, lucky shirt.*

I put my hand on her waist. "Let me make the spill up to you. Let's get out of here and find some food."

Her head drops, her eyes, I'm guessing, on where I'm touching her. I'd like to touch her a whole lot more. On repeat.

"Drive-thru tacos and then you can drop me off at home," she says, meeting my gaze before she pushes off the wall, the spill on her dress forgotten. "I Ubered here."

I do a mental fist pump and follow the sway of her ass.

Elliot's jaw drops when I ask him if he's cool catching a ride home later, and after Harper says good-bye to her friends, we take off. I open the passenger door of my jeep and check out her tanned legs as she sits. If there were a dark-haired poster girl for California, it would be Harper. I hurry to my side and climb in.

We haven't been alone since the night we slept together, so I turn to confirm she's cool with this. I've no doubt she doesn't do anything she doesn't want to, but I need to be sure.

She's slipping off her heels.

Okay, then.

I notice a T-shirt on my backseat and reach for it. "It's not much, but if you want to put this on, here you go."

"Thanks."

Rather than put the shirt on over her dress like I assumed she would, given the chill in the air and the wet fabric, she grabs the hem and pulls the dress up and over her head. I am so fucking glad Elliot threw out that bet. Her tits are on full display, perfectly round with rose-colored nipples, the skin paler than the rest of her sun-tanned body. The tiny scrap of material between her legs is red and lacy. My pants are immediately too tight.

"Uh…"

She tosses the dress over her shoulder and pulls on my tee. "What? You've already seen me naked."

I watch as she tugs the material down until it reaches the middle of her thighs. The awesome visual is gone way too fast for my liking. However, she looks gorgeous in my shirt, too. She reaches for her seat belt, snaps it into place, and turns her head.

"Are you going to keep staring at me or drive?"

That's my cue to start the car. I readjust my jeans before getting us on our way.

The car ride is silent after that, but the saying *cut the*

tension with a knife is definitely applicable. This girl confuses the hell out of me. "Can I ask you something?"

"No."

"Seriously? What's your problem?"

She twists to face me. "*My problem?*"

I didn't mean to sound accusatory, and that isn't exactly the question I wanted to ask, but I feel like I'm on the defensive here.

"Sorry. I meant what's your problem with me? I can't figure out what I did to deserve your hostility all the time."

Her eyes briefly close. "It's not you, it's me."

I burst out laughing. She did not just feed me that clichéd line of bullshit. Like that would get her out of talking. I *know* she can talk. When we were together, she talked about her swim students, how much she loved college in Oregon, and her favorite way to eat In-N-Out.

She pushes me in the biceps, and that only makes me laugh harder. "You're such an ass."

"*I'm an ass?*" I ask incredulously. "What did I do?"

"You're laughing at me."

"No, I'm laughing at what you said."

"It's the truth," she says quietly.

"Harper, look—"

"Could we please just stop talking? I don't want to explain myself, and I don't want you trying to figure me out. Okay?" She turns so she's back to facing forward, her gaze out the windshield.

"Okay." But there's no way I'm letting her go hungry. I hit the drive-thru and order us tacos. Three for me and two for her, placed in separate bags. She whispers her thanks.

A few minutes of silence later I whisper, "Harper?"

"What?" she mutters back.

"This isn't over."

Chapter Three

The last time I was in a conference room, I was eight years old and dressed in a matching outfit with my Malibu Beach Barbie. Don't tell anyone, but I've got a bikini on underneath my slim black skirt and tailored aqua poplin shirt this time, too. I had a Supergirl moment this morning, my imagination running wild with me quickly taking off my clothes and jumping into a pool because I was needed.

I'm not totally ridiculous. There *is* a pool downstairs.

And I don't know. It just felt right.

This conference room, however, is smaller than the one when I was eight, and I'm not sitting in my father's lap. I'm sitting *at* the table, and all eyes are on me. We're on the second floor of the recently renovated two-story building that serves as headquarters for MASF. So far, I'm kicking ass, if I do say so myself.

"All great ideas for the campaign," Brad says to me. Then he asks his two PR people to run with them and write the copy for several thirty- and sixty-second PSAs. "I'd like to shoot on the next three Saturdays," he tells his production manager. He hands out more direction to the others around the table, then dismisses everyone with a thank-you.

"Harper, if you don't mind waiting a few minutes, there's one more team member I need you to meet."

"Sure." I gave notice at the coffee shop last week and trained a new person yesterday, so my boss said no worries on returning, which means I've got the whole morning free. Mornings I'll now need to use for the next month of Saturday swim lessons. It pains me to have to move my students for more than just my cousin's wedding, but hopefully it's understandable. I'll toss in some extra lessons free of charge to make it up to them, and maybe plan an end-of-the-summer pool party.

Which reminds me, I need to find a fake wedding date.

"Hey, sorry I'm late," a deep, familiar voice says from across the room.

No way. No way. No way.

I look up, and all the air in the conference room is squeezed out while the door slowly swings shut behind the one guy in the entire universe I least want to see.

Yes way.

"No problem," Brad says. "Thanks for coming on board last minute. I really appreciate it. Harper, this is Levi Pierce, your cameraman. Levi, meet Harper McKinney. She'll be featured in our PSAs. You two will be working together a lot."

The smile Levi gives me is a direct hit to my heart, and it stupidly flutters. "We've met," he says. "Hi, Harper."

"Hi." I do not smile back. But when Brad gives me a funny look I read as, *Is this going to be a problem?* I add, "It's good to see you again."

Levi raises his eyebrows.

Those are the nicest words I've said to him since we spent the night together.

"How do you two know each other?" Brad asks.

"Mutual friends," Levi answers quickly and easily. I'm grateful he leaves it at that. He takes the seat next to me, and I'm immediately drawn to his masculine, just-showered scent. It takes effort not to lean into him. *Fuck.*

"Brad? Sorry to interrupt. Can I see you a minute?" a man asks, poking his head into the room.

Brad nods to the guy and gives him a "sure" before turning back to me. "If you'll excuse me, I'll be in touch later today, Harper. Thanks for coming in."

"Thank *you*," I say, thinking I should follow him out the door, but I don't. If Levi and I are going to be working together, we need to get on the same page.

"This is a nice coincidence," Levi says as soon as Brad is gone.

"Nice" is not the word I was thinking. Here's my problem: I like Levi. He's the first guy since my high school boyfriend, Joe, I've spent time thinking about. And a guy is not where I want my thoughts to stray. Liking someone engages more than brain cells. It changes your beats per minute and leaves you vulnerable, and I never want to feel that open to heartache again. I remind myself, however, that this is an important job opportunity, so if I have to play nice, I'll play nice.

"I didn't know shooting PSAs was your thing." Music videos, television shows, and YouTube stuff is what he does. I may keep our exchanges to a minimum, but I do listen to what the people around me say.

"It's not. Brad is my brother-in-law, so I'm doing this as a favor to him. The cameraman he had lined up canceled this morning."

Shit. Make that super nice.

And this bit of information also adds to my heart

condition because… "You're Axl's uncle?"

"I am. You've met him?"

"Yeah." Axl is four, and all he talks about is his Uncle Vee and how Uncle Vee takes him to see the doggies at the "shetter" and when he's five, Uncle Vee is going to give him one.

"Cool kid, right?"

"The coolest."

Levi turns his chair, crosses his arms, and catches me with those golden-brown eyes of his. He is insanely good-looking. His dirty blond hair is longer on top and stands straight up in a tousled but perfect way. Sexy stubble lines his square jaw. His plain white tee stretches across a broad chest and strong shoulders.

"Careful, Ham. This civil conversation might give me the impression you like me or something."

Ham.

Harper Annabelle McKinney.

My older brothers called me Ham when I was little and still do on occasion. Levi heard it and decided he'd do the same. We were three years old at the time. From age three to seven, we were inseparable. Our moms met at a Mommy and Me swim class. That's right. I learned to swim with Levi. There are pictures of us naked together in the pool, at the beach, and in the bathtub.

The night we hooked up was the first time I'd seen him since we started second grade at different schools. When we realized who we were to each other, we'd fallen into effortless banter, the sexual attraction intensified, and the ease with which we fell into bed was more fun than I'd ever had.

"Why is it important that I like you? Because we had sex? News flash. You don't have to like someone to fuck them." I know I sound crass, but the way Levi is openly staring at me as if I mean something more than I should is making me edgy.

He continues to study me, and the more he looks, the faster my pulse races.

"Would you quit looking at me like that?"

"How am I looking at you?"

"Like you want to bend me over this table and fuck me again." Even if I wanted a repeat performance—which I don't, not really, okay maybe—there's no way it can happen now that we're working together. This job means everything to me, and I can't be distracted. If this opportunity falls through, I'll have no choice but to accept my dad's offer. Levi might have his professional life sorted, but I can't say the same for mine.

"Actually, I was picturing you sitting on this table while I buried my face between your legs." He leans forward, elbows on his knees. "I remember how much you *liked* my tongue there."

I push my chair back to put some distance between us. His words make me want his face there again, and I hate him for it. "I'm easy to please," I lie.

"I doubt that."

"Trust me."

He laughs, the jerk. I'm not sure if his reaction is because he finds me amusing or he doesn't trust me. Thinking he might doubt my integrity really bothers me, but it's my own fault. I've led him down this path because I don't want him knowing me. He's already scaled the wall around my heart farther than any guy since I was sixteen, and I need to knock him down. Just because we had the best sex of my life and he's taking up space in my head doesn't mean he's the one to break me of my single-girl mentality.

"Well, sex is off the table," I say, mentally high-fiving myself for the pun. "Now that we're working together, we should keep everything professional."

"On Saturdays, yes. The rest of the week, no. Let me take you out to a movie."

"*What?*"

"You heard me."

"And you obviously haven't heard me. I don't date."

"But now you've got this"—he gestures down his body, lingering at his crotch—"to consider, which is arguably unlike any other."

"Because you have a recurring rash?"

His lips twitch, one side slightly higher than the other. "Because I've got muscle in all the right places."

I roll my eyes. "Cocky much?" The truth is he does have a mouth-wateringly great body. Biceps that bulge, a chest and abs with ridges I traced my fingernail along, a round, tight ass.

"You loved my cock—"

"I did not."

"No? You don't remember saying, 'Oh my God, Levi, I love your cock' while I—"

"Shut up. Do not say another word about that night." I stand up. Why is perspiration trickling down my sides? Because having a conversation with him is impossible. Not because he flusters me. "That night was a mistake, and I would appreciate it if you never brought it up again. I have to go."

I don't believe that love happens instantly, but all those other words that have to do with love? I felt every one of them the night we spent together. Which was why I pushed him away the next morning. I could fall for this boy, and it's the very last thing I want.

If I'd thought we could just be friends, I would have given him my phone number like he'd asked.

He puts a hand on my arm. "It wasn't a mistake."

I look at his grip, gentle but firm. My body heats further

at the memory of him touching me all over, the pads of his fingers tracing his own unique path over my skin.

"Let's talk tonight. I'll pick you up at seven," he adds.

I scowl at him. Is he serious right now?

"To talk about the shoots," he clarifies. "Since I missed the meeting, I thought you could fill me in. Get us on the same page. From what Brad mentioned to me, we'll be grabbing some B roll together, too."

That he assumes I'm available tonight grates on my nerves, but we do need to figure this thing out. No matter how much I wish he wasn't a part of this, he is, and everything has to go smoothly.

"You could talk to Brad."

"I will. But it's a good idea for us to kick around our thoughts, too." He lifts his hand like he's about to cross his heart, but drops his arm instead. "No ulterior motives."

I'm not sure I believe him. "Fine."

"Great." He gets to his feet and opens the conference room door for me. "See you later."

I nod before I casually walk off. I will not let him see how much he rattles me.

For the rest of the day, my nerves are all over the place, and I can't stop thinking about life and where I'm supposed to fit in the universe. More than anything, it's important to me that I make a difference. After Joe, I was numb for a long time. I didn't show it. Not even to the therapist my mom made me see for two years because she didn't have the words to help me. Mom wasn't entirely to blame. I let my family and friends see only what I wanted them to see: I was fine. Sad, but fine. It's weird how combining those two feelings can trick people. I still live with fear and remorse, though. So much so, that I own those feelings now. They're a part of who I am deep down.

Tragedy stole my love of the water and love for myself. I

credit Teague with helping me get back in a pool. I couldn't fool her. She saw right through my *fine*.

Which is why when she texts me later that day that this Friday is Elliot's birthday and we're all going out to celebrate, I only *contemplate* telling her I feel the flu coming on.

Sounds good, I message back, then toss my phone into my small shoulder bag. It's a few minutes before seven, and I want to meet Levi at the curb in front of my aunt and uncle's house. My decision has nothing to do with keeping him out of proximity to a bed. Or couch. Or table.

With a shake of my head, I clear my thoughts and walk around the pool then the side of the house. The sky is a soft blue. Palm tree fronds look down on me and sway with the warm summer breeze. I don't think anything of the voices I hear in the distance until I turn the corner and see my mom and Levi standing on the driveway, talking beside her car.

I jump back, out of sight, debating whether to join them. I hadn't realized my mom was here. She was most likely doing wedding stuff with my aunt, which means she's feeling nostalgic, and whatever she's saying to the six-foot-two hottie, I probably won't like. I peek around the house.

He's opening the driver's side door for her. She smiles up at him as she sits and says something that makes the corners of his annoyingly sexy mouth lift in a grin that reaches his eyes. This isn't good. I should have barged into their little reunion before they exchanged too many words.

Mom backs her Jaguar out of the driveway then waves out the window. Levi waves back. It's a wave of conspiracy.

"Whatever my mom said to you, you need to disregard it."

Levi turns at my approach. "Hi, Harper."

I wait for him to comment on my order, but he doesn't flinch or say anything further. This only ratchets up the tension in my shoulders. I'm the one in charge here. Not him.

"Hi, Levi," I finally say.

"Greetings really shouldn't be that hard."

"They aren't, usually."

"It's the face, right?" He makes a circular motion with his finger in front of his nose like I don't know which face he's referring to. It's kind of cute, dammit. "I've been told it renders women speechless."

No doubt, but it has zero effect on me. Zee-row. "Whatever. Did you hear what I said?"

"You want me to ignore your mom."

"Yes." I wander over to the iron bench on the grass. I cut the bottom of my foot on a piece of plastic from a broken pool toy earlier today, and it hurts, even in my comfiest pair of flip-flops.

Levi sits next to me, close enough that our thighs touch. He's in well-worn jeans. I'm in shorts. The denim does nothing to curb the warm sensation his touch spreads up my leg. "Wouldn't you like to know what she said before you issue a command?"

"No."

"So you'll never know if I heed your advice or not."

I send him a dirty look.

"She was very happy to see me. Said she has fond memories of you and me in the buff. Then she said we should get naked again."

"Jesus." I cringe and shake my shoulders. "My mother has no filter sometimes." I push the image of Levi naked out of my head. Not easy with him right next to me.

"I'm messing with you." He bumps my knee with his. "She didn't say that."

"Ass." I push him in the arm. He doesn't budge.

"She *did* say she's ecstatic we're dating, and how happy she is I'm your date for your cousin's wedding."

"Shit." Of course my mom would jump to a conclusion

like that after what I told her. "Why didn't you correct her?"

"It didn't seem like the right thing to do."

"The right thing to do? You lied to her!"

"No, I just didn't correct her. For all I knew, you'd told her about us."

"There is no us!" He is seriously grating on my nerves. I don't anger easily, but Levi Pierce presses all my hot buttons.

"There's an us now, Ham."

"No. There isn't. And you are not my date for the wedding. We are not dating. Not now. Not ever." Taking Levi to the wedding is a dangerous idea, so no way is it happening. I have a clear picture of my future, and it does not include a relationship. I plan to make my own way, play by my own rules, and be wildly successful all by myself.

Levi shrugs and says nothing.

I hate that I wonder what he's thinking.

The best things in life are FREE!

1. Swimming
2. Roasting marshmallows with Teague (we've got enough bags to survive a zombie apocalypse)
3. Walking along the beach
4. Visiting the animal shelter and stopping at each enclosure for petting
5. Breathing in the smell of chlorine and sunscreen
6. Collecting sea glass
7. Reading
8. Taking a nap!
9. Texting my brothers in emoticons (they hate that)
10. Binge-watching Friends
11. Volunteering
~~12. Thinking about Levi~~

Chapter Four

LEVI

I rub at my eyes and stare unfocused at the email twisting my stomach into knots. I've been accepted into a two-day seminar with Leo Gaines. The event had slipped my mind, given I applied months ago and hadn't heard anything. The class is limited to ten, the opportunity may never come around again, and the only way I can attend is if I bail on my brother-in-law. Not that I would bail on him. I'd find another cameraman to take my place, but this still causes two problems. One, Brad is already stressed out and I hate to add to it. Plus, he's always had my back. And two, it puts me out of touch with Harper.

Weirdly, when I showed up at MASF the other morning, I was seriously thinking about telling Brad I'd find someone else for him. I know nothing about shooting PSAs. My skills have been honed on music videos, short films, and television programs, and I'm concerned about capturing the look and feel he has in mind.

Then I saw Harper sitting at the conference table. Beautiful, surprised, irritated, a little breathless. And I stuck with the job. This makes me a total ass, I know, but you don't live with Elliot. He's decided Operation Harper is the best thing since cronuts. And since I didn't seal the deal last weekend, he's convinced he's got the bet won. Now *my* pride is rearing its ugly head.

But more than that, I want to be with her. I want to make her feel so good she forgets what day it is, what frustrates and pains her. Because that's what she did for me. For one night, I completely forgot about everything and lived in the moment with the hottest, funniest, most intuitive girl I've ever met.

I should tell her. I should come right out and tell her I don't want to date her, either. I just want to have sex. But I don't trust her not to take that information and somehow use it against me.

She's not Kayla, man.

She's also not a random girl.

Whenever I'm around her, I fall into easy friendliness. A byproduct of our night together for sure, but also of our bond as kids, I think. Someone I was close to as a child can't be an awful person like my ex.

I rub the bridge of my nose and slip my eyeglasses back on. The seminar is for two Saturdays. Twelve full hours with my favorite director. Twelve hours to talk about the craft of filmmaking and be inside his head. To make a connection that has the potential to advance my career in staggering ways.

People go a lifetime without spending one minute with their idol.

Fuck.

An RSVP is required by tomorrow to confirm my spot. The seminar starts next week, so I could shoot this weekend with Brad and Harper and have plenty of time to find a replacement.

A *ping* alerts me to a new email. It's from Brad. I open it. He's grateful and happy to have my help with the PSAs. The production schedule is attached, and I've set his mind at ease. He trusts me. He knows he can count on me.

It takes me all of two seconds to click back to my invite and respond so I can stop dwelling on it. Family always comes first. Without them, I'd still be under Kayla's dark cloud. My parents, happily married for thirty-five years, are always my biggest supporters. My sisters and their husbands, most especially Brad, are there for me 24/7. I'm a son, brother, brother-in-law, uncle, and friend, and I'm grateful for all of it.

"You are not going to believe what happened tonight," Elliot calls out. He's walked into the house and said those words at least a dozen times in the last year alone. He rounds the corner into the kitchen with a satiated smile on his face, which tells me a good meal and a couple of after-work drinks are part of what happened. He works his ass off in corporate finance, and the stories he's shared about after-hours are straight-up *House of Lies*.

"Michaela, the hot as hell HR supervisor visiting from New York I told you about?" He pulls off his loosened tie as he sits at the table across from me. "She took off her shirt and had me eat sushi off her stomach. Laid herself right out on the table and told me to go for it. So I did."

"You and everyone else?"

He leans back in his chair, clasps his hands behind his head. "Just me."

I take my glasses off and put them on the table beside my computer. "Why aren't you at her hotel, then?"

"You think I didn't close the deal?"

My roommate and best friend has the worst poker face ever. "She's on her way here? Need me to set a little mood lighting for you?" I tease.

"I got it, Romeo. You just worry about yourself."

"Nothing to worry about."

"Yeah?" He looks around the kitchen. "I don't see a gorgeous brunette hiding anywhere."

I think about the highlights in Harper's dark hair, the summer sun having woven lighter streaks through the soft strands. Then I think about Elliot's description, and I want to claim her as *mine* in this weird competition between us.

"You can call off the bet," Elliot adds. "Take your defeat and pay up." He says this lightly, but he's got a fucking scorecard with our bets on it, and another win for me will bring us to a tie. Christ, we're childish douchebags sometimes. But this bet isn't going to hurt anyone. Quite the contrary, with the plans I have for Miss McKinney. So I feel okay about winning this one.

"The bet's still on," I say.

"You sure?"

"Positive." I've got plenty of time left to charm the pants off her.

"Good luck, then."

I smile. I don't need luck.

"I wonder where—" The doorbell rings, and Elliot explodes out of his chair. "That'll be for me." He swaggers out of the kitchen without a glance back. I listen as he greets Michaela, she giggles, and they make their way to his bedroom. He's been on an unusual binge of hookups lately, probably because work leaves him little time for a relationship.

Smart man. Relationships will ruin you.

Even knowing this, my mind charges right back to Harper. To relieve some of the contemplations I can't seem to get rid of, I grab a piece of plain white paper out of the printer, a pen, and write her a letter I have no intention of sending.

Dear Harper,

Since I have no plans to actually tell you all the things I'm feeling, writing this seems like a good idea. Believe it or not, it's the first handwritten letter I've ever written to a girl. Wait. I take that back. It's the second, right? I think I remember giving you a note when we were five and we got different teachers for kindergarten. It went something like, C U LATR HAM, and included a picture of a dog because I knew you liked them.

I'll spare you any drawings this time, but the sentiment is still the same. I want to see you later. I get that you don't want to date, and I'm cool with that. I don't, either. But I think we could be friends with benefits. Cliché, I know, but the fact is our best friends are dating, so we'll be around each other. The more important fact is we're incredible in bed together. Don't deny it. And please don't deny me the pleasure of your naked body a second time. Maybe a third or a fourth. I'll let you decide the number, just give me one more, at least.

The truth is, I think about you all the time. I like you. And I'm pretty sure you like me, too, even though you're unwilling to admit it.

So let's not overthink it. I'd like to have your beautiful, sexy, responsive body underneath mine. Please say yes.

Sincerely,

Levi

PS Your mom loves me so that should count for something. Unless you count that against me, then forget I mentioned it.

Chapter Five

I jinxed myself, and it's all Pants Charming's fault.

I blow my nose for the hundredth time, then toss the tissue into the small, overfilled wastebasket Teague left beside the couch. I woke up this morning with the summer cold from hell and have spent the entire day on the couch watching Netflix. I can't remember the last time I took a sick day, but I have to be well for tomorrow. I'm even more miserable at the thought of telling Brad I'm in no shape to be on camera.

On the coffee table, next to my feet, are cold medicine, ibuprofen, cherry-flavored throat lozenges, a bottle of water, a bottle of orange juice, and my PSA scripts. I only got them this morning, but a killer headache has prevented me from concentrating on them for longer than a minute. I close my eyes and try to relax the tense muscles in my forehead. There isn't a lot of copy to memorize, and it's information I already know, but there's a rhythm and timing to it that I have to practice.

Rest and fluids will make me better, Teague said in her don't-argue-with-me voice this morning and again a little while ago. She tried to stay home with me tonight, but I insisted she go out for Elliot's birthday and have fun. The misery I'm feeling does not need or want company.

When an incoming text sounds on my phone, I pull my arm out from under the blanket and pick it up. It's Teague. *I'm having soup delivered. Be nice and eat it. XOXO*

I should have known she wouldn't leave me alone. I am a little hungry, so I'll be nice and do as she asks. Especially if it's chicken soup from Nate 'n Al's. I pick up the jar of Vaseline and put some under my raw, red nose, then settle back into the couch for a quick nap before my dinner arrives. More than anything, my worries about tomorrow have drained the energy from me.

I've just dozed off when there's a loud knock on the door. I start to get up, but the door opens, and I hear, "Hey, Harper, don't get up. It's just me."

Me. The "me" with the too-tempting voice that immediately causes tingles in places I don't want them.

I'm going to kill my roommate. No, not kill her. Torture her. What in the world was she thinking sending *him* to deliver my soup? I slump back into the couch pillows.

The door clicks shut.

"Leave it on the table, and you can go," I say. I hope he heard me. I can't talk very loud, and my back is to him.

Of course he doesn't listen. Levi rounds the couch, soup bag in hand. I feel his eyes on me, so I look up. Why, oh why, does he have to be so attractive? He smiles. I frown.

"Hi," he says.

"Hello," I croak, giving him his greeting in hopes he'll put down my food and go. *This* is obviously what Teague meant by *be nice.*

"I come in peace with your favorite soup." He steps

around the coffee table and sits next to me, pulling the jar of Vaseline out from underneath him. Oh, right. I look like a hot, shiny mess. *Great.*

Unfortunately, he just looks unfairly hot in ripped light blue jeans and an ivory button-down with the sleeves pushed up to his elbows. I tear my gaze away from the forearm eye-candy.

"How did I get so lucky?" My grumble turns into a coughing fit.

Levi hands me the bottle of water. After a few sips, I'm better. Sort of. I'm starting to think Levi might kill me with kindness. "Teague was going to leave the bar and bring it to you, but I told her I'd do it."

"You shouldn't have."

"The blonde at the bar would agree with you."

He left someone interested in him to come see me? Why? And why does the thought of him with another girl bother me? I grab the bag of soup out of his hands. "Mission accomplished, so you can go back to Blondie now."

"It's tempting, but I came here for a reason."

"To torture me?"

"There is that." He takes the paper bag back and lifts the container of soup out. I watch him unwrap the plastic around the carton, remove the lid, and place the white plastic spoon inside.

"Are you going to blow on it for me, too?" I ask with sarcasm.

"I'd rather watch you do that." He passes me the soup as his eyes dip to my mouth. My scoff immediately vanishes, and I shiver at his blatant interest. I know from experience he likes to watch. He knows from experience I like to be watched.

I drop my gaze to the soup, ignoring the sparks of attraction that always detonate when we're near each other.

"What are you doing here, Levi?"

He turns his whole body so he faces me, one leg tucked under the other, which shouldn't be unnerving, but it is. I concentrate on ignoring his easygoing position in order to take my first bite of chicken noodle yumminess.

"When Teague told me you were sick, I figured you'd be worried about the shoot tomorrow."

"I'm not," I lie. "I'll be fine in the morning." I hope. I hope. I hope.

"Whether you are or not, I wanted to tell you I've seen the production schedule and thought you might feel better knowing we can shoot around you tomorrow."

I drop the spoon in my soup. "Shoot without me?"

"Brad wants a lot of footage to use later, too, and some of that is just with the kids."

I get that. I do. But several of the kids participating are my students, and I guess I feel protective of them. I don't want them in the water without me, even though I recruited all good swimmers. They're still young. And accidents can happen and—

"It's okay," Levi says. He takes the soup from me and puts it on the coffee table.

My hands are shaking. *Fuck*.

"You're still the spokesperson." He catches my hand before I tuck it under the blanket and laces our fingers together. "No worries there."

I should yank my hand free, I really should, but I don't because, even though I don't want it to, it feels nice inside his. No one has held my hand in a really long time. And the truth is, I am worried. I don't understand why it's okay for me to do the PSAs, but not get further commitment about the ambassador job.

"Brad is really happy to have you on board. I didn't know he coached you."

"For two years."

"You won a national and world championship with him."

I was the underdog both times, and winning made me feel invincible. This isn't a conversation I want to have, though. I don't reminisce. And I don't deserve any kind of reverence. "Brad talks too much."

"He also told me the reason he's interested in you for this job is that you know firsthand what it's like to lose someone to drowning."

My world tilts off its axis. There's always this underlying anticipation of more happening between Levi and me, but now that he knows about Joe, I'm angry, scared, and ashamed all over again. Levi's sympathetic eyes don't help. I can't allow myself his comfort. If I do, I risk getting too attached.

I yank my hand free and get to my feet. The blanket falls to the floor. "It's time for you to go."

Instead of standing to leave, he checks me out. His gaze slides down my body, then back up, and I'm furious at myself for liking the attention. I forgot I'm wearing my tiny, gray cotton boy-short panties and a white lace cami that barely reaches my belly button, so I can't blame Levi for his delayed response. A guy sees a girl in her underwear, and he has to pause. His eyes linger on my pierced navel, then on my chest long enough to make my nipples harden before he comes back to rest on what I hope is my angry face. My head and nose are so congested it's hard to express myself properly.

"You done?" I ask.

"Not even close." He says this like it's a foregone conclusion, and his light brown eyes stay glued to mine as he stands. "But you should finish eating and get some rest."

"I don't need you to tell me what to do." I walk to the door and open it, ready to usher him out as quickly as possible.

When he reaches my side, he stops. "I know what it feels like to lose someone."

My mouth opens, but no words come out.

"Not the same way," he clarifies, "but there's some fucked-up shit in my past I pretend isn't there, too. If you ever want to talk about—"

"I don't."

He studies me so intently my legs shake. "If you ever want to talk about it, let me know."

"Don't hold your breath."

"I wouldn't dream of it where you're concerned." He smiles. The more prickly I am, the nicer he is, just to annoy me, I'm sure. Then he wraps his hand around the back of my head and kisses my forehead. It's the sweetest move a guy has ever put on me. Levi's lips are warm—soft, but firm, and when they're close to mine, everything seems better. He pulls away much too soon. "Later, gator."

I sag against the doorframe and watch him walk away. That was…that was…I don't know what that was, which is a very bad thing. He's disarming and lethal at the same time. I'm the way I am for a reason, but I wonder about his confession and whether it has anything to do with his ex-girlfriend. Months ago, before Levi and I hooked up, I happened to be at his house with Teague. He was holed up in his room with "Kayla" the entire night, but Elliot and Mateo talked about what a bitch she was and how Levi would be better off without her. At the time, I'd paid very little attention. I didn't even register his name, or have any idea he was my childhood friend. I don't know what happened to end the relationship for good, but I recall hearing she'd "screwed with his head" for the last time.

I close and lock the door, and once I'm back under the blanket eating my soup, my thoughts drift to Joe. Memories of him preoccupy me the rest of the night. I wonder if we'd still be together. Engaged or married, even. Losing him messed with every part of me in ways that still hurt. Which is why I keep my no-relationship policy firmly in place, and why I have to feel better tomorrow.

• • •

I don't feel better. If anything, I feel worse. But I'm here at MASF's headquarters to do what I can. The kids are in the Olympic-size pool, laughing and splashing—exactly what Brad wants them to do. I count the number of children repeatedly, watch for signs of tiring or apprehension, and take slow, deep breaths to keep myself calm. I'm not the only one with eyes glued to the pool.

This affords me brief peeks at the cameraman. Levi is sexy when all he does is move from point A to point B. But Levi is sexy *and then some* when he's behind his camera. He's in total command, confident, and completely at ease and patient when the kids don't follow directions. In board shorts and a well-washed blue surf tee, with light stubble on his jaw, he's ridiculously distracting. The other women around the pool, most of them the moms of the kids, can't keep their eyes off him, either.

"We good?" Brad asks Levi.

Levi gives a thumbs-up.

"Let's break for lunch," Brad calls out, then directly to the kids he says, "Fantastic job, you guys."

One of my students, Zoe (who coincidentally is Levi's next-door neighbor), climbs out of the pool and walks directly over to Levi. He sets his camera down and kneels to her level. She puts her small hands on his shoulders and says, "Did you get me good?"

"I sure did," he tells her.

"Should I do anything different?"

"Zoe, you're perfect just the way you are."

That earns Levi a giant smile and, if I'm not mistaken, a

blush. I think little Zoe might have her first crush. Can't say I blame her.

She drops her arms and runs off to join the rest of the kids, parents, and crew.

Levi notices I'm not rising from the bleachers and strides over to sit next to me. I was half hoping to be left alone, but the traitorous other half is happy for the handsome cameraman's company. It's the first chance we've had to talk today. He slips his sunglasses from the top of his head over his eyes. I keep my attention forward, on the pale blue chlorinated water glistening under the afternoon sun.

"How's it looking?" I ask when Levi remains uncharacteristically quiet.

He turns his head so our sunglasses meet. "Beautiful."

Goddamn him. I don't blush like six-year-old girls, but I'm pretty sure I just did.

I didn't just think about Joe last night. I thought about Levi, too. They're the only two boys I've been close to. Joe wrote me love notes. He brought me flowers he picked from his momma's garden. He played his guitar and sang to me. He moved from a small town in Texas to Beverly Hills the summer before our sophomore year of high school. To say he stuck out would be an understatement. At six-foot-four with honey-blond hair, cornflower-blue eyes, and a down-to-earth attitude unlike anyone else's in the 90210 zip code, every girl instantly wanted to date him. That he played football like a champion made every guy immediately respect him.

On the first day of school, he sat next to me in English. He wore a cowboy hat. He took it off and put it over his heart when our teacher walked into the room. Then he turned to me and introduced himself. I was toast.

We dated for the rest of the school year. I wanted to have sex with him after two months. God, how he made my heart pound, my blood burn through my body, and desire unfurl inside me everywhere. The simplest touch from him made it hard to breathe. But we were only fifteen, and his momma had told him some things shouldn't be rushed, so we did everything we could think of but have intercourse.

We were both busy that year. Between football, then baseball, for him, swimming for me, and schoolwork for both of us, there were stretches when we were lucky to steal kisses. He loved to come watch my swim meets. Was in awe of how I moved through the water, mostly because he'd never learned to swim. He'd had a bad experience as a child and feared the water. We had plans for me to teach him over summer break. And we had plans to lose our virginity a week before school let out—on my sixteenth birthday. I loved Joe so much, I wanted forever with him.

Levi drew me pictures of dogs. He once brought me a worm he dug out of the dirt in his mother's garden. He didn't sing or play an instrument, but he told me I smelled like bubble gum. That was thanks to the bubble bath I insisted my mom use. We were young, and I remember hating him for swimming faster than me. But I also remember loving him, like little girls do. He was the one person I always wanted to play with.

Which is why I dislike being around him so much now. I made up my mind a long time ago never to let a boy inside my heart again. It's not Levi's fault I feel this way, but he is the biggest threat to my vow, and that's why I'll push him away until he gets the hint I'm no good for him.

"The footage, too?" I say, ridding my head of memories best left in the past. For the next few weeks while we're working together, I'll try to be cordial and accept his compliments.

"Absolutely. I'm very good at what I do." The cocky tone of his voice tells me he's talking about more than filming.

I most definitely know the other things he's good at. *Do not let his flirting get to you.*

I'm grateful when I have to sneeze. By the third one, I've shaken Levi's other talents out of my head. When I open my eyes, Brad is looking in my direction from across the pool. I'm not sure if it's my cold or the fact that I'm sitting with his cameraman, but he doesn't appear happy. Shit.

"I think I'll grab something to eat and let Brad know I'm good to go," I say, sliding off the aluminum seating. I didn't eat breakfast, and while I'm not really hungry, I realize belatedly that keeping my distance from everyone isn't smart.

"You sure you feel okay?" Levi is at my side, damn it, his shadow eating up the space next to mine on the concrete.

"Honestly, I feel worse not being in the water, so…"

"Let me check with Brad and see if we can grab some underwater footage."

"My raspy voice won't cut it?"

"Not today."

"Okay." I peek at Levi out of the corner of my eye. He's all business as we head toward the group. It's a total turn-on.

I grab a sandwich and bottle of water and join the kids while Levi talks to Brad. The two of them sit with other crewmembers out of earshot. It's a hot summer day, and even though we're under a large pop-up tent, a few of the kids complain about being tired. Brad notices and announces that the kids are done for the day. He shakes hands with all the parents and fist bumps every child as they say their good-byes. I stand and give hugs.

"It's you and me," Levi says in my ear, his hand on my waist. "Meet me in the shallow end in twenty."

There is no reason why those words and innocent touch should affect me, but they do. I'm winded and I haven't done a thing.

I've already got my suit on underneath my loose, cotton dress, so I sit down facing the pool with my legs outstretched. Brad takes the spot next to me.

"You sure you feel okay to get in the water?"

"Positive."

"I understand you and Levi have more than mutual friends in common," he says out of the blue, and I press my lips together. What did Levi say to him? "My wife remembers you. She said you and Levi were inseparable when you were young. Around Axl's age?"

My panic evaporates. *Not Levi.* But my head is down, eyes on my knees when I say, "Yes, that's right." If I remember correctly, Levi has four sisters several years older. They were sweet to me, treated me like I was special. I've only seen Brad's wife from afar, but her name is Amelia, which makes her the oldest, I believe.

"Levi's fond of you."

"Okay." I'm not sure how else to respond to that. I have a working relationship with Brad now, not a personal one, so this is a weird topic of conversation. Is he trying to play matchmaker or something? I glance up and notice Levi is looking at me, not the camera equipment, from across the pool.

"I'm telling you that because, as his brother-in-law, I feel I need to step in."

I gape at Brad. Uh, what? "There's nothing going on between us." Okay, there's a little something, but I can ignore it.

"He looks fine and acts fine, but he's not in the right frame of mind for another relationship. Not yet."

My head spins a little, wondering what happened between Levi and his ex to cause Brad concern months later. It must have been bad. "There's nothing—"

"I'm not blind, Harper. I see the way you two look at each other. But please do me a favor and don't encourage him."

Brad says this nicely, not like I'm out to snag a boyfriend, and my initial annoyance softens. I could even look at it as a compliment. "You don't have to worry. I'm not. I won't."

"Thank you."

"I'm going to jump in the water now." I thumb toward the pool. Brad nods with a big-brother smile. I'm not sure how to process our conversation, and don't want to dwell on it, so I quickly pull off my dress, slip off my flip-flops, and dive into the water. I swim a few laps to loosen my muscles before I take a seat on the concrete steps to wait for Levi.

He and a PA are fitting the camera into a waterproof box. Once that's done, Levi tosses off his shirt and puts on scuba gear. I swim away from the steps to get out of his way, and with help from the PA, Levi and the camera are in the pool.

"I'm going to stand at the bottom in the middle," Levi tells me, "and I want you to just do your thing underneath the water. I would like some long shots of you gliding with your arms above your head, legs together, and a shot where you're fanning out your arms and legs. Other than that, whatever style you want is fine. Questions?"

"Should I look at you?"

"Not during this run-through. After I get what I need, we'll take a short break and then do some takes where you can look directly at the camera. Give some smiles and thumbs-up."

"Got it."

Levi puts his regulator in his mouth and walks down to deeper water. Once I see he's ready, I push off the side with my feet to give me some speed. I'm a little nervous at first, but before I've even made it halfway across the pool, I've relaxed. This is my element. And it's exhilarating. I don't pay any attention to Levi as I do my thing as instructed. In my modest, one-piece USA bathing suit, I cut through the water with barely a ripple. I love the peaceful quiet—the feeling that nothing can touch me down here. It took me a long time to get back to this place after Joe died, so I relish it now.

I have no idea how many laps I've swum back and forth in between catching my breath before I notice Levi give me a hand signal that he's headed to the surface. I follow.

He gets out of the water to check the footage. I'm tempted to ask if I can take a peek, but I don't. It doesn't matter whether I like it or not, so I'd rather be surprised.

We do a second series of shots after that, and I can't help but make some silly faces at the camera. This is fun, and I'm enjoying being in the water with Levi. He hasn't taken his eyes off me.

I don't count this as encouraging him. I can't help that I'm entertaining. When we're finished, we towel off side-by-side and make small talk. We're the only two left at the pool.

"See you next Saturday," I say as I slide my feet into my shoes. With Brad's request in the back of my mind, I need to fly out of here.

"Hang"—Levi's phone rings—"on a second?" He notes the caller ID. "It's Brad."

Just in case it has something to do with the shoot, I wait.

"Hey." Levi holds the cell to his ear. "*What?* The hospital? Okay, yeah…sure, that's no problem… I'll lock up and be right over… Bye."

"What happened?"

"Axl fell out of a tree."

"Oh no. Is he okay?"

Levi runs his fingers through his wet hair. "He will be, but he may have broken his arm and collarbone. Brad is freaking out. He'd just gotten home when my sister was rushing out the door. Axl was at a friend's house. Anyway, Brad asked if I could come over and stay with Lily. He doesn't want to take her to the hospital with him."

I put my hand on his wrist. "Little boys are tough. I'm sure he'll bounce back in no time."

"Come with me?"

"*What?*" I take the camera bag he hands me and put it over my shoulder.

"My niece is hell on two tiny legs. I could use some backup."

"Backup?" I can't keep the amusement out of my voice. Lily is two and he's basically saying he's afraid of her.

"Yes. She's like the Tasmanian Devil in a tutu." He hangs a second black bag over my other shoulder, effectively keeping me with him.

Looks like I'm not running off anywhere yet. "And you want to outnumber her?"

Levi flashes me the most sexy, adorable grin I have ever seen, and there's no way I can stay immune to that. I need to get my ass in my car and drive home, do not pass go, do not be swayed by Mr. Hottie McFarley.

"Two is always better than one," Levi says. "You in?"

Chapter Six

LEVI

"You've got chocolate in your hair," Harper says, raising her arm and running her fingers through the strands near my temple. She smells like the chocolate chip cookies we baked with Lily, and I want to bury my nose in her neck, kiss her, and whisper I want her. This is a side of her I haven't seen before. Gentle, sweet, maternal. She was stunning in the pool earlier. So confident and commanding. She kept me absolutely riveted. Then I watched her bake cookies with my niece and talk about swimming. When she enlisted Lily in a secret "swimja" society, I was fascinated even more.

"Thanks. I'm pretty sure I've got chocolate in my ear, too." Lily's little hands were covered in melted chocolate after she ate two cookies and decided to hold my face and kiss me for making her favorite food.

"Your niece adores you."

"What's not to adore?"

"Where should I start?" Harper fires back.

"You can't give me a compliment and then knock it down, Ham."

She bristles. She hates when I call her Ham, which is partly why I do it. "It was an observation, not a compliment." She also likes to argue with me.

A high-pitched squeal snags my attention, and I turn my head. Lily is chasing a year-old mutt around the dog run at the animal shelter. The second we got here, she had to go play with him. I'm hoping the running around tires her out.

"Thanks for hanging with us," I say. I'm not sorry for using my niece as an excuse to have more time with Harper. I can handle Lily on my own, but I saw an opportunity that put me closer to winning the bet, so I took it. The more time I spend with Harper, the more ammunition I have when Elliot gives me shit about her.

"I'm not sure Brad appreciated me showing up with you."

I lean my arms on the chain link fence and watch Lily skip around the dirt and grass in delight. "Why do you say that?"

"He thinks we like each other and isn't happy about it."

"What are you talking about? Did he say something to you?"

She hunches. "It doesn't matter."

It matters. "He mentioned Kayla, didn't he?" My brother-in-law thinks I'm still fucked-up, and to a degree, I am. But I don't need him butting into my personal life. Especially where it concerns Harper. Not sure why that bothers me so much in particular, but it does.

"Not in so many words, no."

I shift my stance, and my arm brushes hers. It's unintentional, which makes the electricity spreading through my body that much more significant. I like her touch. Her nearness. Something in me comes unearthed. I know she's suffered loss in her past, too.

Lily shows no signs of slowing down, so for reasons I'm not too clear on, I decide to tell Harper about Kayla. My family is always encouraging me not to keep shit bottled up inside. "Kayla and I started dating when we were sixteen, and when she was seventeen, she got pregnant."

Harper's head swings around, her eyes wide with surprise as she looks at me.

"When she told her parents, they freaked. They were ultra-strict and religious and didn't think we were having sex. I was in love with their daughter and would have taken responsibility, but they saw it as ruining her life if she kept the baby. They were also overbearing and cared what other people thought so they packed up and moved to Ohio so Kayla could have the baby in secret and give him up for adoption." I let out a breath. "In that sense, her parents were unselfish. They wanted a couple who couldn't have children to be blessed with one."

"Him?" Harper whispers.

I nod, a little choked up. Somewhere out there is a boy with my DNA. Lily waves to me, and I wave back. "I didn't find that out until college. When Kayla left, they forbid us from having any contact. They made sure she had no cell phone or social media access, so I had no way of reaching her. But we'd talked about going to UCLA together, so in the back of my mind that first week of school, I wondered if maybe I'd see her. Turned out she *was* there."

"Wow."

"We got back together. She was different, but the same, and I wanted to help her."

"What do you mean?"

"She hadn't wanted to give up the baby. She fell in love with him while he grew inside her, but her parents threatened to disown her if she didn't. And afterward, they continued to make her feel bad about herself. She was pretty screwed up when she got to college and took a lot of that out on me. It was my fault the condom broke. Why did I let her go? Why didn't I come after her? Then, other times, she made me feel like I was the king of the world. She told me she never stopped loving me." I scratch the back of my head. "We were on and off throughout college. The off times were on her. She'd do shit and say shit to push me away, but I knew she didn't mean it, and I loved her, so we'd work it out. After graduation things got better. She got a job she really liked, and her confidence grew, and I thought we were over the baby and ready to talk about a future together."

"But that didn't happen," Harper says softly.

"No. Turned out she started seeing someone at work while she was seeing me. For six fucking months. One morning when I got home from an overnight shoot, she told me about him. She said she was in love with him and he was going to help her find our son."

"What?"

I clear my throat. "Yeah. I told her that wasn't right. That in my head our son had a good life with parents who loved him, and she'd better not interfere without their consent. Then I said we were through. About six weeks later, she shows up and says she ended it with the douche and gave up her search and she loves me and made a mistake and would I please take her back. That was the night you and Teague were at our house.

"I knew she was hurting and messed up, and a part of me always wanted to be her hero. I was the guy who got her back to a happy place. It just never lasted long enough. Two weeks later she told me she was pregnant with the other guy's baby."

"Holy shit."

"I haven't seen or talked to her since and have no plans to."

Harper covers my hand with hers. "I'm sorry all of that

happened to you."

I turn my wrist and lace our fingers together. "Thanks. I try not to linger on it, but sometimes when I think about Justin, I wonder *what-if*."

"Justin?"

"Kayla named our son Justin."

"Is that weird?"

"Thinking that if things had gone differently, I'd be a dad right now? Yes. Knowing and wondering about a kid who might look and act just like me and I'll never know him? Definitely. I've felt guilty. Sad. Confused. But mostly relieved that I didn't have to make a decision back then. The truth is I wasn't ready to be a dad, but my parents taught me to take responsibility for my actions, so I would have stepped up."

"You're a good person, Levi."

I rub my thumb over the back of Harper's hand. She's easy to talk to. Always has been. "Thanks, Ham. You're a good listener." A piece of me wants to pull the I-told-you-my-story, now-you-tell-me-yours card, but that's not why I confessed to her. I shared without much thought, really, obviously needing to get it off my chest after Brad poked at my past. Do I trust Harper with my story? Fuck, I don't know. If someone had asked me yesterday, I would have said no.

She slips her hand out of mine. "Should we find Axl a puppy now?"

"We should." Lily has finally turned her skip into a sit on the grass, and the dog is licking her face. "I'll get the little monster."

"You tricked me, you know."

I glance at Harper with a *what, me?* expression while I open the gate to go grab Lily.

"Lily is an angel," she says, her full lips twisting into a small, knowing smile. It's the first genuine smile she's given me since our night together. I smile back, feeling like shit. I did trick her, because I've got a bet to win. I remind myself it's not hurting anyone. That when Harper and I do land in bed together, it will be because she wants it, too.

"Hey Lily-pad, let's go find a puppy for your brother." I pick her up and hold her close to my chest. She weighs nothing.

"Shudders peese," she says, and I lift her onto my shoulders. Her fingers go right in my hair.

We rejoin Harper and start down the first concrete aisle of enclosures. When I talked to my sister Amelia, they were on their way home from the hospital. Axl did break his collarbone and arm but was feeling okay thanks to some pain medication. He liked his cast but didn't like the sling he had to wear on top of that. When I asked what happened, Amelia said he was trying to save a cat in a tree. *That kid.* I told her if that act of heroism didn't earn him a puppy before he turned five, then I didn't know what did. It took a little more convincing, but I got her to agree. "Can you get one already potty trained?" she'd asked. I told her if there were no puppies, I'd do my best.

I feel Lily's body go limp. "She asleep, isn't she?" I ask Harper.

Harper looks over my head and nods with another small smile. Fuck, she's beautiful. I tighten my hold on Lily and move my attention back to the dogs. We finish walking down the first aisle and round the corner to the second.

Right there on the left, my wish is granted. "That's the—"

"That's the—" Harper says.

"One." We finish the last word at the same time.

Sitting with his—or her—nose against the fence is a bulldog puppy. Harper drops to her knees and immediately starts petting the pup and cooing. "He is the cutest thing ever," she says.

I kneel beside her. I keep one arm around Lily and let the

puppy sniff the knuckles of my free hand. Another couple with a young child walks up behind us. "This one is ours," I say nicely.

"His name is Gus, and he's eleven weeks old," Harper reads from the sign on the chain-link gate. "Hello, Gus," she says with affection. "How would you like to come home with us?"

Axl is going to lose his mind when he sees this dog. "Stay with Gus, and I'll go do the paperwork?"

"Okay." Harper doesn't take her eyes off the puppy. "Wait." She stands and reaches for Lily. "Let me take that weight off your shoulders while you do that."

"Thanks."

She puts Lily on her hip, guiding my niece's head to her chest. "You lucked out finding a puppy today."

"Things happen for a reason," I say.

A flash of pain crosses over her pretty face before she turns away. "You're lucky today, too, Gus."

"Hey, you okay?"

"Of course. Why wouldn't I be?" She spares me a quick glance. "Go buy your nephew his puppy."

An hour later, Gus and Axl are sitting on the kitchen floor of my sister's house getting to know each other. Amelia and Brad look on with smiles. Lily is in her highchair kicking her feet and waving her hands in excitement, Cheerios flying this way and that.

I glance over at Harper to find her eyes on me. She quickly looks away, hoping, I'm sure, that I didn't catch her. But I did.

The game is most definitely on.

Top Ten words to say out loud that make me happy:

1. Swimja (translation: swim ninja) ~ Swimjas are the best kind of ninjas!

2. Discombobulate ~ Grandpa Bob's favorite word.

3. Kerfuffle ~ When I'm feeling silly, I also like to say fuffleker.

4. Shenanigans ~ Even thinking this word makes me happy.

5. Mojito ~ Not on my list of preferred beverages, but I love ordering them for friends.

6. Winky tinky ~ I have no idea what this means, but I use it if I have to curse during my swim lessons. My students think it's hysterical.

7. Gobbledygook ~ When I was young, I called our Thanksgiving turkey this.

8. Thingamajig ~ Who doesn't love a thingamajig?

9. Kumquat ~ I'm not sure I'd be able to pick this out in a lineup. LOL Yeah, I just cracked myself up because I have no idea what one looks like.

10. Pants Charming

Chapter Seven

I fumble with the small heart locket I'm trying to put around my neck. It's because I'm running late and in a hurry that I have trouble, I tell myself.

"Hey," Teague says, walking into our Jack and Jill bathroom in her robe. "You've been trying to put that on for five minutes. Let me help."

"Thanks." When her fingers find the clasp, I gather my hair off my neck and stare at the silver locket situated against my bare skin. Maybe I shouldn't wear it.

"There. It looks really pretty, Harp. I haven't seen you wear it in a while." She tilts her head to the side so it touches mine and admires the necklace's reflection in the mirror.

"I'm not sure what possessed me to put it on tonight."

"Were you thinking about him today?" Teague asks softly.

"More than usual, I guess, yeah." Joe gave me the necklace for my sixteenth birthday. His gift was the hardest one to accept when a week after my party I sat down with my family to open my presents.

"Then it's good you put it on." She kisses my cheek and walks back to her room, leaving me to contemplate if that's true. For a long time, I didn't open the locket, thinking I'd be devastated all over again to see a picture of Joe and me together. Eventually I caved and looked inside. It was empty, which disappointed me on some level, but relieved me, too. Rubbing the smooth metal between my fingers now, I wonder if Joe meant for me to put a picture from my birthday party inside it.

"Whose house is the party at again?" Teague calls out, saving me from my troubling thoughts.

I let go of the locket and square my shoulders. I didn't put the necklace on to bring me down. "The maid of honor's. You remember her. Her boyfriend is the chef." *The party* is a wedding shower-slash-bachelorette-slash-bachelor party for Colleen and George.

Teague pokes her head into the bathroom. "Got it. Rochelle, right?"

"Right." I pick up the curling iron and run it through my straight hair. "I wish you were coming. I'll probably be the only one without a date." This shouldn't bother me. It's a party. I'm good at parties, with or without a date. But for some reason, there's a huge knot of apprehension sitting heavily inside my chest.

Teague pops back into the doorway. She's half dressed in a cute little black skirt and pale pink bra. "Whoa. Back up there, sister. Since when did this turn into a date thing?"

"Since the wedding got moved to next month. Tonight is a couple's party of everything rolled into one, including the bachelor party."

"Let me get this straight." Teague slaps a hand on the doorframe. "There's going to be boys at this party?"

"That's what I'm told."

"And you're not bringing one."

"Nope."

"Because?"

"I don't need one."

Teague disappears for a minute then reappears wearing a cute sleeveless top that shows a hint of cleavage. "You do in this case."

I put the curling iron down on the counter. "Why?"

"Because it's the polite thing to do."

"How do you figure?" I finger comb my hair until the large, loose curls cascade down my back.

Teague leans over the sink and looks in the mirror to apply mascara. She and Mateo have dinner plans tonight. "The party is for couples. That means if you show up without a date, Colleen is going to feel awkward. Especially since you're a bridesmaid *and* her cousin. And if she's uncomfortable, then she won't have as good a time."

"I don't think she'll care."

"She'll tell you she doesn't mind, but she really will. Brides want everything, including showers and bachelorette parties, to be perfect. Plus, on top of having wedding worries, she's got pregnancy hormones making her act like an unreasonable person a lot of the time."

"Fuck." Teague's right. I should have thought about Colleen and not myself in this situation. "I don't have time to ask someone to go with me now."

"I've got a guy," Teague offers, her lashes now spectacularly long. "But you're not going to like it."

"It's almost seven o'clock on a Friday night. I can't be picky at this point. Wait. Since when do *you* have a guy?" I cross my arms over my chest. Before Mateo, my sweet best friend had sworn off getting within five feet of a penis.

"Since Mateo."

"Oh no. I'm not taking Levi or Elliot." Elliot will make a big deal of it, and I don't want to give him any wrong ideas. And Levi...all week I've thought about him. How amazing he is with a camera. How devoted he is to his family. I can't believe he shared so much about his ex with me. Every time we're together I learn more about him, and the more I learn, the more I like. Which, in a normal girl, would make her happy. But I'm not normal. I haven't been since my sixteenth birthday. What I feel for Levi scares the shit out of me.

Teague puts her hands on my shoulders. "This is just a few hours, Harp, nothing more."

We look each other in the eye, and both know that's not the case with Levi. I've told her about him. Not every little thing, because even though she's my best friend and the closest thing I have to a sister, I don't allow myself to be that vulnerable with anyone.

I don't tell her that if anything bad happened to Levi, I'm not sure I could deal with it.

"How do you know he doesn't already have plans?"

"*He?*" She drops her arms and smiles innocently.

"We are not having this conversation again." The one where she tries to sell me on a relationship with her boyfriend's best friend so the four of us can live happily ever after together. And I don't mean Elliot. Not that there's anything wrong with Elliot. He's hot in a business-suit, corporate way, if you like that sort of thing.

"I have no idea what you're talking about." She picks up the mouthwash and pours a little into the cap. "So, Levi. I don't know if he has plans tonight or not, but he owes me a favor."

This is news to me. "For what?"

She pours the contents of the cap into her mouth and swishes it around. A few seconds later, she spits the mouthwash out into the sink. "I can't tell you."

"Seriously?"

"Seriously."

"Never mind, then." I turn and march into my room to slip on my heels. There is no way I want to get in the middle of a favor from Levi. Actually, I guess I would be the favor, which is worse.

"Harper," Teague says, trailing behind me. "Don't be so…"

"So…?" I bounce down on the foot of my bed and reach for my shoes.

"I don't know. Proud? Let me at least give him a call and see if he's available."

"Why won't you tell me about the favor? I tell you everything."

She raises her eyebrows and looks down her nose at me. "That's almost true." She spins around and takes the spot next to me, bumping my hip. "But that's okay. And this is one of those things I can't tell you."

"Fine. Call him." I'll just ask Levi what Teague did. A couple of drinks, a few accidental touches, and he'll spill.

"Be right back." She pads away in her bare feet in search of her phone, I assume.

I fall back onto my bed, eyes on the ceiling. This is a mistake. It's bad enough I have to be with Levi for the next two Saturdays while we film. I hate feeling like I have no control around him, like my emotions are out of my reach and closer to his. There's more than attraction between us, and I can't let myself go there. I'm not sure what's going on in his head, but I'm worried that if we do hook up, it won't be so easy for me to say never again.

For the hundredth time, I wonder if I should be over Joe's accident. My mom thinks so. She says hearts break, but they eventually heal. But how is that possible when I can't forget the sight of Joe's cold body? His blue lips. The smell of his soap mixed with tequila and chlorine, and the devastating agony of holding him in my arms, helpless and guilty. I never should have taken him near the pool that night. If we'd gone anywhere else, he'd still be alive.

How does a person ever process being up close to death? One night and my life changed forever.

"Levi is on his way over," Teague says, strolling into my room with an extra bounce in her step.

I sling my arm over my eyes. "Of course he is," I mumble.

"He did have plans, but he said he could get out of them." She lifts my arm away from my face and gazes down at me. "It's not a big deal."

"It kind of is."

She tilts her head then lies down beside me. "What if you just turn off your brain, have some naked fun, and leave it at that."

"I'm pretty sure I said something similar to you about Mateo, and look what happened."

"True. But I wanted to fall in love. You don't. Not yet."

"Not ever." I sit up. "But you're right about tonight. It is about fun and making sure Colleen has a good time, nothing else." I can be around Levi and not be bothered by feelings.

The doorbell rings and Teague pops to her feet. "That's Mateo," she says excitedly.

I follow her toward the front door, veering into the kitchen for an apple. I need something to do while I try not to think about Levi and hanging out with him tonight.

Mateo is lip-locked with his girlfriend the second he sees her, one hand on her ass, the other on the back of her head. I clear my throat. "Hi, Mateo."

He continues to kiss the shit out of her for another minute before looking up with a grin plastered across his face. He glances over Teague to meet my gaze. "Hey, Harper."

"Nice greeting."

"Can't help myself."

"Just be sure you don't steal *all* the air out of my girl's lungs."

Teague spins around wearing a blush. It's adorable how my best friend still turns every shade of pink when there's an eyewitness to anything physical between her and Mateo. "We're gonna go," she says. "You're good, right?"

"I'm good. You two kids have fun tonight. Don't do anything I wouldn't do."

Teague's cheeks turn even pinker. With Mateo, there's nothing my best friend won't try. She 100 percent trusts him and is devoted to him. He's devoted right back. The two of them are adorable and nauseating at the same time.

I toss my apple into the trash then fiddle with the tray of appetizers I finished making before getting dressed. Tonight's theme is "A Perfect Pair" so I made lobster mac and cheese. I put small servings in shot glasses and topped each one with toasted breadcrumbs. I've paired them with a couple of bottles of buttery chardonnay. I totally googled this combo. I know nothing about wine, but being that mac and cheese is my specialty and I love lobster, it was an easy pick. I've also got a bottle of sparkling apple cider just for Colleen. I can already picture her sad face when she doesn't get to drink with everyone, so hopefully this makes her happy.

A few seconds before Levi knocks, I have the feeling he's right outside the door. Worse, jitters slide down my spine like this is a first date. Which is ridiculous. This isn't anywhere near a date. It's a favor, and the lesser of two evils, I quickly decide. The decision calms me down. Slightly.

"Come in!" I call out, walking around the kitchen counter.

Pants Charming lets himself inside with an ease and confidence that sends a strange thrill through me. That he looks drop-dead gorgeous in jeans, a beige-colored fitted designer tee, and stubble on his angular jaw, doesn't help. "Hi," he says, closing the door behind him.

"Hi." I search the room for my purse, hoping he doesn't notice how much his being here affects me. "We need to hurry. Mind grabbing the tray of appetizers and the bag of wine on the counter?"

"Not at all."

"So, I hear you owed Teague a favor." I can't help saying this now rather than later. If we can get the matter out of the way, maybe I can relax. Not that being close to Levi elicits calm inside me.

"Looking for this?" he asks instead of answering me.

I turn to find him standing by the kitchen table holding up my purse. He's also smiling. He wears smiles like he's got a million of them to give, but more than that, his face is filled with warmth. Intimacy. It's impossible not to be taken with him when he looks at me with familiarity and hot-blooded desire.

"Yep." I zero in on my small bag, putting all my focus on the outside pocket. "Thanks." I wonder if I can get through the rest of the night without looking at his face again.

"Nice outfit. Sorry I'm not more dressed up."

"No worries." I don't dare glance back up at his expression, but I guess he's looking me over. Tonight's attire is a short, pale-blush raglan-sleeve body-con dress. Levi's shirt and my dress go nicely together. You could say they're a perfect pair.

Which is not what I'm thinking. Not. Not. Not.

He clutches my purse to his chest when I reach out to snag it. My eyes jump back to his. I'm close enough to get a whiff of his body wash and notice his hair is slightly damp. Was he on his way to another date when Teague called?

"Do you mind?" I say, suddenly mad at him for everything. It's his fault I burned my finger on the pot of boiling water earlier. It's his fault I ran out of shampoo in the shower. And it's his fault I left my car lights on the other night and needed my neighbor's jumper cables.

He arches his eyebrows. "Are you tapping your foot at me?"

"Maybe."

"You were too far away." He says this like I know what he's talking about.

"What?"

"You were too far away," he repeats. "And I minded."

I grind my teeth and tug my purse free. "You are not allowed to let things like that bother you."

"Then you're not allowed to look so hot in a dress."

"I can do whatever I want." I twist around before he catches a glimpse of my mouth stretching into an unwelcome smile.

"But I can't?"

"Nope." I'm about to pick up the tray of appetizers when Levi traps me against the kitchen counter, his front to my back and his arms on either side of me with his hands on the stone worktop. I freeze.

"Last I checked, it's a free country." His warm breath fans my ear, which shouldn't be a big deal, but somehow it has me squeezing my thighs together. "Which means I'll do whatever I please."

He smells so good. Looks even better. And when he couldn't care less what I say in these entertaining situations, I want him to *do* me. Thankfully, he backs away before I forget myself. I use the space to steal a moment and close my eyes, rubbing my necklace between my fingers.

"I've got this," I say, lifting up the lobster-mac tray. The Levi-effect is mostly gone now, thanks to my birthday reminder. "Would you please take the wine?"

"Sure."

We talk about basic stuff on the drive to the party. It's nice, but not exactly relaxed. I'm hyperaware of his hands on the steering wheel and the way his shirt molds to his shoulders and biceps. I'm ready to leap out of the car when we reach our destination. By the number of cars parked in front of Rochelle's house, we're one of the last to arrive. "Hey," I say before we head right inside through the large, white-painted front door, "you never told me why you owed Teague a favor."

Levi thinks about it for a second. His expression is hard to read. "That's not why I'm here."

"No?"

"No." He's adamant about his answer but doesn't elaborate. "Come on. Sounds like there's a lot of fun going on without us." He opens the door, and we're quickly swept inside, all thoughts of favors forgotten.

Colleen's eyes widen when she sees Levi at my side. "Hi!" She gives me a hug then waits for me to introduce her. George wanders over, and the four of us fall into easy conversation. "I'm really glad you brought someone," Colleen whispers in my ear while Levi and George talk about baseball. "I was afraid you wouldn't."

I have to admit when couples are pitted against each other for various games, I'm glad I brought someone, too. I'm as competitive as they come, and apparently, Levi is, too.

Right now, for example, we're sitting beside each other on a small loveseat in the living room. We're ready. Eager. We each have a paddle in our lap. On one side are the words *I have.* The other side says *I have not.* I glance at the rest of the couples spread around the room. I have no idea how this game is going to go, but I'm excited to play.

"Okay," says Rochelle, the uber-organized hostess standing in the center of the room. "First question. And remember, you have to be honest with your paddles and score sheets. Here we go… Have you ever had sex in the backseat of a car?"

I don't have to even think about my answer. I lift my paddle and show Levi "I have." His paddle also reads "I have." Yay! Not that he's had sex in the backseat of a car, but because we both answered the same way. I give us a point on our score sheet for question number one. Couples get one point when their paddles match and zero points if they don't.

"Have you ever spent the night sleeping by the toilet?" is Rochelle's next question.

Levi has. So have I. We get another point. "One too many Madras?" he asks, remembering my drink of choice.

"No, actually. Tequila shots. What about you?"

"Sadly, no alcohol was involved that night. Or maybe not so sadly, since I have spent an hour or two praying to the porcelain god before, and it sucks."

"Explain," I say. "The sadly part," I clarify. I understand the rest.

He gives me a cute little half smile like he *was* about to explain the praying part. Smartass. "It was a stupid April Fool's joke."

I motion for him to continue. I need more info than that.

He sighs like the incident embarrassed him once, but it doesn't anymore. "Mateo and Elliot reversed the lock on my bathroom door, and I had to sleep in there all night. Made a pillow out of a towel and slept on the floor."

I laugh. "No bathtub?"

"No," he says with an affable grin.

Rochelle clears her throat. "Have you ever gone commando?"

Once again, Levi and I answer the same way. As I give us another point, I wonder if he's commando tonight. I picture him shirtless, wearing low-slung jeans, the top button undone, his arms out to the side with his hands gripping the doorframe to my bedroom. I'm lying on my bed, waiting for him. The image is so vivid, I startle when he says, "Ham?"

Shit. I missed the next question. "Sorry. What did she say?" I whisper.

"Have you ever been skinny-dipping?"

I have not. Levi has. Damn it. No point for us. "You've never skinny-dipped?" he asks incredulously.

Before I can tell him no, Rochelle says, "Have you ever eaten food that fell on the floor?"

I'm kind of ashamed to admit this, but yes, yes, I have. So has Pants Charming, which makes him even more endearing. We tap paddles. It's a paddle bump. "Five-second rule," we say at the same time. I'm around kids all the time for my swim lessons, so obvs. And he's got nieces and nephews, so it makes sense.

We also get points for the next three questions:

Have you ever faked being sick to stay home from school or work? Yes, we have.

Have you ever broken a bone? Nope, neither one of us.

Have you ever been awake for two days straight? Paddle bump!

"What did you just say?" Levi asks, the corners of his mouth lifting to a lethally sexy angle.

Fuck. I said "paddle bump" out loud. "I asked what kept you awake that long."

He tilts his head and drops his chin, an okay-fine-we'll-play-it-your-way move that earns him yet another smile from me. "Axl's birth. He's the first grandchild, so we were all at the hospital, and I couldn't leave or even close my eyes in the waiting room until I knew everything was okay. Amelia didn't have the easiest pregnancy, and her doctor had said the delivery could be difficult, so my mom was especially anxious. I kept her occupied by playing Words With Friends. What about you? What kept you up?"

"A bet in college with a guy friend. It turned into a big

fraternity-sorority thing with his friends bringing him Red Bull and mine bringing me Mountain Dew. He dozed off before me."

"What did you win?"

"Bragging rights. And he had to dye his hair our college colors, which looking back, wasn't even the slightest big deal. School pride and all."

"So you're a betting girl," Levi states, an unfamiliar note in his voice.

I shrug.

"Last two questions," Rochelle announces, drawing my attention. I'm kind of sorry the game is almost over. It's been fun learning more about my date. I mean Levi.

"Have you ever had a sex dream?"

My eyes meet Levi's before we show our paddles. A total accident. I meant to look somewhere else, but those milk-chocolate orbs are magnetic or something. It's annoying. And arousing. Because right now he's eye-fucking me. Does this mean his sex dream was about me? I hold his gaze. Two can play this game. I've had a sex dream about him, too. More than once, even. Take that, Pants Charming.

His eyes move ever so slightly to check out my paddle. "Looks like we get another point."

"Looks like."

"Who's gotten points for all the questions?" Rochelle asks, relieving me from Levi's hold. I look around the room. None of the couples answer. "Who's only missed one?"

"Us!" I answer.

"Us, too," Colleen says.

It's weird that we're tied with my cousin, since we're *so* not a pair, Levi and me. But the game really comes down to luck, nothing else. Levi and I aren't soul mates or anything. Colleen raises her eyebrows and shoots me a WTF look. *I know!* I shoot back. *Who would've thought?*

Rochelle straightens her shoulders. "Okay, then. Last question. Have you ever been naked with the opposite sex in public?"

I know for a fact Colleen has been to a nude beach and there were men there, because she told me in great detail all about their dick dangles. So, the question is, has George stripped with any females nearby? I'd bet my first-place medals he hasn't.

Once again, Levi and I make eye contact. His shine with amusement, and all of a sudden we're laughing. Softly at first. Then louder. Harder. We raise our paddles to show the room we've got this.

"What's so funny?" Colleen asks, her voice light even though her paddle doesn't match her fiancé's.

"Levi and I have been naked together," I manage to eke out through my laughter.

"When we were little," he adds.

"A lot," I giggle.

I've laughed more tonight than I have in a long time. It's nice. And as the party people around us stand, move about to grab another drink or more food, and fall into group conversations, the boy I learned to swim with keeps me to himself with talk of favorite movies. He rattles off film after film, who directed and starred in them, and how much they grossed. He asks me to name the one movie I can watch over and over again. *The Wizard of Oz*, I tell him. I've seen it at least a dozen times. When he talks about cinematography in both classic and present-day motion pictures, his eyes sparkle with passion for filmmaking.

Sometime after midnight, we say our good-byes to Colleen and George. As we walk out to the car, I've got the bottle of champagne Levi and I won. He opens my door, waiting until I'm seated to circle around to his side. He's been attentive all night. And I've liked it.

Before he puts the key in the ignition, he looks at me. The car's dome light is enough to see his face clearly as he reaches over to brush the pad of his thumb gently across my cheek. "You had an eyelash."

It's no less than the tenth time he's touched me tonight, but now that it's just the two of us in the small confines of his jeep, I shiver at the brief, innocent gesture.

"I had a fun time tonight," he says, pulling his hand back.

"Me, too. Thanks for coming with me on such short notice."

He turns the engine on, a smile evident in his profile. That I'm the reason for his happy face feels good. The last guy I made grin slyly like that was...

"You saved me from meeting up with Trixie, so I should be thanking you," Levi says, and I immediately latch onto those words. Trixie? Nanny Trixie?

"Oh?" It's the only word I can get past the lump in my throat. I hate lumps. It was obvious at the bar a couple of weeks ago that Trixie liked him. And how stupid am I to think tonight was anything other than a favor? I forgot myself more than once during the party, but I won't let it happen again.

"She's a nice girl, but she doesn't know how to take 'I'm busy' for an answer. Plus, she's friends with Kayla." He makes a left on Wilshire, driving us away from Brentwood.

His ex and Trixie are friends? Do they still see each other? I wonder how Levi would feel if he saw Kayla again. Pregnant. Or with a baby. She'll always be this weird, painful reminder of his past.

"Looks like I did you a favor tonight, too, then."

"You definitely did."

We stay quiet for a bit until I slip the bottle of champagne from between my legs and place it on the floor. We're about to pass the Electric Fountain, lit up and glowing in hues of green and blue, when Levi says, "I know it's late and we start shooting in what, eight hours or so, but you up for a little more fun first?"

I should say no and get a good night's sleep. Tomorrow, or rather today, is important, and after being sick last weekend, I need to be in top PSA shape. But one glance over at Levi, his hair tousled and sexy, his eyes alight with mischief, and I can't say no.

"What did you have in mind?"

Chapter Eight

LEVI

Sex. That's what I have in mind. I really want Harper in my bed. Or hers. Actually, the backseat of my car will do just fine, too. Anywhere I can get under that sexy dress of hers. She's had me semi-hard all night. She smells like summer, laughs like no one's listening, and she's got this way about her that keeps my interest nonstop. She's been a great distraction from thinking about what I'll miss at the seminar with Leo Gaines tomorrow. And it's that, combined with my desire to do something with her she's never done, that has me wanting to play a little longer before I take her home.

I make a quick left onto a small residential street off Santa Monica Boulevard, then pull a U-turn and park near the Electric Fountain. This late at night there's no one around the recently restored historic fountain illuminated by a changing pattern of colored lights.

"What do you say we open that champagne then skinny-dip in the fountain?" I ask, releasing my seat belt. That I'm dying to see her naked again might have something to do with my suggestion, too.

Harper searches my eyes for clues I'm serious. I help her out. "Unless you're chicken."

With a straight face, she unclicks her seat belt, picks up the bottle of champagne, and proceeds to pop the cork like a champ. She takes a swig, her full lips wrapped around the bottle, her eyes never leaving mine. My dick twitches as I imagine her gorgeous mouth sucking me deep. Full disclosure: I've been picturing this every damn night for the past two months.

"Your turn." She hands me the bottle as her tongue licks across her full bottom lip. If she's trying to torture me, it's working.

Our fingers brush when I accept the Dom Perignon, and once again, the small, effortless touch isn't enough. I take a small gulp of the sparkling drink, mindful I'm driving. When finished, I pass it back. "So, your cousin said something interesting to me tonight."

"Shit."

I laugh. The harder Harper tries to keep me at arm's length, the more her family tries to draw me in. "Since you're sitting at the head table during the wedding reception, she wanted me to know I'll be sitting with your brothers."

She chokes on the champagne. "What the hell? I never RSVP'd you were my plus-one."

"Your mom did."

Harper's head falls back against the seat, chin up, eyes closed. "That woman is impossible. I'll tell them you're not coming to the wedding."

"I don't mind."

"I do."

"All right. Whatever you want."

"That's it? Just like that, you're not coming now?" She

shifts positions, drawing her legs up so she's sitting on them and facing me. I hadn't noticed that she'd slipped off her shoes.

"I don't want to make you uncomfortable around your family."

"You don't do that."

"You sure? I think I do."

"No. You don't. Not even a little. But…"

"But what?"

"I did tell my mom I had a date so she wouldn't bug me about it. I was planning to find a random guy to go with me, so I guess since she thinks it's you…" She takes a drink, extends me the bottle.

I put my palm over my heart. "How magnanimous of you."

"I know," she teases. "Don't you forget it."

"So I *am* going to the wedding?"

"Yes."

The champagne tastes much better going down this time. It shouldn't. I'm walking a fine line here, but I can't stop myself. "Is green still your favorite color?" I ask. We continue to hand the bottle back and forth.

"That just came out of nowhere."

"The fountain flashed green, and I figure I should know a few more personal things about my wedding date."

She glances out the passenger window. "It's pretty, isn't it? And yes."

"Mine is brown, in case you were wondering."

Her eyes—my specific favorite shade of brown— reconnect with mine. "Netflix or HBO?" she asks.

I love that she asked me a question like that. Being a cameraman, of course I enjoy television as much as film. "Both are sick."

"I'm obsessed with *Stranger Things*."

"Agreed. It's awesome."

"Remember when we fed Milo cereal for breakfast?" She wipes the back of her thumb down the corner of her mouth to catch a drop of champagne. How she made the leap from television to cereal, I don't know, and I find myself wanting to figure out everything about her.

"Cap'n Crunch's Crunch Berries." It was my favorite as a kid. We poured my dog, Milo, a huge amount, added milk, and made a big mess on the kitchen floor when we overfilled the bowl.

"And it turned his tongue—"

"Blue," we say at the same time and crack up.

Harper's smile is radiant. Mesmerizing. A carefree and beautiful expression she doesn't share often enough. When she belches, very unladylike, she puts her palm over her mouth, mutters, "excuse me," and laughs harder.

The temperature in the jeep rises while we grin at each other. We laughed like this the night we slept together, and I'm pretty sure she's remembering that right now, too. She hands me the champagne then tucks her hands under her legs as she quiets. It's deliberate, like she's trying to keep herself from touching me. I stare at her mouth. Slide my gaze down her neck to the soft, delicate skin at the base of her throat. Continue the once-over to her round, pert tits. Her dress hugs every inch of her body in a sophisticated, sexy way that makes it hard to concentrate on anything else.

I lean forward, hoping my intentions are clear. I've been aching to kiss her full, pink mouth all night. I'm afraid if I ask, she'll say no, so I'm going for it.

She doesn't move, doesn't meet me half way. *Shit.* I'm about to pull back, when she cants her head, giving me the okay. Thank God.

Our noses touch first. Her long lashes sweep down. I keep my eyes open as our lips touch, tentative at first because

I don't want to blow this. She could change her mind, push me away at any moment.

Her lips press more firmly against mine, then she sighs in surrender, giving me the final go-ahead. I love the breathy sound so much, my control snaps. The champagne bottle slips through my fingers to the floor mat at my feet. I cup her face in my hands. The kiss escalates quickly after that. Tongue, teeth, and the taste of Dom mix with Harper's one-of-a-kind flavor. I lick inside her mouth, explore with long, thorough strokes, devour what is mine tonight.

I groan when her hands slip under my shirt. She's warm, soft…needy. She lifts the material up and over my head, momentarily breaking our connection. I'm ready to resume where we left off, but get mouth-blocked when she puts her fingers to my lips. "Let's do this," she says playfully, then opens her door to slide out of the car. "And bring the champagne!"

Operation Skinny-Dip is apparently in motion.

I'm out my door and chasing her down the short path to the fountain two seconds later. It's quiet and still, the air chilly. I try to recall if I have a sweatshirt in the backseat so I can wrap her up afterward.

She waits for me at the back of the fountain. It's a large circular design with a sculpture of a Native American man in the center.

"How many times have you done this?" She takes the champagne from me and sips.

I never thought drinking directly from a bottle was a turn-on until now. "Skinny-dip in general, or skinny-dip in this fountain?"

"In general."

"Twice." I've got my shoes and socks off and am working on my belt. "I was surprised to find out you've never done it, especially given how much you love to swim."

She puts the champagne on the tiled brim of the fountain

and shrugs. "This happens to be one of the few things I haven't experienced."

All of a sudden, I have a feeling there's a good reason why she hasn't, and it bothers me to think she's doing it now only because she doesn't want to admit defeat. "We don't have to."

"You chickening out on me?" Her tone is back to playful, and whatever pensive vibe I briefly got from her is gone.

I look around. It's one o'clock in the morning, we're alone, and while we're close to a pretty big intersection, I don't see a car, and I'm not about to give up the opportunity to get Harper naked. "No way."

"Good." Hands on the hem of her dress, she pulls it up and over her head. Her bra and thong follow. She gathers her long, wavy hair and ties it in a knot on top of her head. No modesty. No fear. She's wearing nothing but a silver locket around her neck. The piercing in her belly button sparkles. She is spectacular.

This is definitely the best idea I've had in a long time.

"Hurry up, slowpoke." She flashes me a quick smile, her tongue darting out before she spins around and shows me her incredible ass as she steps into the water.

I drop my pants and boxer briefs.

"Fuck, it's cold," she announces.

"I can make it better." I leap into the fountain, making a splash. She squeals and splashes me back. We're standing in two feet of water, so I figure the best way to warm up is to jump around and have a water fight. I tease her with "You splash like a girl!" To which Harper says, "I am a girl! You splash like a baby!" To which I say, "Is that the best you've got, Ham?"

After a minute, Harper visibly shivers. She's cold—not to mention, we shouldn't press our luck out here. The base of the fountain hides us from clear view of the main road, but there is a house a couple hundred feet away, and we haven't been exactly quiet. "You ready to run back to the car?" I ask.

"Yes!"

We turn so we're shoulder-to-shoulder to climb out of the fountain and immediately freeze. Standing a few feet away, arms crossed over a hefty chest, an amused but tough expression on his mustached face, is a police officer.

"Shit," I mumble and jump in front of Harper to hide her nakedness. She probably doesn't care, but I don't want anyone else seeing her.

"Fuck," she whispers from behind me.

I reach my right arm back to wrap around her waist and cover my junk with my left hand. She tucks herself against me, her tits pressed against my skin, her arms holding on to my middle.

"Why don't you kids put your clothes back on?"

"Yes, officer," I say.

I help Harper out of the water, trying to keep her from view. My back is to the officer, my focus on her and getting through this situation as quickly as possible.

In my periphery, I'm aware of someone else approaching. Then I hear laughter. And not just any laughter. But a familiar snicker I know well. I glance over my shoulder.

My brother-in-law, Tim, is standing beside the other cop, his arms crossed over his chest, and a big, toothy smile on his face. He doesn't usually work the graveyard shift, so I'm surprised to see him. Happy, too. Mostly. He'll let me and Harper walk, but no doubt I'll be the butt of the joke—no pun intended—for the next few family gatherings. Maybe more.

"Hey," I say.

He raises his eyebrows. "Hey, bro."

"You know these kids?" Officer First On The Scene asks.

"I know the male perp."

I roll my eyes. So it's going to go like that. I turn back to Harper and try to block her from view, but it's impossible to shield her completely. "That's my brother-in-law," I whisper, hoping to ease some of the anxiety on her face, but her eyes widen instead.

I watch as she slips her dress back on over her head. The stretchy material clings to her more than usual, given her wet body, and she struggles to smooth it down. She pulls on her underwear next then folds up her bra and holds it in her hand. "I'm good," she says quietly, but she isn't. Her lips are in a thin, disturbed line. Her breathing is a little ragged. For a girl who I thought didn't take anything too seriously, she is seriously upset right now, and I need to fix this.

"I'm sorry," I say sincerely. Really fucking sorry that I've made her upset. I pull on my pants, tucking my underwear in the pocket then stuff my socks in my shoes and pick them up.

"You kids twenty-one?" the officer with the mustache asks. He's holding the bottle of champagne.

I look at my brother-in-law. *Seriously?* my expression says.

"Yes," Harper answers.

"ID?"

"In the car," she says.

"You two know indecent exposure is a misdemeanor?" Mustached Cop asks.

I glare at Tim now. Joke's over, dude. Yes, we were skinny-dipping in a public place, but no harm, no foul, and if he doesn't say something to his partner in the next five seconds, I'm going to tell my sister, Hadley, about the time he—

Tim cracks up. The other officer, too. "Thanks, Dwight," Tim says. "I've got this."

"Did you see the look on his face?" Dwight asks. I assume he's talking about me.

"Priceless," my douche brother-in-law says. They must have planned this when my back was turned to shield Harper. Speaking of Harper, I glance at her. While I've relaxed immensely, she's still frowning. Her arms are crossed over her chest. She's shivering.

"Can we take this to the car so I can grab Harper a sweatshirt?" I ask.

"Absolutely," Tim says. Dwight walks ahead of the three of us.

"You're an ass," I tell Tim.

"And you *were* breaking the law, my friend."

"Are we in trouble?" Harper asks.

"Nah. Just wanted to have a little fun with my brother-in-law. Harper, is it? I'm Tim."

"Hey," she says.

We get to my jeep—the police car is parked right behind us—and I reach into the backseat for the sweatshirt. Harper quickly puts it on. It falls to the middle of her thighs, and I feel better now that she's covered in something more substantial.

"So, what preceded this case of indecent exposure?"

"Would you knock it off?" My eyes shift from Tim to Harper and back to my brother-in-law. Harper is mangling the bra in her hands. It doesn't take a genius to see that, despite our luck in this situation, she's still not happy about it. She wants this to be over with. I do, too, more for her sake than mine.

"Seriously," Tim says, his attention on me. "I didn't know you were dating anyone."

"We're not dating," Harper is quick to say. While true, it bothers me hearing her say it with such conviction.

"This isn't one of those bets with Elliot, is it?"

"No," I'm quick to answer this time. It's the truth. Skinny-dipping was all my idea. If I wanted to just sleep with Harper, I would have taken her straight home. That I didn't is something I'll think about later. "We were at her cousin's bridal shower and a game of Have You Ever led us here."

"So I can write this up as your first offense, then?"

"You're hilarious," I deadpan.

He grins. "Tell you what, I'll let you two go with a verbal warning."

Like I ever doubted that. My brother-in-law is a damn good officer and takes his job very seriously, but a quick skinny-dip isn't a big deal. If he'd caught me doing something really criminal, he'd have handcuffs on me. He'd hate it, but he'd do it. The guy is the most upstanding person I know. "Thank you, officer," I say respectfully.

"Don't mention it."

"Good idea." Let's definitely keep this between us and not my nosy sisters.

"Oh, I didn't mean *I* wouldn't be mentioning it."

"Tim, come on. Isn't there some kind of cop-offender confidentiality thing?" I know. Stupid question.

He laughs. "Even if there were, we're family." He wraps his arm around my shoulders. "And you know your sisters like to get all up in everyone's business."

Shit.

"Bring Harper home safely, then yourself." He gives a casual salute. "Good night."

I open the car door for Harper before going around to my side. Tim and his partner wait for me to pull away from the curb before they do. A second later, Harper breaks the uncomfortable silence between us and goes off like a firecracker on steroids.

"I cannot fucking believe you did this to me!"

"Me? We both agreed to this. *I* didn't do anything to you."

She rolls her bottom lip between her teeth. "You're right," she relents. "It's just…"

"Just what?"

"Your brother-in-law saw me naked!"

"He's a professional. I don't think he was really looking."

He absolutely was. Harper's body is a thing of beauty, but I don't think she'd appreciate me mentioning that.

She pushes me in the arm. Yeah. No. And all of a sudden, my emotions are up, down, and sideways, because I hate that Tim saw all her soft, tanned skin, her perfectly round breasts, her—

"He's going to tell your family."

"It's not a big deal."

"Not a big deal?" she practically screams. She fidgets in her seat, brings her hand to her mouth to bite her nail, then thinks better of it and drops her arm. "What is Brad going to think?"

Ah, that's what's really bothering her.

"He's not going to want me to be his ambassador if he finds out."

"Harp—"

"Do not tell me I'm overreacting!" Damn. I *was* about to say that. "This is my life we're talking about, and I really want this job, and now I've screwed it up." She stares out the window, tension filling the car even though her focus is outward.

"I'll talk to him. Make sure things are right."

"No." She turns her head to look at me. "Please don't. I'll figure out a way to tell him myself." Her body completely deflates. "This is the worst..." She trails off abruptly and angles her face away from me.

"Day ever?"

She doesn't answer. I reach over to take her hand, but she moves it out of my grasp. "I'm sorry," I say again, unsure what else I can do to fix things.

I feel like shit that this happened, but I didn't do it on purpose. And I get that she's pissed, but I can talk to Tim and negotiate with him to keep what happened to himself.

"Could you please just stop talking." Her voice is flat,

annoyed. She's not asking me. She's telling me.

The streets of Beverly Hills are deserted, so I've got her home a minute later. She spares me a glance over her shoulder as she opens the car door before I even come to a complete stop. "Good night."

"Hang on. Let me walk you to your door." The strain between us sucks, and I need to make it better.

"No," she says firmly. "I'm fine."

"You're not."

She pauses. "Okay, fine. You're right. But I need to be by myself right now, so please leave me alone." The door slams, and she's gone.

I watch her jog away until she's out of sight. It bothers me, letting her go when she's upset, and I have the strong impulse to chase after her. *She told you to leave her alone.* I'm usually the kind of guy who respects a request. But with Harper, doing what I'm told will get me nowhere. I'd rather fight with her than let her slip away.

My decision is made for me when I notice she forgot her shoes. The shiny gold heels are my in. She'd want them returned to her right away, wouldn't she? She may need to wear them tomorrow. Yeah, that's the stupid thing I tell myself as I climb out of the car.

She'll probably want to punch me when she finds me on her doorstep.

Wish me luck.

Chapter Nine

HARPER

I want to take a hot shower then climb into bed with my face buried in my pillow. Tonight was too much. Everything about it. Just. Too. Much.

Teague texted me earlier to say she was spending the night at Mateo's so I don't need to worry about waking her. I can leave lights on and bang around and not pretend that everything is okay.

I make it as far as the hallway when there's a knock on the door.

He came after me.

There's a second knock.

Shit. I've been standing here freaking out over the possibility that I've lost my chance to work for MASF, and unsure whether I want to answer the door. A big part of me is glad he's here. Another part of me is mad. I told him to leave me alone, and he didn't listen.

Rationally, I know it's not his fault we got caught skinny-dipping, but it's much easier to be mad at him than admit tonight was great. That everything about Levi is great, and I had a really good time with him.

Goddammit.

I open the door.

"Hey," he says. "You forgot these." He shows me my shoes. I'd completely spaced out about them.

"Oh." *That's* why he's here. I'm such an idiot. Our fingers brush on the handoff, thawing the chill in my hand, and I toss the heels somewhere to my right. They make a *thud* when they hit the hardwood floor. "Thanks."

"I thought you might need them for tomorrow."

It takes me a few seconds to respond to that, the tension at seeing Levi on my doorstep melting away. I think he's nervous. It's a side of him I haven't seen before. "At the pool?"

"Right. We're shooting tomorrow. So, that's not the reason I'm standing here."

"No?"

"I just really needed to see you one more time."

My heart beats faster without my permission.

"Not to make sure you're okay. You set me straight on that score. But to make sure you got inside safe and sound."

"I did."

"I can see that." He takes a step back. "And now that I have, good night."

"Wait! Do you want to come in for a minute?" What am I doing? Danger! Danger! He came. He saw. I got my shoes back. I was supposed to say good-bye after that. Apparently my brain doesn't care about permission, either.

"Sure."

He grazes my arm as he walks into the guesthouse. All these accidental touches make me want to throw caution aside and go at it on every surface in my house. I close the door and turn around to find him facing me, his arms at his sides. I lean back against the door with my palms flat on the wood behind my butt. Less than an hour ago we were naked together, so the memory of Levi's cut, lean frame is still very fresh in my mind. (And FYI, even in cold water, he's really well hung.) I had to fight the urge to run my hands over his chest and abs, drop down to my knees, and give him a blowjob. Thank God I didn't. "Fellatio in a Fountain" is not a story I want circulating around his family.

My unbidden thoughts remind me how much Levi protected me tonight. How he tried to hide my naked body from view and gave me his hoodie to keep me warm. Family or not, getting caught by the cops is cause for anxiety.

He moves closer.

He helped me at the fountain more than he knows. The last time I had to talk to police officers was when Joe drowned. One of the officers from that night had a mustache, too, and I was suddenly in my backyard again, watching them bag Joe's body and carry him away.

I hate those memories. Hate them so much.

Levi's care and safeguarding tonight got me over them quicker than ever before. I'd felt completely alone the night of Joe's accident, but tonight I wasn't isolated. Not for one second.

I think that deserves a proper thank-you. We both know I didn't invite him in just to talk. I push off the door, erase the distance between us, and when I'm standing right in front of him, I jump up. He catches me with a surprised but happy grunt as I wrap my legs around his waist, cross my arms behind his neck, and fuse our mouths together. This is more than gratitude. I want to forget, and he helps me do that with nothing more than a kiss. It's the reason I once again break my rule of keeping kisses to a minimum.

His kisses are earnest. Enthusiastic. They're openmouthed, delicious, and send waves of pleasure through me. Not to mention, his hands are warm and possessive. One is cupping my ass, the other is pressed between my shoulder blades to keep us anchored, and it feels so good. Having his hands anywhere on me feels so good.

I curl my tongue around his to savor the taste of champagne and desire, and slide my fingers through his soft hair. He's moving us somewhere. It could be anywhere for all I care, I'm so lost in his kiss. His mouth moves over mine with a sureness and a rightness that makes me dizzy, in hot need of so much more.

He sits me on the kitchen table and hikes my dress up so he can stand between my legs. His hands roam. They slip underneath the sweatshirt, up my sides, over my breasts, around the edge of my panties.

It's not enough. I'm desperate for skin on skin. I gently bite his lower lip to slow his wonderful invasion of my mouth. God, his unhurried kisses are just as powerful as his fast and furious ones. Maybe even more so because they feel like a beginning with no end.

Stay out of your head, Harper.

We break apart so I can lift the hoodie off. His brilliant light-brown eyes wander over my face and body for several charged seconds. I'm about to peel my dress off, but then he's undoing the knot on top of my head, freeing my hair to let the damp strands fall down my back and around my shoulders. He gazes into my eyes as he twists several ends of my hair around his finger. I hold his stare. He has this way of keeping me right here with him, unable to look away, even though a part of my brain is telling me to run like hell.

"I know you don't think so, but tonight was pretty perfect," he says.

"I can think of a way for you to make up the not-so-perfect part."

"Yeah?"

"Uh-huh." I start to undo his belt buckle. "It starts with fewer clothes."

He stills my progress, covering my hands with his and sliding his tongue back inside my mouth. I'm useless at fine motor skills when he kisses me, so I abandon his belt and simply wrap my arms around him.

We make out until we're both breathless, and Levi steps back. I could stare at his face for days. The square jaw, always covered in light stubble. Full lips, the bottom one just a little bit more so. Straight nose. Golden-brown eyes a shade darker than his hair, which turn downward the tiniest bit in the corners. Emotion sparkles in them, and I'm sure my own feelings of want and caring are reflected back. I blink to rid any warmness betraying me.

"I'll see you tomorrow," he says, surprising me.

"You're leaving?"

"Sleep calls. You have a long day in a few hours."

"Sleep here," I blurt out, then immediately wish I could take the words back. I hate that I sound needy, like his walking out the door will leave me lonely. It won't.

It will.

It won't. I'm used to being on my own. I *like* being on my own.

He pauses his backward steps. "I...I need to be ready for tomorrow, too. Next time?"

That's not the answer he was supposed to give after kissing me like he couldn't imagine ever stopping.

And who made him in charge of sleepovers? Not me. There is no way I am ever making that invitation again. Doesn't he realize how hard that was for me? "Probably not," I say with childish certainty. I'm over him. Over every single thing about him. I was happy before he walked back into my life, and I'll be even happier when we're done working together and I only have to see him occasionally because of

Teague and Mateo.

"I've missed my chance?"

"Yep." I know I'm not being reasonable right now, but it's that or admit my true feelings.

He is not supposed to smile at that. Why is he not eating his words and changing his mind? He reaches behind him to open the door. "We'll see. Sweet dreams, Ham."

I slide off the table, ready to push him out the door and slam it shut. "Oh, they will be."

"Mine, too. Later, gator."

"That's the dumbest good-bye ever!" I say as he disappears around the door. I immediately close and lock it. I'm mad and confused. And horny.

So horny. I march to the shower and take care of myself. That I picture Levi's hands and mouth on me while I do so is only natural. The guy is hot.

Nothing else.

Dear Harper,

Walking away from you tonight was one of the hardest things I've ever had to do. I meant it when I said it was a perfect night, and if I'd stayed, it would have been for the wrong reason, tainting our excellent time together. I've gotten myself into something I need to get out of before we go any further. Before I follow through on all the things I want to do to you. Because I want you to know that when I bury myself inside you, it's for no other reason than to bring us both pleasure.

There's another reason I backed off, though. I don't want emotions interfering with what we know is a physical thing. We like each other's bodies, and what happens when we touch, so having angry sex, or make-up sex, or whatever the hell it was we were about to do because of the whole police thing, isn't smart. I'm sorry you were put in that uncomfortable position tonight, but I am glad I was your first skinny-dipper. You're gorgeous, Ham. And so full of life. Did you know you shine brighter than the moon? You do. And that your tan lines are ridiculously sexy? They are.

So I guess what I'm trying to say is, give me another chance. You know you want to and that you won't be disappointed. (Remember how much you loved my cock?) We're fighting a losing battle if we think we can keep our hands off each other. Fate has brought us back together for a reason, don't you think? You probably want to tell me off right about now, but instead, tell me yes.

I promise to do that thing with my tongue you like so much.

Sincerely,
Levi

Chapter Ten

Saturday's shoot goes well. Copious amounts of coffee get me through the morning. A Mountain Dew at lunch gets me through the afternoon. For the most part, I ignore Levi. I do what I'm told, keep my distance from him during breaks, and spend extra time in the pool swimming laps or playing with the kids. Being in the water is my safe place.

More than once, Brad looks at me quizzically. Like he senses something is off. Something is. I feel like shit for disregarding his request not to encourage Levi. Last night I threw myself at the cameraman in an attempt to encourage all sorts of things. I'm angry with myself for acting so stupid and letting my emotions get the better of me. It was unprofessional. Out of character. Whenever I'm around Levi it's like I'm someone else. Someone I don't recognize or know how to deal with.

And since he's the one who put a stop to it, I obviously misread his signals. Only, that can't be right. He was definitely into me, if his kiss is anything to go by. His mixed signals are making me crazy.

Then there's the skinny-dipping incident. I don't want Brad finding out at a family dinner I got naked with his brother-in-law during the time we were shooting the PSAs. So I have to come clean. Soonish. When he asked for a sit-down next week, I decided that would be the perfect time to confess my R-rated indiscretion.

When shooting ended for the day, I took off without a glance back. I had to get to my parents' house. My mom makes a monthly family dinner for my brothers and me, and short of bleeding to death, there is no acceptable excuse for missing it. We sat around the kitchen table eating pasta primavera, and for once she bugged my brothers about their love lives instead of bugging me. I enjoyed every second of it—until she mentioned Levi's name, and how happy she was that I had a date for Colleen's wedding, and how maybe I'd catch the bouquet.

I might have spit my water across the table at that little remark.

Now it's Sunday afternoon, and my happy, in-love roommate and best friend's plans for a backyard barbeque and Ping-Pong tournament are in full swing. She's weirdly excellent at the sport and is soundly defeating everyone. Mateo is cooking burgers on the grill while watching his girlfriend with pride.

I'm lying on a lounge chair next to our friend Madison, soaking up the hot August sun. "Hey, how was your date the other night?" I ask her.

Madison sighs with despair. "It sucked. The guy talked nonstop about his T-shirt business and nothing else. He didn't ask me one question about myself." Two months ago, Madison left her cheating fiancé at the altar. This was her first date since then.

"At least you're putting yourself out there. That's huge, and I'm proud of you."

"Thanks. And get this—at the end of the date, he gave me one of his shirts. It said GILF on it. Like that was going to get me to agree to a second date with him."

I laugh. "Girl I'd Like To Fuck? You gotta give the guy props for going for it.'"

"I handed it back to him and told him to give it to a girl who found it complimentary rather than desperate."

"*Nice*," I say. "Any news on the job front?"

"No," she says, sounding utterly hopeless. "Unfortunately, planning one's own wedding isn't a very useful skill for a résumé, and even if it were, the epic failure of the wedding probably negates all the work I put into it."

I turn my head to look at her. "You'll find something. You're smart and kind and personable, and you just haven't found the right match yet."

"Thanks for saying that." Madison smiles and shifts her attention back to the pool. I note her gaze lands on Elliot and lingers. *Interesting.* He and two of my old coworkers from the coffee shop are standing in the shallow end talking with red plastic cups in their hands. Levi is in the water playing with Zoe while her mom, Abby, watches from a chair. Mateo's sister, Isabel, is floating on a raft in the deep end and texting nonstop on her phone.

For the tenth time, Levi's sunglasses meet mine before I'm fast enough to look away. To stop this crazy impulse to survey his every move, I put my chair flat and roll onto my stomach. "I'm going to close my eyes for a few," I tell Madison. I undo the string of my bikini top so I don't get a tan line, take off my shades, and sink into the chair cushion more fully.

I'm not sure how much time passes, but when I open my eyes I find Levi in Madison's chair. He's lying on his side, head propped in his hand watching me. "Hi," he says.

"Hi."

"Good nap?"

I lift my arms from my sides so I can tuck my hands under my cheek. I've no desire to get up yet. Staring into Levi's gorgeous butterscotch and gold-flecked gaze makes me half think I'm still dreaming. Yeah, there's no escaping him no matter how hard I try.

"Uh-huh."

"Guess what, Harper?" Zoe says, popping her cute little face over Levi's shoulder. She's wearing his sunglasses and a big smile.

"What?"

"I beat Levi in a race across the pool."

"That's awesome."

"He said I must have had a good teacher, and I told him you were my teacher!" She puts her small hand on his arm. "Maybe you could take some lessons, Levi. Harper, do you teach big boys?"

I can't help it. I grin. Levi grins. He hasn't stopped staring at me, which is both annoying and flattering. What is his deal? Today he's in the mood to shower me with attention? "No, I don't," I say, "but maybe I can make an exception for Levi."

"Zoe," her mom calls from around the pool. "Come get your burger, sweetie."

Zoe scrambles off the lounge chair next to Levi's. "Bye," she calls over her shoulder before skipping away.

"We should start as soon as possible," Levi says. "It may take me a while to learn everything I need to from you." His teasing is insanely attractive, and I do enjoy a good flirt, so I'll play along.

"What kind of everything are we talking? Freestyle? Breaststroke?"

"You can put those at the top of the list, yes." He traces his finger from my shoulder to my elbow, sending a zing of electricity through me.

I don't know what we're doing, but I don't want it to stop. He has a way of making me forget why I should keep my distance from him.

"My schedule is kind of full at the moment, so I'm not sure when I can *fit you in*." I really should stop flirting with him. Things were so much easier—and safer—when I merely tolerated him for the sake of our best friends.

"I can wait for *when*." His eyes slip away from mine to watch his finger trace down my side. "Especially since I know how tight that fit is." He needs to stop touching me.

I silently pray he never stops touching me.

"Your skin is so soft," he says, his tone seductive.

I close my eyes. I'll let him do this just a little bit more. Some tortures are sweet.

"You left in such a hurry yesterday, I didn't get a chance to confirm Friday's location shoots with you. Brad's got permits for the Annenberg Community Beach House pool and Stoner Park Pool in West L.A. We'll grab some beach shots, too."

He moves all his fingers across my back in a light caress that feels amazing. I think I maybe purr. In the past, when it came to guys, it took zero effort to forget about them. I'd have some fun and never give them a second thought.

Levi Pierce is impossible to forget. He's also maddening, infuriating, irritating, and the reason my body hums even when he's not near.

All excellent reminders to keep myself in check. "I've got lessons until two on Friday. Does that leave us enough time?" I reluctantly open my eyes. It takes me a moment to blink away the sunspots. "I'm sorry. I didn't realize that day was set already."

"I can't do any other day, so we'll make it work." He draws lazy lines and squiggles over my warm skin.

"You have another shoot?"

"Yeah."

"I bet the talent will be a lot easier to work with."

He laughs. "No doubt."

"Hey," I argue.

"I didn't say I liked easier better, Ham, just that I agreed with your assessment. At the moment, there's no one I'd rather have in front of my lens than you." His voice is soft and sun-drenched, the epitome of a summer compliment.

His looks, his attitude, his kind words—no matter how hard I try, I'm helpless against them. "I could probably reschedule my lessons so I'm done at eleven on Friday. Would that be better?" He didn't say my time constraint was a problem, but I'm thinking it is.

"It would. Thanks."

He continues to lightly rub my back, and I'm so relaxed my eyes drift shut.

"Can I ask you something?" he says.

"Sure." He's got me feeling very agreeable at the moment.

"Who drowned?"

My eyes shoot open. My heart jumps into my throat. He tried this once before and it didn't work. What makes him think it will now? I sit up, crossing my arm over my chest to keep my top in place. The quick movement makes me light-headed, and it takes a second for my vision to clear. Twisting I say, "Mind tying me?"

He finds the strings dangling at my sides. "I'm sorry. I didn't mean to upset you." The simple act of tying my swimsuit shouldn't feel intimate, but somehow it does. He's putting me back together slowly but surely, in more ways than one.

"You didn't. I just don't want to talk about it."

"I get it."

I spin back around. "What do you get?" For a moment,

I'm lost. Lost in his tanned, well-defined bare chest. I'd been so focused on his face while lying down I'd failed to notice his body. His nipples are round and flat, the color of cinnamon. A light dusting of freckles covers his muscled shoulders. My gaze dips to his abs. The muscle there is sinewy enough to look sexy, not burly.

He smirks when I look back up. Then he returns the inspection, running his eyes over me while I watch. I'm furious when my nipples point at him.

"I'm hungry." I start to stand.

"Me, too." There is no innuendo as he stops me with a hand to my wrist. I plop back down, my nerves mixed up because he obviously has something serious to say. "But I'd like to answer your question first."

"Go ahead." I look down at my lap.

He gently takes my chin between his thumb and finger, lifting my face to meet his warm, sincere eyes. "I know that you don't want me getting too close."

"Good. I'd appreciate not having to remind you of that again." I sound unfriendly and coldhearted and don't like myself for it, but I'm not going to apologize for being this way. This is who I've practiced to be. Levi's efforts are wasted on a girl like me. My walls are not coming down.

"Here's the thing," he says pleasantly, like my tone and disposition don't bother him in the least. "I think you need me."

"I don't," I huff.

"You do."

"Oh my God." I lean away from him so that he drops his arm. "I thought Mateo was the one with the big head. Boy, was I wrong. I don't need you. I don't need anyone."

A smug smile takes over his full lips.

"Why are you smiling at that?"

"You just proved me right. When someone says they

don't need anyone, it absolutely means they do and they're afraid to admit it."

"That's bullshit. It means I'm independent and happy to figure things out on my own." I put my sunglasses back on. I don't want him seeing any hint of the truth. That I'm the kind of hurt he can't fix. No one can. That he thinks I need fixing hurts, too. I'm good the way I am. Truly. It's only when I'm with him that I wonder if I am missing out.

"I'm not refuting that."

"Can we just stop talking, please?" I ask for, like, the tenth time over the past couple of weeks. I push to my feet.

He stands, catching me around the waist when I wobble from getting up too fast. Our hips line up, my chest brushing his. Tingles shoot down my spine. I can't read the expression on his face, but I know one thing for sure. The two of us together is a recipe for disaster.

Chapter Eleven

I could tell you I'm over my ex, but that would be a lie.

Not a complete lie. I'm over her in that I don't ever want to talk to her again. I don't ever want to see her again. And I don't ever, ever want to touch her again.

But I'm not over the feeling of betrayal. Of being used and discarded like I mean nothing. I trusted Kayla. Worse, I trusted myself when I was with her.

So whatever is going on with Harper and me is scary as shit. I've been telling myself the bet is harmless, but I don't think it is anymore. Kayla pushed me away and pulled me back, over and over again, and Harper is pushing and pulling, too. But it feels different. She's not doing it to hurt me. She's doing it to protect herself.

The problem is, if I let it go on too long, it will hurt. I know this, but I can't bring myself to walk away. She's the bait on a hook, and I'm the fish struggling between hunger and denial.

It's obvious whenever we're together that sex is something we can agree on, though, so maybe I should stop obsessing over what brought us to this point and just go with it. Only, for some effed-up reason, the thought of her treating me like a hookup and nothing more grates on my nerves. I think of her underneath me, my cock buried deep, her cheeks flushed with pleasure, and her eyes heavy with arousal, all the damn time. We didn't just screw the night we spent together; I moved inside her with slow, committed thrusts. She responded by grabbing my ass and moaning how nothing had ever felt so good. True that. My toes actually curled when my orgasm barreled down on me.

"You might want to do something about that wood problem, my friend." Elliot slaps me on the back, reminding me that, Jesus Christ, I'm at a backyard barbecue and there's a six-year-old present.

I step around the built-in bar to block the view below my waist. I walked over here for a refill on my drink, not a semi tenting my shorts.

"She's still not into you, huh?" Elliot opens a bottle of beer, pours it into his cup, and tosses the bottle into a recycle bin. "Can't say I blame her with that tiny pecker."

"Fuck you."

He laughs. "No, fuck her, or lose the bet."

"I'm calling off the bet."

"Too late to call it off now. But you can admit defeat and pay up." Elliot says this in a brotherly way, but he's bouncing from foot to foot, happy as hell by the prospect of winning.

The thing is, I'm fairly confident Harper and I will end up in bed again no matter what. The attraction is there a thousand-fold, and we like each other, whether we admit it or not. I said no the other night, but I'm not strong enough to say it a second time.

"I've already been with her." I'm not sure why I tell him

this.

Elliot chokes on his beer. "You slept with Harper?" There's a tiny measure of hurt in his voice, either because I hadn't told him, or because it wasn't him. I'm not sure which.

"A couple of months ago. Before I met her as Teague's roommate."

"Wait. Is she the girl you said blew your mind and then blew you off?"

"Yup."

We turn our attention to the Ping-Pong table where Harper is playing against Teague. It's no contest. Teague is kicking Harper's sweet ass. She's kicked everyone's ass, but Harper's is the only one I can't pry my eyes away from. Thank fuck she's wearing white drawstring shorts over her red bikini bottoms, or I'd be in more serious wood trouble.

I go on to tell Elliot how we knew each other as kids, too.

"So why does she hate being around you?" he asks.

"Good question." I wouldn't call it hate anymore, but there's always tension between us, and I have no idea why the fuck that is. What's that saying? There's a fine line between love and hate? Maybe she hates liking me, which still begs the question. Why? Who hates the guy who gives you orgasm after orgasm? *It's not you, it's me*, she said in the car the night Elliot tossed out the bet. I shouldn't have made light of it.

Elliot turns to look at me. "You want to find out, don't you?"

"Yeah."

"Bet's still on."

I'm about to protest when he continues. "Think about it. You're still not right, bro. Kayla's in your head. And Harper's not going anywhere, since she's best friends with Teague. So as long as the decision is ultimately Harper's, what better way to keep the relationship only about sex?" He scratches his jaw. "You're welcome."

"I can't believe you don't want the win right now."

He opens his mouth to say something, but before he can, a bright pink Ping-Pong ball hits him in the side of the head.

"Sorry!" Harper shouts. "My bad."

"You can say that again," Elliot calls back. He throws the ball to Teague.

Harper ignores his teasing and goes back to the ready position, bouncing from side to side. She's the hottest, most adorable thing I've ever seen. Until I glance down at her tits covered in tiny triangles of red material, and then she's the hottest, sexiest thing.

She catches me checking her out. My bad, but I don't care.

"Good luck," Elliot says with a squeeze on my shoulder before he takes off back to Harper's friends from the coffee shop. What the hell just happened?

I stay where I am to watch the Ping-Pong game. Harper and Teague talk smack and laugh the entire time.

Mateo bounds over to the bar to snag a couple bottles of water. "Hey," he says. "You good?"

"I don't know, dude. Girls are confusing."

"You mean Harper, don't you?"

I side-eye him. "Am I that obvious?"

"It's been pretty hard to miss. Plus, it's really difficult to tune out Elliot's chant about how he's going to win the bet with you."

"Why do we let him live with us?"

Mateo laughs. "We could change the locks."

"That would go over well." I rub the back of my neck. "I never should have taken the damn bet."

Something in my tone or expression makes Mateo put down the water bottles. "Talk to me," he says.

The guy does have experience with giving advice. He surprised the hell out of Elliot and me a few weeks ago when he told us he was the Dating Guy, morning radio's most popular advice guy on love and dating. He went by the name Bennett and used a British accent so no one knew his real identity. Meeting Teague put an end to his single life and an end to Bennett. Some new guy is doing the reports now, and he isn't half as good.

Teague belts a hit over the Ping-Pong net. Harper swings and completely misses it. "Jeez, Tea, could you hit that any harder?" she teases as she retrieves the ball.

I tell Mateo about my childhood friendship with Harper, followed by how we hooked up a few months ago. He admits he knew about our one night because Teague mentioned it.

"Oh my God, my aim sucks," Harper says as her ball sails into the pool. "But at least I got four points this time." She puts her paddle down on the table. "I think you're slipping Ms. Ping-Pong Princess." Zoe retrieves the ball and tosses it to Harper. "Thanks, Zo."

"So, got any advice for me?" I ask my friend.

"Follow your instinct," Mateo says. "And don't second guess yourself." The guy has known me since junior high and is smarter than all of us, so I'm taking the suggestion to heart.

And right now my inclination is to follow Harper into the guesthouse. "I'm just going to—"

"Go." Mateo lifts his chin in recognition, noticing where my eyes have wandered.

I let myself into the cozy bungalow and close the door. Harper is standing in the kitchen looking inside the refrigerator. Her ass is wiggling to a song only she can hear. I wonder whether, if I watch her long enough, I can name that tune. She hums a few notes, but I'm still clueless. I'm also acting like a total perv standing here unannounced.

"Hey." I step toward her.

She spins around, her hand flying to her chest. "Jesus Christ, you scared me."

"Sorry. Got caught up in the view."

It's often difficult to notice her flush with her sun-kissed complexion, but pink stains her cheekbones at my admission. "What are you doing here?" she asks, closing the fridge with her hip and abandoning whatever it was she wanted.

"Following my instincts."

Her eyes widen. She swallows. "And what are they telling you?"

I close the distance between us. "To talk less and act more." Fantasies of fucking her right here, right now, crowd my mind. The air heats, thickens, as does my blood when I notice her pulse flutter at the base of her neck. Despite our conversation earlier, for the past two hours we've been dancing around each other like it's foreplay.

She grips the edge of the counter, arms bent at the elbows. I like to think it's for support because I make her legs weak. When we're toe to toe, her chest rises on a slow breath. "By act you mean touch, right?"

"Do you want me to touch you?" I ask.

"No." Her eyes, glittering with lust, say otherwise.

I wait a beat.

"Yes."

"Turn around."

She complies without arguing, which tells me she's also operating on instinct and really wants my hands on her. Her surrender is potent, a gift I'll make good on until she comes all over my fingers.

I put my hands on her small waist and start with a kiss to the shell of her ear. The contact earns me a breathy sigh, and I imagine her full, pink lips are parted. Her head falls to the side, giving me better access. I breathe her in, the scent of sunscreen, chlorine, and woman filling my nose as I kiss under her jawline.

"Where? Where do you want my hands?" I whisper. Blood pounds through my veins in anticipation of her answer.

"All over. Please, Levi, touch me all over." She wiggles her ass against my front, making my dick instantly hard.

I slide one hand up to her tit and the other inside the front of her shorts. I run my finger over her stiff nipple while I cup the rounded flesh. The feel is sensational, and I'm pretty sure I could come in my board shorts just from playing with her tits.

She arches her back, pushing her chest up, seeking more from my fingers. I knead, pinch her nipple.

"I can't believe how good that feels," she says.

Then she switches tactics and tucks her hips, giving me better access to the space between her thighs. I rub over the small scrap of material covering her sex, feeling her flesh swell under my palm.

All day I've stared at her little red bikini and imagined taking it off her. I kiss the delicate slope of skin where her neck meets her shoulder as I untie the knot at the top of her spine. The material falls away. She moans when my hand returns to scrape over her exposed nipple while I simultaneously massage her clit.

I glance down her front. I fucking love her tan lines.

She grinds against my hand, inviting more. I'm happy to oblige and slip underneath the nylon of her swimsuit bottoms. Jesus, she's wet. I push a finger inside her, find the spot I know drives her crazy. My hands work in tandem while I suck and kiss her nape, her jaw. She's completely at my mercy, the sexy sounds she makes telling me she's enjoying this.

My hands work her inside and out until her body goes taut, and then she's moaning.

Vibrating.

Falling apart in my arms.

"Oh. My. God." Each word is ripe with gratification, with pleasure that fills my chest with pride. I like making her feel good. *This* is what we do to each other.

I slow my hands as she comes down from her climax. Once she's lax and I notice her grip on the countertop ease, I wrap her in my arms, nuzzle her neck, and say, "I really like feeling you lose control."

"I think you should do it again." She twists around and goes straight for the tie of my board shorts. No preamble. No delay. Everything in me tightens. I can't wait to sink inside her hot, welcoming body.

I lift her up onto the counter. Her quick fingers keep working on my shorts.

"There's a knot," she rasps, impatient with the strings.

My dick is so hard, I'm surprised it can't break the tie. "Let me help." I try to focus on the task, but her tight, gorgeous nipples are so close, I want to rub my tongue over them. I bend to take one in my mouth just as there's a knock on the door.

"Levi?" The door to the guesthouse opens.

I straighten. Harper's hands fly up to cover her breasts.

Teague peeks around the frame. Her eyes widen when she sees us. "Oh, uh, shoot. Sorry. I..."

"Get in here," Harper says. "Before you draw attention. Levi's decent."

She steps all the way in, her face red with embarrassment. "I'm really sorry to interrupt, but Cane's here, and I wouldn't have bothered you except that he can't stay long."

"Great. Thanks. I'll be right there."

Teague smiles and disappears, leaving the door slightly ajar.

A brief look of disappointment passes between Harper and me. If we hadn't been interrupted...

"Who's he?" Harper asks, tying her bikini top back in place.

Not wanting to share until I had something concrete, I haven't mentioned the guy to anyone. Teague knows because she set it up. And if it works out, I'll owe her a hundred favors.

"'He' is Cane Bertin, a professional kiteboarder."

Tiny lines crease the corners of Harper's pretty, dark, green-brown eyes. She wants further explanation. A weird tightness fills my chest at knowing she's so interested, but more than that, the ache is because I want to tell her. I reach around her to wash my hands in the sink.

"Teague set it up for me. When I told her I loved to kiteboard, she mentioned her brother, Luke, had recently photographed Cane. Cane is one of the best in the world, so of course I'd heard of him. I'd also heard he was getting a crew together to make a film in Australia. I jokingly asked Teague if she could hook me up, and she took me seriously and told her brother about me. Luke put in a good word, and Cane was interested in talking. He's in town for a couple of days and here to meet me tonight."

"Wow."

I run my hands over a dishtowel to dry them. "Yeah." What's really "wow" is Cane is Leo Gaines's best friend. What's that saying? When one door shuts, another one opens?

"That's amazing, Levi." God, I like when she says my name. "I hope it works out. How long is the shoot?"

"I'm not sure. A couple of months at least. I do know it doesn't start until November."

"Well, get out there and talk to the man." She grips my upper arms and turns me toward the yard, then swats my butt to move me along.

When we get to the door, I push it shut, turn *her* around, and trap her against the white painted wood. All of her tanned, luscious skin stands out. Her pink, pillowy lips, too. I take her hands in both of mine, raise her arms above her head, and crush my mouth to hers. She kisses me back, her fingers lacing tighter with mine as I press our hands against the door. We nibble, suck, taste. It takes Herculean effort to back away.

"Go out with me next Sunday," I say. We'll be done shooting for MASF then, and fuck, I guess I want to take her out. Dinner. Some flirting. Then my mouth on every inch of her.

"Like a date?" She's flushed. Breathless. "Because I don't—"

"You can call it whatever you want."

"I don't want you to think—"

"Look at it as prep for the wedding."

"The wedding! I forgot that was coming up." She thinks for a minute, like she's calculating how far away the big day is. "I can't next Sunday. My parents are having a pre-wedding thing at their house."

I do a quick mental rundown of my schedule. She seems semi-agreeable, so I don't want to let her off the hook. "Monday then?"

"That's going to be a really busy week, but the rehearsal dinner is on Thursday night." She bites her lip. "Do you want to go with me?"

Shit. I think I'm working that night, but I'll try to get a replacement. "It's a date."

"Not a real date."

I brush my lips over hers one last time. "It is if you want another orgasm."

Chapter Twelve

Cruising the grocery store aisles when hungry is a terrible idea. I came in to buy cumin, which is in the spice aisle, but my growling stomach led me down the cookie aisle, the frozen food aisle, and now the cereal aisle. A box of Cap'n Crunch is balanced precariously on top of my other extra food items in my hand-held basket.

One tiny forgotten essential to the chili mac and cheese sitting in a pot on my stove and I'm Girl Gone Junk Food Wild. It's not enough to combine two of my favorite comfort foods into one delicious meal. I need the solace of sugar, too.

That I was rude when talking to my brother on the phone earlier and he asked if it was "that time of the month" makes me grab a box of cinnamon Pop Tarts. Can't a girl just be hormonal over a boy? Yeah, I'm not just hungry. I'm *that* kind of hungry.

I delicately slip the box into my basket so nothing falls out. I've never needed food to make me feel better before, and I'm pretty irritated about it. Levi has me completely off my game. I can't stop thinking about him. Tomorrow's shoot can't get here soon enough. I miss him, and I'm mad about that, too.

The feel of his tanned, hard body against my back while he fingered me is still so fresh, my legs grow weak just thinking about it. *Stop thinking.* I shake my head and take a step forward, but immediately still. A chill steals over me even though I'm suddenly warm all over.

"Harper?" April says. "I thought that was you."

"Hi," I manage in return. Holy shit. April is two feet away. Close enough to reach out and touch. She looks prettier than I remember. She looks happy, for which I'm grateful. She also makes my heart hurt. I think I'm going to be sick.

"Hi." She wraps me in a hug, knocking the Cap'n Crunch cereal out of my basket. I quickly bend to pick it up. Bad move. My head gets light. My stomach roils.

I haven't seen Joe's sister since she graduated high school, a year before I did. She went back to Texas for college. Her parents followed shortly thereafter, wanting to be close to their only living child, among other reasons, I'm sure.

She and I were good friends until Joe died. Until I pushed her—and everyone else—away.

My throat feels like I drank glue, my vocal chords sticking together. She smiles at me with warm blue eyes that remind me so much of her brother's, I'm about to puke. Even after all this time, I can't look at her without sadness. Shame. Apology. I swallow to force down the terrible taste in my mouth.

Joe's family didn't once blame me. At least, not out loud. After a full investigation and autopsy, his death was ruled an accidental drowning. I wish it had been me to fall into the pool. I wish that so badly.

"How are you?" she asks amiably.

I clear my throat. "I'm good." I notice the basket in her

hand is filled with vegetables and bread. "Are you living here again?"

"Yes. I'm a physical therapist at the UCLA Med Center in Santa Monica. What about you? Are you done with school?"

"Yes. I'm…" I can't bring up swimming or anything to do with it. I just can't. I don't want to remind her, not that seeing me doesn't bring back awful memories anyway, but at least we can pretend to have a normal conversation for a minute. "I'm doing some charity work until I figure things out."

She nods. "How's your family?"

Shit. Fuck. My heart hammers. It's my fault her family isn't whole when mine is, yet she has the decency to ask that question. "Good, thanks. How are your mom and dad?" I adored Joe's mom with her southern accent and southern charm. She welcomed me with open arms and an open mind, always interested in my swimming and my thoughts on life. She liked to talk, something my mom didn't, and I often found myself sitting at her kitchen table for hours after school while I waited for Joe to get home from a practice.

"They're really well." She puts her hand on my arm as if she senses my discomfort. Of course she does. I'm sure the entire freaking store does. "Happy and keeping busy."

"That's good. Will you tell them I said hello?" And I'm sorry. Still so, so sorry. My mom's pained voice echoes in the back of my mind. "I can't imagine how devastating it is to lose a child," she said when she didn't know I was listening.

"I will. And I'd love to get together with you for coffee or lunch or something."

"Umm…"

"Here," she says, pulling a business card out of her purse. "Call me when you're up for it, okay?"

"Okay. Thanks." I tuck the card in the front pocket of my shorts.

"It was nice seeing you."

"You, too," I say as she walks past. Her parting words don't sound rote, but I have a hard time believing them. Strangely, I *am* happy I saw her—healthy, smiling, carefree. It sets a piece of my mind at ease.

The other pieces are still in distress.

I get my feet to move toward the checkout lines. Maybe Teague is right. Maybe the bitterness and pity from people who know about Joe and me is all in my head. But she doesn't know how many times I heard, "It's such a tragedy," and, "That poor girl."

If I could quiet the noise in my head, I would. But the shit there is powerful. *Except when you're with Levi.* He's pain relief and happiness, flutters instead of stings. But it's hard for me to accept those things when I'm not sure I can handle them beyond short bursts.

When I get home, Teague is stirring the chili mac and cheese. "Hey," she says, her back to me, "did you have to go to more than one place for the cumin?"

I dump my three bags of groceries on the counter.

Teague twists around. Her knowing eyes go soft as she nudges me out of the way with her hip. "Go sit. I've got this."

"Thanks." I sink into the couch. It's not often I let my best friend take care of me, but I'm tired. Really tired of keeping everything bottled up inside.

"Here." Teague hands me an oatmeal cookie a minute later. It's the soft, chewy kind. The hard ones don't taste as good.

I eat the entire treat. Teague eats hers. Then I say, "I saw Joe's sister at the store. She's living here again. I almost puked on her shoes."

Teague tucks her hair behind her ear and shifts to face me with her legs crossed in front of her like she's about to meditate. She got home early from work today and is wearing the cutest J. Crew top and black shorts. "Almost is better than doing it."

"She was really nice and wants to get together sometime." I pull out her card from my pocket. I need to get it off my person.

Teague places it on the coffee table for me. "That's not a bad idea."

I squeeze my eyes shut, but it doesn't help. A tear leaks out of the corner. Goddammit. Teague instantly folds my hand inside hers. She knows better than to make too big a deal of this.

"April took the first step, so maybe you can take the next one," Teague says quietly. "You're not to blame, Harp. It was an accident."

We've rehashed this so many times that I don't want to do it again. I love Teague, but I realize she isn't the person to help unburden me more than she already has. She's the perfect Band-Aid, but she can't give me a new perspective.

Maybe April can.

Or Levi.

He's opened up to me, and I know he wants me to reciprocate. My fear is that if I tell him about Joe, he won't look at me the same way—like I'm someone he approves of, a girl he likes to be around because she's worthy of his attention.

I brush away the moisture on my cheek. "When I get the ambassador job, I'll call her." That will give me time to work up the courage to tell her how I turned the worst day of my life into something good.

"How soon do you think you'll hear about that?"

"I don't know. I'm meeting with Brad next week, so hopefully he'll have some news for me." I need to find out something. My dad has been pestering me about his movie.

"Speaking of next week, I'll be gone Tuesday to Sunday instead of Wednesday to Monday."

"Abandoning me in my time of wedding need."

"*Harp.*"

"I'm kidding. I'm just jealous that you get to be in Costa Rica with your boyfriend while I'm trapped here in bridesmaid hell."

She narrows her eyes. "Did you just admit you're jealous I have a boyfriend?"

"What? No. I'm envious of your distance from the wedding." It's the truth. Maybe not the *whole* truth, but the truth.

Teague continues to stare at me. I break eye contact first. "You are," she says with surprise and joy.

"I am what?"

She traces tiny circles in the air with her finger pointed at my chin. I bat the gesture away. Undeterred, a slow, certain smile takes hold of her face. "It's Levi. Don't even try and lie. I did catch you guys in the middle of something last weekend."

"Would you lower your voice?" I have no idea why I ask that. It's not like Levi is hiding in the next room.

Her smile grows impossibly wider. "Oh my gosh! Harper! This is huge."

Yes, he is. The outline of his cock through the thin material of his board shorts is thoroughly imprinted on my mind. Not to mention, every time I even think about how he felt pressed against my ass, my sex clenches. I want him inside me so badly it's gotten to the point where my vibrator isn't enough to get me off. I need the real thing. And not just any thing. Levi's thing.

"Stop. It's not—"

"You're blushing. You're ducking blushing!" My roommate and "ducking." She can't bring herself to say "fuck" no matter how often I tell her she's a grown-up and it's okay. I cuss like a sailor. She talks like an elementary school teacher.

Maybe that's why I can never keep anything from her for very long. "Fine. He made me come with his fingers."

"Did you kiss him again?"

She knows all about the night I spent with Levi and the night we went skinny-dipping and she knows, to me, kissing is super personal. I don't generally let a guy lick and suck inside my mouth like Levi did, and vice-versa. "Yes."

"And you want more." There's no question mark in her voice.

"Yes, but—"

"No buts. Just go with it. As long as I've known you, you've only ever had lukewarm feelings toward guys who are interested in you. You need to explore these new red-hot waters with Levi. Who knows where they'll lead."

"Hopefully to fucking."

"Don't do that. Don't make it just about that."

"That's all I want."

"Wrong. You're just afraid to admit that you really like him and have more than a physical connection going on."

I run my finger over the frayed edge of my shorts. "It doesn't matter."

"It does. He matters to you. I know he does. And don't try to tell me that's bullcrap. I see the way you look at him."

"He's gorgeous. Of course I'm going to look at him."

Teague's eyes crinkle in frustration. "You know what I mean. He's more than good-looking, and after everything he went through with…" She trails off. Her eyes slide away from me.

"What? Say it. After the way Kayla treated him, he doesn't deserve to be treated badly by someone like me?" I pop to my feet and stride into the kitchen to stir the chili mac and cheese.

"No!" Teague is right on my heels. "You don't ever treat people badly, Harp." She wraps me in a hug from behind while I stand at the stove. "You have an incredible heart. But you only play it safe when it comes to relationships, and that can shatter the people who care about you."

"Exactly. Which is why everyone is better off if I keep my distance. Now can we please change the subject?"

Teague puffs out a breath. "You are really frustrating sometimes."

"I know," I say with apology in my voice, hoping that earns me some forgiveness for my bitchiness. Teague only has my best interests in *her* heart, and I appreciate it even when I don't act like it.

"Will you do me one favor?"

I don't answer right away. If I say I'm going to do something, then I do it. "Yes."

"Give yourself a pep talk once in a while. Something like, 'you're a good, kind person, Harper McKinney, and you deserve happy things.'"

Sounds easy, but I know it won't be. "Okay."

"Thank you."

There's a knock on the door. "Who's that?" I ask.

Teague shrugs. "No idea." She pads over in her bare feet to check it out. As she does so, the phone sitting on the counter rings. My aunt or uncle is calling.

"Hello?" I say into the receiver.

"Hi, Harper. How are you?" my aunt asks.

"I'm good. How are you?"

"Stressed! Hey, I just sent a flower deliveryman back to you. He's got a gorgeous bouquet for Teague."

As if on cue, my roommate squeals in delight.

"Thanks, Aunt Betsy. She just opened the door."

"Tell her Mateo has good taste, and we'll miss the two of them at the wedding."

"I will. I'll see you Sunday, if not before." We may live only a few hundred feet away from each other, but we rarely have a face-to-face.

"Sounds good. Bye, sweetie."

"Bye."

Teague deposits a gigantic vase of pink flowers on the kitchen table. Roses, daisies, and peonies in her favorite color equal delight times a thousand on her face. She plucks out the card. As she reads it, she blushes, and smiles so hard I bet her cheeks hurt.

I find some of the tension leaving me. I'm happy she's found someone who loves her and treats her like she deserves to be treated. It's the uncomfortable stab of jealousy in my chest I'm not so happy about. I've never been envious of my friends' relationships before. I rub my breastbone, wishing the feeling away.

"They're gorgeous," I say.

"They are. I love them." She puts her nose in the bouquet and takes a big sniff. When she lifts away, her eyes are glassy.

"What's wrong?" I abandon the wooden spoon I've been using to stir our dinner.

"Nothing." She fans her face with her hand. "It's just Mateo and I got in a fight this morning, and he wanted to apologize. Harp, I love him so much it's scary sometimes."

"I know." Hence the reason I will not let myself fall in love. I can't be vulnerable to hurt again. Can't risk losing someone. I won't recover a second time. "But he loves you, too, Tea, just as much."

She nods and takes in the flower arrangement again. There's got to be three-dozen blooms in there. I'm curious what she and Mateo fought about, but it's clear it doesn't matter, so I don't ask.

We take our big bowls of chili mac and cheese outside to eat. There's a tiny breeze that brings the smell of oranges with it. Our neighbor has a large tree that hangs over the fence. My aunt loves the free fruit and makes fresh OJ for my uncle on the weekends. As the sun drops away, Teague tells me about her upcoming trip. I'm grateful she's in a talkative mood so I can mostly listen. The pool glistens behind her, catching my eye often, and leading my mind to Joe.

And Levi.

Joe.

Levi.

Levi.

Levi.

It's not until hours later when I'm lying in bed that I realize he pushed out all thoughts of Joe. That's never happened to me before. Ever.

I cover my face with my pillow. I'm in serious trouble.

Happy Pants!
    *Because how can you not be happy when wearing HP's?
Go with me on this...*

    *Fabric so soft it feels like I've stepped into a tub of silk
and cashmere*

    *A secret pocket filled with a lucky gold charm—like the
stamped penny I got from the zoo when I was little and carried
around with me for months. I won the spelling bee that year!*

    *No matter how often I wear them, they never need to be
washed, so they never shrink and they always smell fabric-
softener fresh. They're also totally stain resistant!*

    *Other features worth mentioning:
They come in denim, white, and black.
They make my ass look spectacular.
They also make me look five pounds lighter.
Too tired to put on my PJ's? No worries. They can be
sleepwear, too. And they don't wrinkle!
They're never too tight, so I can eat all the junk food I
want.*

    *Name they go by: Levi's. Fuck. I can't even think about
pants!*

Chapter Thirteen

Levi

"I don't know what to do with you," Harper says.

It's a damn shame we're in public, because I can think of a few things.

She hides a smile, but she's got this expression—a tiny crease in the right corner of her mouth and a twinkle in her eyes—that I think means she's smiling on the inside, so I readily grin at her in return.

"I can give you a list."

"Really?" she asks with teasing curiosity. "And what would be on this list?" She sits across from me at the poolside table where I've been waiting the past few minutes. We're at the Annenberg Beach House to film, and I've brought her In-N-Out for lunch.

"If I tell you, I'll have to let you do them." We both unwrap our burgers.

She laughs. "*Let me?* What makes you so sure I'll want to?"

"Because you know I like to reciprocate." I nod to her lunch. "Got you a two-by-four, no onions, with an extra toasted bun to help it soak up excess burger juice, just how you like it." Two-by-four means two patties and four slices of cheese.

"You remembered all that?" We talked about our favorite burgers the night we spent together.

"I remember everything you've said to me."

That earns me another inner smile before she ducks her head and lifts the hamburger. "Thank you."

"You're welcome." We eat in easy silence, sharing the fries I pulled from the takeout bag and placed between us.

I've missed her the past few days, way more than is smart. The good news is I had a great talk with Cane Bertin last Sunday. We hit it off so well, I left the party with him to grab a beer and meet his producer. The film is a great opportunity to do something different, and I'm hopeful he'll want me to shoot with him in Australia. He's locking down plans in the next few weeks and said he'd be in touch. If I get the gig, I'll be on location for two months, which sounds great. It's exactly what I need.

We finish eating, and Harper leans over the table to kiss me on the cheek. "That was really good. Thanks." She stands, trash in hand, ready to toss it. "And now you can cross that off your list."

I'm pretty sure she means the barely-there press of her lips, which isn't anywhere near the X-rated activities playing shot-by-shot in my head. "No way, Ham. Cheek kisses don't count." Without thought, I grab her around the waist. She leans into my body like she's been waiting all week to get close to me again. It's not the reaction I expected, and I forget the kiss I was about to put on her cheek to prove my point. I aim for her mouth instead.

The kiss is short, but so damn good it takes super human

effort to pry my lips from hers. It's Friday, the sun is shining, I've come off a long four days of work, and all I want is to have some fun with this incredible girl, but duty calls first.

"Fine," she concedes. "That was much better than the kiss I gave you. But there will be no more of that. We're here to work."

"Has anyone ever told you you're bossy?"

"Maybe. Now, where to first?"

We start in the pool. The lifeguards help keep an area free of other visitors until we ask a few parents if they'd like their kids involved. I've got release forms with me and hand them out while Harper meets her young company. She's super vigilant with them even though they're all good swimmers. She's had a watchful eye on everyone in the pool since we got here, actually.

I get the footage I need, some of it choreographed, some unrehearsed. Sixty minutes of film I think Brad will be happy with.

Harper and I walk down the sand to the ocean next. There's no red bikini today, but her red one-piece reminds me of the female lifeguards from *Baywatch*, only Harper is way hotter. I'm hyperaware of her. Every accidental brush of her arm or meeting of our eyes makes my dick twitch.

And hell yeah, I pictured her in slo-mo, running down the beach.

"Have you ever lifeguarded?" I ask.

"I did in college. Went through the certification process my freshman year and worked at public and private pools until I graduated."

"Did you have to make any saves?"

"A couple." She visibly tenses with her answer.

I quickly try to lighten the mood. "Any fakers? Guys who just wanted your attention?"

That question doesn't help *at all*. She digs her feet into

the sand and stops abruptly. "Why would you even ask that? That's a terrible thing for a guy to do, and it could take attention away from someone who might really need it. I'd punch a guy in the face if he pulled a stunt like that just to get me to notice him."

"I'm sorry. I didn't mean to be insensitive. I thought I was giving you a subtle compliment, but I see how I screwed that up." I start walking again. I'm an idiot, given she lost someone close to her to drowning.

"I'm sorry, too," she says, falling in step beside me. "I didn't mean to be so defensive. It's just that I take water safety super seriously and don't like to joke about it."

"I get it. I was out of line."

"A little, but don't worry about it." She elbows me. "Let's forget about it, okay, and have some fun the rest of the day and with the rest of the shoot. This job means everything to me, and I've only got today and tomorrow left to prove I'm the right ambassador for MASF."

Fun has been on my mind, and if Harper's relaxed she'll come across much better on camera. "Fun it is," I say.

I set up my tripod and light kit in the hard-packed sand out of reach of the tide. When I'm ready to shoot, Harper does cartwheels, writes *Be water safe!* in the sand, and skips in and out of the waves. She's playful, energetic, dazzling. She makes my job easy. Once we get everything I think Brad wants, we hop in our cars and she follows me to the Stoner Park pool.

"This place is great," she says as we enter through the wrought-iron gate surrounding the pool area. "I had no idea this was here until Brad mentioned it."

The setup is sweet. Half the pool is a traditional design with deep water and laps designated for swimming, while the other half is designed like a water park—shallow with a slope entry. There's a giant sprinkling mushroom and several smaller, colorful shapes that spout water. Take a few steps across the concrete and you can ride down a bright blue waterslide into a small pool.

For families who don't have a swimming pool in their backyard, or can't afford trips to the large SoCal waterparks, the facility is available for a couple of dollars. Two lifeguards stand watch on their chair towers.

Harper gives me some scripted dialogue with the pool in the background then I set her free to share her own words as she wades around the spraying structures. She recruits some kids with their moms' permission, and I shoot over an hour's worth of footage.

We finish at closing time for the public facility. Once I have my gear put away, I pull off my shirt. It's my turn to get wet.

"Thanks again for your help," I tell the lifeguards standing with Harper at the pool's edge. Then I scoop her into my arms and carry her toward the mushroom.

"Hey!" she protests, but wraps her arms around my neck.

"You were amazing today," I say. "Everything you said and did, and the way you interacted with the kids, especially with that teenage boy, was fantastic. His entire attitude changed after you talked to him."

"He really listened, didn't he?"

"You're an easy person to get caught up in."

She touches the tip of her nose to mine. "Is that so?"

"It is."

"Hmm. Are you going to do something about it?"

"This." I step into the spray of water raining down from the mushroom. Harper squeals at the initial cold shock. I suck in a breath. The sun is on the downslide, so we weren't exactly in need of a cool shower.

Once we're on the other side of the stream, cocooned by a three-hundred-sixty-degree sheet of water, Harper slides down my body. She gazes up at me, droplets clinging to her eyelashes, a look of admiration on her face.

"You were amazing today, too, you know."

"You think so?"

"Uh-huh." She traces a finger down the center of my chest. "I like how you operate your equipment."

It's too bad we aren't hidden from view, because I'd like to insert my equipment into hers. She glances down, noticing the power she has over me. It's ridiculous how often I think with my dick when I'm around her. Her eyes jump back to mine and lock. I slip into their depths and back to our night together, when we clicked in a way I never have with anyone else. The teasing. The talking. The laughing. The phenomenal sex.

I groan when I feel her hand on my cock over my board shorts. My shaft thickens. Fuck, that feels good.

"Let's get out of here." I lift her wrist, my dick protesting instantly.

"Where to?" she asks, lacing her fingers with mine as we step through the water.

"My house is closer." I've dreamed about having her in my bed, her hair fanned out on my pillow, her arms above her head as I thrust inside her. I adjust myself inside my shorts. This isn't about the bet anymore. It's about her and me.

"Closer is good," she practically purrs.

We dry off with the same towel while sharing intense, appreciative glances. Her body is lean but curvy in the right places. I could admire it all day. She slips on a sheer white cover-up and adds Chap Stick to her luscious lips.

"I hope Brad likes everything we shot today," Harper says on the walk to our cars.

"I'm sure he will."

"I know PSAs aren't your usual thing, but do you think these will stand out and get the campaign the kind of attention

Brad has in mind?"

"I think they're going to blow every other PSA out of the water."

She chuckles. My pun worked.

"They're going to be different than your run-of-the-mill public service announcements and that's Brad's intention," I continue. "Any time something is different, it gets noticed. Not to mention, he's got the hottest swimmer alive delivering his message."

I load my gear into the back of the jeep, and I'm about to walk her to her car when my phone buzzes with a text. I glance at the screen. It's Cade, so I pull up the full message. He wants to know if I can send my demo reel to him tonight. Shit. I thought I had a little more time to finalize it. The pro athlete is taking a chance on a guy like me with zero documentary experience. I think that's part of my appeal, though. Like Brad, Cade wants something different. And I really want this job, so...

"Sorry. It's Cade. He needs me to send him a demo of my work right away," I tell Harper.

"Oh. Okay. I guess I'll see you tomorrow then." She twists around, but I catch her before she takes a step. There's a sudden chill in the air I don't like.

"Hey."

Her teeth dig into her bottom lip.

"You should be really proud of what you did today."

She slips her arm from my hold, slides her hand into her bag. "Thanks."

I snag her key fob from her fingertips, unlock her car, and open her door. She climbs into the driver seat. "Good luck with the demo," she says.

It feels weird between us as we exchange pleasantries like acquaintances, but I don't have time to fix the problem, whatever the problem is. I obviously wanted this night to go differently.

"Drive safely," I tell her.

"You, too."

With Friday night traffic, it takes me forty-five minutes to get home. When I pull onto the driveway, my stomach clenches in dread and alarm. There's a familiar white car parked at the curb. I contemplate backing out and speeding away, but Kayla's already out of her car and standing at the end of the drive waiting for me. I'm not surprised my ex is ambushing me here. She knows Mateo and Elliot hate her and will get in the way of whatever she's come to tell me.

"Hi," I hear her say as I hop out of the jeep.

I stumble when I look at her. She's wearing a long, light blue cotton dress, and my eyes dart right to her rounded stomach. She's got to be around six or seven months pregnant now. For a minute, I'm back in high school closing my eyes at night and wondering what she looks like with my baby growing inside her. Did she look like this?

I shake the unwelcome memory away.

"Hey." I keep several feet between us.

"How are you?"

"I'm good. You look well." I might loathe her, but I can be nice.

She drops her head and rubs a hand over her belly. "Thank you. This pregnancy hasn't been as easy as—" Her focus jumps back up to me. "Thank you."

I knead the back of my neck. "What's up, Kayla? Why are you here?"

"I need your help."

"Sorry. I'm not available to help you anymore. That's the guy who knocked you up's problem."

"What if I told you that was you?"

I flinch like she slapped me in the face. "It's not me." What the fuck kind of game is she playing now?

She takes a step onto the driveway. "It could be."

"No. It can't. We were broken up when you got pregnant." I back away. She has this ability to trick me into believing untruths. "I need to get inside, and you need to work your shit out with your boyfriend."

"Husband."

"Congratulations." I breathe a sigh of relief. That is the best piece of news she's ever given me.

"He's leaving me."

"Not my problem." Does it make me a pussy that I want to scream for Mateo or Elliot to come outside and help me get away from her?

"I can't do this by myself again, Levi. I just can't." Her bottom lip starts to tremble. Tears fill her eyes. "I told him about us, and that's why he's leaving."

"What are you talking about?"

"He didn't know about the couple of weeks you and I got back together, and now he thinks the baby might be yours."

"The baby is not fucking mine!" My body is shaking. It's been months since I've seen Kayla, and I want her gone. I want to rewind the last five minutes and drive past my house when I see her car. She has no right to stand in front of me and plead despair. She is fucking crazy if she thinks I'm going to buy into her web of lies again. "Sorry," I say. She's cowering, and that wasn't my intention. "I didn't mean to yell."

"What's going on?" Elliot says from behind me.

I look over my shoulder and whatever my best friend sees on my face must be bad because he steps between Kayla and me. "I told you never to come back here again. Get in your car and go. Now."

"This doesn't concern you, Elliot," she says, swiping a tear off her cheek.

"Levi *is* my concern, so go back where you came from and leave him the hell alone."

"You'd send a pregnant woman away?"

"Do you need me to drive you? Let's go." Elliot takes Kayla by the elbow and steers her toward her car. He'll do it. He'll drive her away to save me further grief and then take an Uber back.

She wrenches free and jogs up to me. Her arms go around my neck. I'm stunned by how fast she moved, but not by how much I hate having her body up against mine. The feel of her swollen stomach makes my skin crawl.

"Levi, please. We need to talk."

I gently grab her arms at the same time as Elliot, and we pry her off me. "We don't, Kayla. Talk to your husband."

Elliot's eyes go wide when he hears that. He keeps a hold on her and has to practically drag her to her car. She shakes her head and shouts at me. "Levi, I still love you!" "Please don't do this!" "This could be our baby!" "We're not over!"

Lies. All of it. She's fucked things up with her husband and thinks she can come running back to me. I scrape both my hands over my head and watch Elliot put her in the driver's seat. He says something to her I can't hear, but she settles down then closes the door and drives away.

"You're not moving out," Elliot says when he reaches me. How did he know I was thinking that? "I took care of it."

"How?"

"I told her the next time she showed up here, I'd call the police, and it didn't matter if she was pregnant or had a baby in her arms. I also informed her you'd get a restraining order. She's fucking crazy, man. You can't believe anything that comes out of that girl's mouth."

That's what scares the shit out of me.

Dear Harper,

When I was ten years old, I had a pet turtle. My dad put together an aquarium for her. She was semiaquatic so we put a big rock in her enclosure, a heat lamp to keep her warm, and of course, water so she could swim. She liked to eat lettuce, carrots, and mealworms, and she liked it when I fed her in the grass in the backyard.

I could watch her swim for hours. Just like I can watch you.

I know that sounds weird. But I got her during a time when I needed a friend. My grandfather had passed away, and it hurt how much I missed him. Spending time with my turtle helped.

The past few months have been a different kind of hurt, but from the moment we reconnected, being around you has helped. This is probably the worst analogy ever, but you have to admit it's an interesting coincidence that the two things that have helped me the most both love the water. For the record, you are much better looking, softer, and smell better.

Right now you're probably asking yourself, "Is he drunk? High?" The answer is a little of both. But if your ex showed up saying shit you didn't want to hear, you'd need a mental break, too. I hate her, Ham. Really hate her. Does that make me a bad person? That I didn't see what kind of girl she is makes me doubt every decision I've ever made.

My chest feels like she's kicked me in the balls all over again. I know my balls aren't in my chest, but you get my drift, right? Of course you do. Because there's something about you that makes us copacetic, or whatever that word is that means like-minded.

Sincerely,
Levi

Chapter Fourteen

If not for Colleen, I wouldn't be here.

My emotions have been so jumbled up lately, that this is the last place I want to be right now. Sunday brunch is in full swing, with thirty or so close friends and family members gathered to celebrate Colleen and George. I sit at a linen covered table on the grass and stare at the smooth surface of the swimming pool. Big floating flower balls of white roses decorate the water, making it something different. Something beautiful. Ever since the night Joe drowned, whenever my mom entertains out here, she includes the flower balls, as if adding something pure and simple will erase the ugliness of what happened.

It helps her forget, and she hopes it helps me, too, so I tell her it does.

"Here you go," Colleen says, taking the seat next to me. She passes me a mimosa in a champagne flute.

"Thanks, Leelee. Cheers." I clink my glass to her pure

OJ filled crystal.

"Cheers."

"So, this time next week you'll be a married woman."

"And on a plane to Cabo thanks to Teague. She arranged the most amazing trip, and I can't wait to get away with George. The past month has been insane, and my mom and I are about ready to strangle each other."

"You should've eloped to Vegas."

"And rob my mother of throwing her only daughter a wedding? I'd be dead," Colleen says with mock outrage.

I flinch at that last word. Rather than let my cousin see how her innocent comment unnerves me, I down my mimosa.

"Are you okay?" she asks.

So much for hiding my heartache. I plaster on a fake smile. "Yeah. I'm a little warm, that's all." The weatherman did predict a heat wave for the next few days.

Colleen lays the back of her hand on my forehead. "You don't have a fever."

"Thanks, Mom," I tease. "This is a sun issue." And location issue. I don't have a problem being inside the house. Good memories live there, strong enough to push away fleeting moments of grief. But I'm at my limit for sitting poolside.

Snapshots of the night Joe drowned start to seize me, and wherever I look, I can't erase them. I jump to my feet. "I'm going to grab some water. Can I get you one?"

Colleen's attention moves across the grass as she rises. "Please."

"Help!" someone shouts. "I need help!"

My heart leaps inside my chest. I follow Colleen's gaze. Benjamin, my uncle's business partner's son, is slumped over at the edge of the pool. His feet are in the water, and his mom is hugging his back to her chest. Ben is a teenager.

I don't think. I run to their side. Muscle memory takes

over. It's been a while since I've had to rescue someone, but I'm trained to take action. I gently pull Ben from his mom, laying him back on the ground then pulling his feet out of the water so he's in a face-up position with his legs straight. I scan the area to make sure it's safe and no one is in jeopardy of falling into the pool. "Ben? Are you okay? Are you okay?" I tap his shoulders and get no response. "Did you see him pass out?" I ask his mom. "Was he eating anything? Feeling okay earlier?"

"He was f-f-fine," she says between a sob. "I saw him with a handful of grapes a few minutes ago, and I came over because I noticed he was clutching his throat."

I check for a pulse and breathing and find neither. Looking up, I see my brother, Carson. "Call 9-1-1," I tell him.

"On it," he says, standing above me with his cell phone in hand. Carson explains the situation to the emergency dispatcher as I open Ben's button-down shirt and start chest compressions. I'm aware of more people surrounding us, more concern, more whispers.

"Tell them he's unresponsive, and I've started CPR," I say. I count my compressions out loud. When I get to thirty, I open the airway to give breaths, but before I do, I look in the back of his throat for a grape. Seeing nothing, I give two breaths then repeat compressions.

"Twenty-eight, twenty-nine, thirty." I open the airway, look inside his mouth again. Nothing. Give two breaths.

I continue with another round, and this time when I look in the back of his throat, I see a grape. I do a finger sweep and get the object out. Ben makes a sound and blinks his eyes open.

Relief swamps me. I help him sit up. The next few minutes go by in a haze. Ben's parents can't thank me enough. Other friends and family give their support and praise. I'm stuck in the middle of a small crowd, and I break out in a cold sweat. I need to escape before I have a panic attack in front of everyone. All of a sudden, I'm back to the worst night of my life.

I come to with pain on the side of my head. Pushing up, I lightly rub my fingers across the sore spot. Lying next to me is a big decorative rock with the words SOAK UP THE SUN written in bold black letters. I must have hit my head on it. I blink away my confusion then glace down at myself. I'm half undressed. It all comes back to me.

Joe!

Frantic, I look around, praying his big, beautiful body is beside me, but it isn't. My gaze rushes to the pool, and I choke back a scream. Joe is floating in the water, facedown. I hurry to my feet, swaying with dizziness, but don't care. Oh God. Please, please, please. *I jump into the water. "Joe! Joe!" He's in the deep end, so I'm unable to stand. My head is throbbing. My heart is pounding. I turn his body over. "Joe!" He doesn't respond. I have no idea how long he's been in the water, but his face is sickeningly pale. I don't think he's breathing.*

I kick as hard as I can and swim with him toward the shallow end. "Joe." My voice is raspy, my limbs tired. Once my feet touch the bottom, I check for a pulse. There isn't one. "Joe, Joe, please wake up." I'm crying. Bawling. I need to get him out of the water and start CPR.

"Harper?" I'm vaguely aware of someone saying my name. Where am I? I'm not at the pool anymore. I'm in my room...

I can't stop shaking. My hands, my shoulders, my legs, my lips, my whole body won't stop trembling. I don't know what to do about it. I wrap my arms around myself, but I still keep shivering. How long will I be stuck like this?

"Here, sweetie," my mom says, returning to my bedroom with a glass of water and a sleeping pill. I didn't know she took them until five minutes ago. She's given me no choice in

the matter. She says it will help my body shut down after the traumatic event I just experienced. I wish it would erase my memory, too.

She sits beside me on the bed and watches me swallow the sleep aid. I can barely get it down, my throat is so raw from the screams and sobs I couldn't stop until she brought me inside the house.

Joe drowned.

I am never going to see or talk to him again.

Never touch, laugh, kiss, or smile with him again.

The pain of that is unbearable. My heart is shriveling. With each passing minute, the beats wither. I think that's why I'm not crying anymore. Or talking. I don't have enough energy.

Mom takes the glass from my hand and helps me to lie down. She tucks the covers around me, kisses my forehead, and says she loves me and will be back to check on me. She turns out the light, but leaves the bedroom door open. She walks down the hallway, looks over her shoulder toward my room, then goes down the stairs.

I curl into a ball. When will I stop vibrating with sadness and hate? I did this. It's my fault Joe is dead. He wanted to come up to my bedroom to have sex, but I said by the pool would be more romantic. As usual, he let me have my way.

And now he's gone.

"Harper? Hey." There's a hand on my shoulder, puncturing the bubble I'm in. "The paramedics are here."

I blink back into focus. Everything is bright again. Colleen helps me to my unsteady feet. Sweat trickles down the middle of my back. It's hard to breathe. "Go," she whispers. "Get out of here." One look and she knew I needed to disappear. I slip away from the scene. I'll call my mom later to apologize for leaving early.

The pain from that night follows me to my car and I hate

it. Normally, I can cope, but today got to me. Ben got to me.

Instead of driving the few blocks home, I find myself driving the few miles to Levi's. He seems to be the only one who can help relieve my grief, and having his strong arms around me sounds really good right now.

I'm halfway up the walkway to his house when the front door opens. Elliot is on his way out. "Hi, Harper," he says, surprised to see me. "What are you doing here?"

"Hi. Is Levi home?"

"That depends. What are you here for?" His tone is lighthearted, but I'm in no mood for jokey Elliot.

"Is he here or not?" I snap.

"Yeah. He's in his room." He looks at me funny then reaches behind him to push the door open. "Go on in."

"Thanks. Where are you off to?" I ask nicely. I hope it makes up for snapping at him.

"The job from hell at the moment."

"Don't work too hard," I say as I pass him into the house.

"Yeah, that's not going to happen, but thanks."

I venture down the hallway to the open doorway of Levi's bedroom. He's sitting on his bed with a laptop on his outstretched legs. His back is against a leather-upholstered headboard. His head is down. He's wearing eyeglasses and concentrating on something so he doesn't notice me. For a few uninterrupted seconds I watch him, the only sound his fingers on the keyboard.

When he senses me and lifts his head, I'm at a loss for words. He is super sexy in his black-rimmed eyeglasses. I have a thing for guys in glasses. It elevates their irresistible status. Add in the stubble that lines Levi's jaw, chin, and upper lip, the dirty blond hair that is standing up in every direction, and if I were wearing socks they'd be knocked off.

He blinks like he's not sure I'm real.

"Hi," I say nervously. Which is unlike me, but I remember

how Levi acted really weird during yesterday's shoot. He was much quieter than normal and didn't make eye contact like he usually does. When I asked if he was okay, he said a simple "yes."

"Hey."

"If this is a bad time, I can go." I take a step back.

"No." He sets his computer on the bedside table. "Stay."

That's all I need to hear. I slip out of my heels, shut the bedroom door, and tiptoe to the bed. Without another word, I climb next to him and lay my head on his chest, my arm over his stomach. He scoots us down so we're lying flat. Wraps his arm around me and holds me close.

I squeeze my eyes shut so I don't cry. This is exactly where I want to be, cocooned against Levi's warm body. For a long time, we don't say anything. I think I doze off for a few. He makes me forget, takes me somewhere outside myself where it's just him and me.

"What are you working on?" I ask in the comfortable silence.

"Brad asked me to edit some of the footage we shot yesterday."

"You're an editor, too?"

"I'm not too bad at it, especially when I've got beautiful talent to work with."

I smile because he can't see me.

"I feel you smiling, Ham."

Damn it. "Can I see what you've done so far?"

"No," he says calmly.

"*No?*" I push up and glare at him.

A smile dangles on the corner of his lips. And God, I love how his eyes turn slightly downward. He took his glasses off at some point while we were resting, so I'm blessed with a clear view of golden-brown tenderness fringed with dark lashes.

"Brad would kick my ass if I showed you, because your opinion doesn't hold any weight, and I mean that in the nicest possible way. His decisions are the only ones that matter, but I promise you're going to like the results."

I stick my tongue out at him then rest the side of my face on his chest again. I guess that makes sense, even though I don't like it. I've got everything invested in these PSAs, since this morning I turned down my dad's job offer. After he cornered me at brunch, ticking off reasons why he wants me to be part of his company, I lost all patience. If I give him even an inch, he'll take a mile. He'll force his beliefs and thoughts and rules down my throat until I choke on them, thus killing any affection I have for the man.

To say he was angry would be an understatement, but he had to get over himself quickly because of all the guests arriving. I'm not sure where this leaves the two of us, and that's my bad, given this week is filled with wedding stuff for Colleen and I have to be around him more than usual. I let out a deep, audible breath. My timing could have been better.

"Trust me," Levi says, clueless to the real reason for my heavy sigh.

"I do." The admission causes a quiver in the pit of my stomach.

"Talk to me, then." He softly rubs my arm. "Why are you here, Harp?"

I don't answer him.

"I overheard someone once say it's better to err on the side of yes," he says. "I get being cautious, but I promise I won't hold anything you tell me against you."

Maybe he won't. Maybe he'll say all the right things, or say nothing at all and hold me tighter. The reasons I stay guarded, though, have nothing to do with him and everything to do with me. If I do this, if I let him in, then I can't hide behind my fear anymore, can I? When I push him away, or pretend none of whatever is happening between us matters beyond a good time in bed, he'll know better.

"I have a better idea." I sit up and straddle his hips, hiking my sundress up so he gets a peek at my white lace panties. This makes me a coward, but I'm Levi's coward, and this is the best I'm capable of giving at the moment.

His hands land on my waist. "You want to wrestle?" he teases.

"Your clothes off."

"Think you can?"

"I know I can." I wiggle against him. He grows hard beneath his thin athletic shorts, the solid ridge of his cock hitting me in exactly the right spot, reassuring me I've got this. I want him inside me, but I'm happy to start with going down on him. There's nowhere else I have to be today.

"Know what I think?"

God, his tone is a combination of sexy and endearing that tugs on more than my desire. If I had the nerve, I'd ask for everything he's thinking. I've wondered what it would be like to get that close to someone again. Could I handle it? Or would I retreat behind a bigger wall?

I slip my fingers under the well-worn cotton of his shirt and smooth my hands up his abdomen and over his chest, enjoying the muscles that shift underneath my touch. He's the one. The one person to make me wonder the most, to think about pressing a soft kiss to his neck and whispering, "You make me feel more than I ever have before."

"You don't have to tell me. I can feel what you think." I grind against him a little more forcefully. We're done talking. It's time for doing.

He cocks an eyebrow and, faster than I expected, pulls my dress up and over my head. Appreciation takes over his expression as he openly stares at my bare body. My nipples snap to attention, turning into hard, achy points. "I love dresses with no bra required," he says.

I return the favor and drag his shirt up to his armpits. He lifts his arms in assistance, and once I've got the shirt over his face, I abandon it to kiss his chest. He chuckles and takes care of ridding himself of the material. I kiss my way to his shoulder, his collarbone, his throat, breathing in his masculine, shower-fresh scent as I go.

"I need those lips up here," he says. "Now."

I'm not one to take orders, but Levi's bossy voice does it for me. I smash my mouth to his. He immediately takes over, leading me in an openmouthed kiss that resonates between my thighs. It's intense, playful, consuming. His tongue does things to the inside of my mouth that sizzle my bones. I want to try for the kissing world record. Kiss Levi for hours and hours straight? Sign me up. Only me.

I push that possessive thought aside as he cups the back of my head. His other hand roams up and down my spine, making my skin quiver.

Then his fingers gently dig into my hip, and he playfully flips me onto my back. I sink into the soft, comfortable bedding with a stupid smile on my face.

His body covers mine, all muscly, strong, protective. When he presses up on his elbows and fixes a hot, irresistible gaze on me, it's official. He can handcuff me to this bed, and I won't put up a fight.

"We're doing this," he says with a low, gravelly voice.

"No argument from me."

"And later I'm buying you dinner."

I'm not sure why that's important to him, but okay. "Can we eat it right here?"

He thinks about how to answer that. He's got me twice more this week, for the rehearsal dinner and wedding, so it's not like I'm going to run after this. I just want to be alone with him. Keep him all to myself.

I roll my head to the side, look out the window. All of a sudden, maintaining eye contact is too hard.

"Sure," he concedes, gently grasping my chin and turning my head back to his so he can kiss me again.

I take his kiss and raise him. I glide my hands down his back, underneath the waistband of his shorts and underwear, and palm his ass, pulling him tighter to my center. I'm a ticking time bomb, ready to get off with him. Foreplay is great, but I feel like we've been doing that for weeks, and more than anything I need Levi moving inside me.

He makes a sound of appreciation inside my mouth before moving his kisses down my neck. The feather-light pressure he uses is delicious and tortuous at the same time. His sexy, barely-there stubble scrapes just right. I wiggle and arch my back. He drops to my boobs and licks and sucks them while his hand starts to expertly rub over my panties.

I run my fingers through his hair, spreading my legs wider.

The pad of his thumb strokes over my clit, lighting up nerves I never knew existed. I'm achy, excited, further aroused. Then he's sliding my panties down my legs, kissing the inside of my thighs, my knees, until he gets to my ankles. He slips the tiny piece of material over my feet and tosses it behind him.

Lying completely naked on Levi's bed detonates goose bumps on my skin. Especially when he stares at me with sexy, smiling reverence.

He stands to his full height and discards the rest of his clothes. I try to look everywhere at once. His broad shoulders, smooth chest, ridged abs. The indentations at his hips that point to the base of his hard, thick cock.

"You aren't beautiful," he says, climbing back up my body, his eyes never leaving mine. "You're more. And as soon as I invent the right word, I'll give it to you."

God, I adore the things that come out of his mouth.

Appreciate them. Want to revel in them. Nothing ever sounds planned or rehearsed. His compliments are genuine. They send butterflies fluttering through the deepest parts of me.

"You're kind of unique, too," I tell him. He's gorgeous, yes, but he's also the first guy since Joe to find a place inside my heart. Yes, he's there, whether I like it or not.

"Kind of?" he asks as if insulted, but his smirk tells me he's not. "Guess I better get busy and prove otherwise."

"You absolutely should do that." I lift my body to meet his, eliminating any space between us.

With my arms around his shoulders, he leans over to grab a condom out of the bedside table. He makes quick work of rolling it on.

We both know how good we fit together, and for a minute he simply teases my opening with the head of his cock. I'm so wet that he easily glides against me.

"Levi," I grumble. He's got way more patience than I have.

"Give me a second," he mutters. "I've been thinking about doing this again for months, and I'm afraid I'll last all of twenty seconds if I don't concentrate."

I cup his cheek. "You've got amazing control. Now, get to it."

"There hasn't been anyone else since you." He brushes a lock of hair off my forehead. "Wanted you to know that."

Swallowing a giant, jawbreaker-size lump in my throat, I say, "There's been no one else for me, either." Then I brush my lips against his and reach my free hand between us, taking him in my palm and guiding him where I need him.

He doesn't hesitate to take it from there.

The second he slides inside me, I lose my mind with pleasure, and all of the crap inside my head washes away. He takes his time, savoring every inch forward, promising an unhurried slow burn that's incredible and unsettling at the same time. He fills more than the space between my legs. He fills the spaces inside me I don't give anyone access to. And if I'm not careful, he'll figure out how important he is to me.

"Fuck," he moans. "I thought I remembered how good you feel, but this is so much better."

I rake my nails over his shoulders, hook my legs over the backs of his thighs. It feels better to me, too, and it's because we have a stronger connection now. We don't just like each other. We care about each other. For a brief moment, I'm back to the night we hooked up, and Levi is fucking me. Only it's more than that. He's moving with measured, steady thrusts with his nose buried in my hair like I'm someone important, not a casual lay. He's making love to me.

Thus the reason I needed to push him away.

Am I going to feel that way again?

Because right here, right now is just as intense. I'm ready to come out of my skin when he fills me completely...and *stops* moving.

"What are you doing?" I ask, rather desperately.

He closes his eyes for a moment, relishing our position. "I know it's cliché, but I could die right now a very happy man."

"Good to know, because if you don't start moving right this second, I'm going to kill you."

His answering grin is going to kill *me*. He's so unbelievably cute and hot and sexy. "Aw, Ham, I love it when you talk dirty."

With that, he dips his head to park his mouth on mine and finally—*finally!*—rocks his hips. We kiss and surrender to our bodies, and it's wild. Lips, tongues, fingers, groans. His mouth and hands are all over me. He scrapes the delicate skin behind my ear with his teeth and moves down my neck to my nipples. He sucks, licks, and teases one while his fingers squeeze and massage the other.

All the while, he's pumping into me, filling me, putting

pressure exactly where I need it the most.

I splay my hands across his broad shoulders, over his biceps. He runs his palm down my side, reaches behind him to curl his hand around my thigh, and lifts my leg. My pelvis tilts to meet his thrusts. I take an unsteady breath. I'm floating toward oblivion, and it never felt so good.

Levi lifts his head, and his beautiful light brown eyes bore into mine in a way that is almost painful. I consider looking away—staring at something else. Anything else. But I don't. I'm caught in the depths of his gaze because it's there that I feel safer than I ever have before.

I cradle his nape and kiss him. It's wet and messy and perfect.

Our bodies become damp with perspiration as we devote our hands and mouths and rhythm to bringing each other pleasure. Keeping us connected, Levi rolls us over so I'm straddling him. I make a slight adjustment, then he plays with my boobs while I move up and down his cock—slowly drag up then sink back down, again and again. It's heady, controlling our momentum. I love the deep, guttural sounds he makes.

We flip positions again. Levi braces himself on his elbows, his warm breath fans my cheek. And then somehow, he buries himself deeper, fills me more completely, and angles his hips so he's pressing against my clit. Hot sparks skitter down my spine. My vision blurs. I go over the edge of bliss, moaning, sighing, and clutching him like I never want to let him go.

"God, Harper," he murmurs against my earlobe. He slams his hips into me one last time before his body vibrates with his own release. He brings me down with him, the waves of my orgasm slowly receding until we both still.

I'm happy when he doesn't pull out right away. I wrap my arms around his back and hug him closer. He lets go of some of his weight, buries his face in the ticklish spot between my neck and shoulder. I wriggle.

He presses up. "Don't move," he says before he withdraws and goes into the bathroom to dispose of the condom. My eyes are glued to his firm, round ass. It really is drool-worthy.

I don't move a muscle—mostly because I'm boneless with satisfaction. When Levi crawls back onto the bed, he's even sexier than when he left. I cover my eyes with my arm. Thirty seconds should not do that to a guy. Fuckity, fuck, fuck, fuck.

He lifts my arm away from my face and kisses the inside of my palm. His tenderness is a little too much, so I slip my hand away in favor of turning onto my side and tracing my finger around his defined chest.

He's lying on his side, too, with his head propped in the crook of his arm. "I never imagined when we were little that we'd end up like this," he says.

"Because we didn't know about *this*, you weirdo." I poke him in the pec. "We were too young."

"True, I didn't know about *this*, but I knew about sex," he says lightheartedly.

I try not to freak out because he just confirmed my unwanted thoughts about this being more than sex.

It was.

It can't be.

"You knew about sex when you were seven?" I tuck both hands under my cheek and pull a face that calls bullshit.

"One night when I couldn't sleep because my mom and dad were making funny noises in their bedroom, I went into Amelia's room and she explained to me that our parents were having sex. She said sex was when a man put his privates into a woman's privates until the woman screamed, but that it didn't hurt."

"That you told me all that sounding like a commercial spokesperson is the cutest thing ever."

Adding to his appeal, a smile twitches at his lips. "If you think that's cute, you should hear how I learned the truth about Santa Claus."

Oh my God. He is too much. And so bad for me. He's cookies, tequila, and Netflix binges, only better. I mean worse. I don't know what I mean! Just that he's lying across from me—gloriously naked!—and looks so good, smells so good, and feels sooo good, that I'm in serious jeopardy of falling hard.

Which will ruin me.

Chapter Fifteen

Harper and I trade takeout boxes of Chinese. I hand over the Kung Pao chicken and she gives me the sweet and sour shrimp. We're kicking back on my bed, and I'm trying really hard not to stare at her tits while we eat. She's not naked, she's wearing one of my T-shirts, but her nipples are poking through. That I had my mouth on them an hour ago doesn't help.

I left the house for twenty minutes to pick up food, but other than that, we've been in my bedroom for the past four hours doing everything we can think to do. I've given her several orgasms, and I'm not finished. My stamina has never been better.

She's talked nonstop in between rounds of sex, leading discussions on food, movies, TV, bucket-list items, and superpowers. It doesn't take a genius to figure out she's doing it to avoid talking about what really brought her to my house. I don't want to ruin this perfect afternoon, though, so I'm good with whatever she wants to discuss. Right now, with beams of early evening light slanting through my window casting her in a gorgeous glow, it's pets.

"...two English bulldogs, an aquarium, and a Labrador Retriever," she says, in between bites of food. The girl has an appetite that is refreshing.

"Labs love the water."

"Exactly. What about you? What pets are you going to have?"

I switch my box of shrimp with the box of tangerine beef on the bed. "You already know English bulldogs are my favorite, too, so definitely a dog, but beyond that, I haven't given it much thought." I bring a bite of the beef to my mouth. "Okay, my turn. Would you rather swim with sharks or swim with crocodiles?"

"From dogs to deadly animals." She gives a little shake of her head in amusement and thinks about it for a moment. "Sharks. Would you rather...eat cow brains or rabbit feet?"

"Is that a real thing people eat? Rabbit feet?"

She laughs and puts her food down. "I don't know. It just came out of my mouth."

"It doesn't matter. I'll go with cow brains since rabbits' feet are supposed to be good luck, and I don't want to jinx any good luck by eating it."

"Good thinking," she says, looking impressed with my answer. My chest involuntarily puffs out.

"Would you rather be covered with bees or covered with flies?" I ask.

Her shoulders wriggle. "I hate flies. Seriously hate. They gross me out. When I was thirteen, a raccoon or some other small animal died underneath our house, and when it decomposed, a million flies got into our kitchen and it was freakishly horrible. It was like a take-over mission by an army of flying, buzzing black insects, and I still sometimes have nightmares about it."

"So, I guess that means you don't want to watch *The Fly* later?" The movie stars Jeff Goldblum as a scientist who makes a teleportation device and tests it on himself only to realize later that a fly was in the machine, too, and the fly's cells start to take over his body. It is fantastic.

"No! Don't even joke about that." She frowns and visibly shivers.

"Sorry. C'mere." I help her crawl into my lap without knocking over the takeout boxes. Wrap my arms around her. She snuggles into me, and it's fucking awesome.

I'd been miserable since my run-in with Kayla the other night, and today with Harper is exactly what I needed. I kept my distance from her yesterday, focusing on our shoot, and felt shitty about it. But with my headspace filled with bitterness, I didn't want to let on that my ex still has the power to affect me.

"How about…would you rather have your back massaged, or your front massaged?" I ask. It's probably clear where this is going.

"Hmm, that's a tough one. I like to be massaged in both places."

"You have to pick one." I slowly pull out the chopstick helping to hold her hair in a messy bun on top of her head. Long, sweet-smelling strands tumble out. I comb my fingers through them.

"I haven't had a back massage in a long time, so I'll go with that. Would you rather kiss someone's feet or kiss their ass?"

"How about I show you?" I pose it as a question, but it's really not. I quickly gather our food and put it on the desk in the corner of my room. Harper sits on her knees in the middle of the bed, tracking me like I'm the most interesting thing she's ever seen.

"Lift up your arms," I tell her when I'm back within reach. She moves in slow motion as she complies, the stretch sultry and flirtatious.

I follow her lead and leisurely help remove the shirt from her beautiful body. She sucks in a breath. "Lie down on your stomach," I instruct next.

She lies with her cheek on my pillow. The arm closest to me is at her side, and the other is bent at a ninety-degree angle with her hand under the pillow. Perfect. I gather her hair and brush it out of the way.

Starting at her shoulders, I rub the tension away. I press the pads of my fingers into the muscles between her shoulder blades, gently pushing her into the mattress. She sighs. Her eyes drift shut. I spend enough time there to work out the small knot on her right side. Then I slowly caress down to the middle of her back. Her skin is soft and warm, but I realize I'm missing something. "Be right back," I whisper in her ear.

I hurry to Mateo's room. He mentioned the other day that Teague left her lotion in his bathroom, and he jacked-off to the smell of it. (Yeah, I told him I didn't need to know that, and now I doubt my logic here, but too late.) The pink bottle stands out amid the few manly products he's got, and I grab it.

Back at Harper's side, I rub some of the lotion into my hands. She startles at my touch. "You falling asleep on me?"

"No," she murmurs. "Just really comfortable." She opens one eye to peek at me. "Why does it smell like my best friend?"

"I'm using the lotion she left here. Thought it might help with the massage." To prove my point, I stroke my palms over her back, gaining some extra glide with the moisturizer.

"Mmmmm...okay."

I rub and knead, hand-over-hand, applying pressure that fans away from her delicate spine. Her back is small, so it doesn't take much to span the length from waist to neck. I sink my thumbs into the sexy dimples just above the curve of her bottom. Her body melts into the comforter.

"That feels really good," she croons.

I smile, even though she can't see me. Having my hands on her silky skin is my pleasure, too. My cock is standing at attention to attest to it.

When I can't take it anymore, and have to touch the exceptional globes of her ass, I rub my hands over one cheek, then the other. I massage with firm strokes out toward her hips. She breathes out loud into my pillow.

The tan line separating her back from her butt is insanely attractive. That she spends so much time in the sunshine in nothing but a bikini validates her easygoing style and dedication to swimming and water safety.

Harper is beyond beautiful, but her real beauty is in her presence. Watching her these past three weeks in the pool with kids, for kids, and about kids, has been amazing. She cares more deeply than anyone I've ever met. She's also friendly, professional, and a hard worker. She isn't afraid to ask questions or make fun of herself.

It's only the times she thinks no one is looking that I notice sadness wrinkle the corners of her eyes. She's keeping something buried deep—something that isn't going to go away if she doesn't talk about it. It's the injuries you can't see on someone that need the most care.

I soften my ministrations and slide a hand between her thighs, tracing small circles on the flesh there. She lazily spreads her legs wider. I drop a kiss on her ass then sit on the edge of the bed.

The smell of her arousal, not to mention the boner in my shorts, spurs me to speed things up. I slide my hand between the bed and her sex. She wiggles against my hand, before lifting her hips slightly to give me full access.

She's wet, and seconds later swollen, as I rub her and

gently pinch her clit. "More," she moans, grinding into my palm.

Happy to oblige, I slide a finger inside her. There is nothing better than feeling her clench down on whatever body part I have inside her. She rocks her hips against my hand and lifts up the arm at her side so she's digging both her elbows into the bed. Watching the sway in her body as she moves to my touch is hot as fuck. I take my free hand and slide it in my shorts and around my dick.

I add a second finger inside her, filling her more fully. She bucks against the added pressure. God, I love watching her get off. Her mouth opens slightly, and full-throated hums spill out. The sexy sounds reverberate down my spine.

Intimacy with Harper is unlike any closeness I've experienced before. My pulse is revving. My nerves are all firing. She does it for me in a big way.

A few more strokes from my busy fingers, and she comes. She doesn't hold back. She's loud, and shameless in the thrust of her hips until she's completely spent and relaxes into the comforter. I free both my hands, hurriedly undress, and have a condom rolled on a few seconds later.

I raise Harper by the waist so she's on her knees then position myself behind her. She lifts up onto her elbows and looks over her shoulder at me. Her cheeks are flush from her orgasm. There's a twinkle in her eyes. A small but potent smile plays across her lips. She wants me inside her as badly as I want to be there.

Earlier, I took her from behind, but something about this moment feels different. I think it's the way she's gazing back at me. With more. More of everything.

I sink into her little by little until I'm balls deep.

"Levi," she groans. She likes it hard and fast when she's one orgasm up on me.

So I give her what she wants. I grip her waist, pull out,

and thrust in. Harder. Faster. But I'm careful, too, deliberate in my movements so I'll get her to the finish line one more time before me. I tilt her hips just so, angle my body against hers just right, and lean forward to suck on the nape of her neck. She's got a spot behind her earlobe that drives her crazy when I put my mouth there.

She clutches the comforter. I use my tongue and teeth, whisper how sexy she is and how good she feels squeezing my cock. We keep this up for a while, and then she straightens, lifting her arms up and wrapping them around my neck. I reach around her to cup and play with her tits. My thrusts slow, but she doesn't seem to mind.

I slide one hand down her stomach to rub the hard, swollen bundle of nerves in the small landing strip of dark curls between her legs. She turns her head to kiss me. It's short, but hot, and then she's back on her elbows.

My hold goes to her waist once again, fingers digging into her soft skin. I pound into her with more urgency. My vision starts to blur; white-hot heat burns through my veins. Then she's yelling, "Yes, right there!" I keep up the pace until her tremors slow and I find my own release, the pleasure so intense I see stars.

I'm never in a rush to pull out of her, so I stay seated until she makes a move to roll onto her back. She's spectacular lying against my white sheets with a thoroughly satiated look on her face. I bend over and kiss her. A slow, relaxed openmouthed kiss that leaves us both panting before I get up to dispose of the condom and wash my hands.

On the return, I grab the two fortune cookies from the takeout bag on my desk. Harper scoots up to sit against my headboard. I offer her first pick of the cookies and get comfortable beside her.

"Thanks." She breaks her cookie in half and pulls out her fortune. "You will find a thing. It may be important."

She looks over at me, a huge smile tugging up the corners of her lips. "In bed." She cracks ups. She can't stop giggling. The beautiful, happy sound should be recorded and used for therapy.

I break my cookie and grin when I read the fortune. "There's been a mix up." I hand her my tiny slip of paper and take hers.

"A man with"—she glances at me—"brown eyes has a surprise for you."

"In bed," I add.

We both burst into a fit of laughter. I twirl several strands of hair hanging over her tit around my finger, brushing the ample skin with the back of my knuckle. She places her hand on my thigh.

After we quiet, she kicks down the covers and crawls underneath them. "I'm tired."

"Okay." I slip under, too, more than ready to fall asleep with her in my arms. It's early, so this might not be an overnight thing, but I'll take it for however long it lasts.

She cuddles right up against me with her head on my chest, a leg tangled with mine, and her palm over my heart. A few peaceful beats pass before she says, "I saved someone at my parents' house this morning. He was choking."

I'm not sure if she wants my praise or congratulations or something else, so I don't say anything. I squeeze her closer, hoping to convey she's truly amazing.

"It brought back a lot of uncomfortable memories for me. I was already out of sorts before it happened."

I kiss the top of her head, silently telling her I'm here if she wants to share more. *Keep going, Harper. Keep going.*

"On my sixteenth birthday, my boyfriend, Joe, drowned."

Fucking hell. On her birthday? Her boyfriend? Pain crowds my chest. My muscles clench. And I'm ashamed to admit jealousy stabs me. She loved Joe enough to carry this with her all these years.

"I'm sorry," I say.

"I was so in love with him. He'd never learned to swim, and I was going to teach him."

I shut my eyes and press my lips together. Her pain is my pain. I wish I could wipe the bad memories away for her.

Moisture coats the side of my chest.

Teardrops.

"Harper…" I try to draw her up, to look at her and comfort her and kiss her, make love to her, whatever it takes to ease the suffering I hear in her voice and feel in her quivers. But she one-arm hugs me to keep me in place. Shakes her head. She doesn't want me to see her as she talks.

"He…he drowned in our swimming pool."

Fuuuccck.

"It was my Sweet Sixteen and my parents threw me a huge party in the backyard. I remember it like it was yesterday—Joe and me dancing to "Just the Way You Are" by Bruno Mars. It was our song, and even though he didn't like to dance, he did with me. He put his hands on my waist. I wrapped my arms around his neck and looked up into his gorgeous face. Everyone else around us disappeared, and then he gave me a quick kiss on the lips. He told me he loved my dress. That it was the prettiest he'd ever seen. Whenever he was close to me, I grinned like a fool. I couldn't help it. He made me feel safe, womanly, loved."

"Ham…" I say softly. Of course he loved her. I imagine a lot of guys did from afar.

"Colleen came up to us on the dance floor."

"Your cousin Colleen?"

She nods. "She smuggled some alcohol into the party and wanted us to do shots with her. I knew she was bringing tequila, so it wasn't a surprise, and she assured me a couple of shots would be fun and harmless. With my strict swimming regimen, I was always super careful about what I put in my body, but it was my birthday and I wanted to break the rules. Have some extra fun.

"The shots loosened us up and we danced and partied and drank more. By the time the cake rolled out, I was feeling lightheaded and happy. After I blew out the candles, Joe and I snuck out of the party tent to go up the stairs to the terrace where the pool was. We were going to have sex for the first time." Her breath flutters against my side. A tear slides down my skin. "It was the perfect night. A full moon and hundreds of stars sparkled in the sky to make what we were about to do even more romantic. I'll never forget the last words he said to me. He said, 'You look more beautiful than anything I've ever seen,' and even though the words were a little slurred, they were so sincere. I *felt* them. Then he told me he loved me. I told him I loved him, too. So much.

"We started undressing as we stumbled around the pool toward the cabana day bed where we planned for this to happen. But with all the drinking...we were too close to the edge of the pool. I lost my balance taking off my heels, and Joe tried to right me. Only he lost his balance, too, and teetered backward toward the pool. I panicked and reached out, thinking to grab his shirt, only he'd taken it off already so all I got was bare chest."

She wipes at her cheek, and I am fucking dying here, at a loss for the right words to say to help her through this.

"I remember him mumbling, 'It's okay, I've got you,' but he didn't. I started to fall while trying to pull him back to me. My vision blurred and heat swamped me. Then Joe's hands slipped off me, and mine off him. I fell and hit my head on a rock and blacked out. When I woke up, Joe was..." She muffles her whimpers with the back of her hand. "When I woke up, I found Joe facedown in the pool. I jumped in, frantic to save him, crying his name over and over again. My heart was pounding so hard, I could barely breathe, but I didn't care. I just wanted him to be okay, but it was too late. He was already gone."

I wrap both arms around her and hold tight. I can't even imagine what that must have felt like. "I'm so sorry," I whisper. There's more I want to say, but I don't think she intended for this to be a discussion. She simply wanted to get it off her chest.

There is nothing simple about this, Levi.

"Thank you for telling me what happened. I'm really glad you did."

She sniffles and gives me a small nod. I don't let go of her, not when her body relaxes and her breathing evens out. And not when she falls asleep. I keep her tucked against me and drift off to sleep, too.

When I wake up, she's gone.

Dear Harper,

> *Thank you for opening up to me.*
> *Thank you for letting me hold you.*
> *Thank you for telling me about someone you loved and how much it hurt when he was gone. I hope it made you feel better, sharing something you've kept bottled up. I'm honored you felt comfortable enough to confide in me.*
> *Your strength shines bright, Ham. I hope you know that.*
> *Most of all, thank you for trusting me.*
> *Your faith in me has renewed my faith in myself.*

> *Sincerely,*
> *Levi*

Chapter Sixteen

I count the blueberries in my muffin. The ones I can see, anyway. Did you know sometimes a blueberry looks like a carob chip? I glance across the conference table at Brad's muffin. Yep, blueberries and carob chips could be twins if covered by the right amount of batter when baking.

I have officially lost my mind.

This is what happens when I'm anxious. I make weird observations.

It's Tuesday morning, I'm at MASF, and Brad had to step out of the room for a minute. We'd only said hello and been served breakfast by his assistant when he had to excuse himself, prolonging the restless energy that is making me fidget and analyze muffins. They *are* the hottest new food item in Beverly Hills, a gluten-free, low sugar, yet tastes-like-heaven baked good that everyone is talking about. I break off a piece of my muffin top and pop it into my mouth.

Wow. It's delish.

"Sorry about that," Brad says, striding back into the room. He sits at the head of the table to my left.

"It's okay." I eat another piece of muffin.

He picks his up. "These as good as they say they are?"

"Uh-huh," I mumble as I chew, and he bites into his.

"You're right," he agrees, returning the muffin to the small glass plate in front of him. "So, I've had a chance to look over all the footage for the PSAs and it looks fantastic. You did a phenomenal job."

"Thank you." My heart is pumping so hard, I'm certain Brad can hear the beats. I hope this means I've got the ambassador job.

"I think they're going to be a big success, and that's why I wanted to meet with you privately."

"Okay."

"In order to bring the most awareness to our cause, we need to figure out how best to get you engaged in the campaign."

"Are you saying I have the job?" I can't hide the excited lilt to my voice.

"I'm saying I want to give you the job, but there is more to it than I think you realize."

"Like what?" I'm not afraid to do whatever is needed to help MASF and reduce the number of people who drown.

"The board is concerned with your willingness to share your past."

Except that. I'm afraid of that. My brows bump together.

"Before our first meeting, I made the board aware that I coached you when you were a teen. I also told them you lost your boyfriend to drowning, but I didn't go into specifics because that's your story to tell." Brad reaches across the table to squeeze my arm. "I know how devastating it was to you, and how much you were hurting back then. You quit swimming and gave up trying to qualify for the Olympics because of it."

I give a strong nod. If I speak, my words will wobble, and I don't allow anyone to hear my vulnerability.

The memory of confiding in Levi flashes through my mind, but I quickly push it away.

"If you agree to be our ambassador, the world is going to want to hear your story, Harper. They're going to *need* to hear it to get our message across."

I blink several times at this requirement.

"So, the board's concern lies with your willingness to open up and share what personally brought you to MASF. Not your competency or likeability or passion. You've got all that in spades, and we're very happy about that. But we've got a list of ways we want you to contribute beyond the PSAs."

"Like?" I manage to say with a clear voice. Sweat trickles down my sides and heat grips the back of my neck.

"Like being a guest speaker at fundraising lunches and dinners. Emceeing and taking part in walks or swim meets. Lending your profile and being quoted in media releases. Helping generate news stories and further awareness for our cause in both the private and public sectors.

"We want someone who is generous of himself or herself and who is passionate about the organization and willing to lend a hand. You fit all of that, Harper, but we'd like to suggest you share your personal story as well."

I pull at the sleeves of my shirt and wiggle my toes to get feeling back in my feet. "I don't know if I can do that," I say honestly. As my coach, Brad was well aware of what happened to Joe and to me. But because I was a minor, my name was never mentioned publicly. Our home address and the details of the occasion were kept secret, but everyone at school knew. My swim friends, when I failed to return, did, too.

It probably wouldn't have mattered if strangers knew. I

shut myself off from everyone and focused only on what was right in front of me. People around me talked, but I did my best not to hear what they were saying. Brad is asking me to speak and listen.

I know what happened is ancient history and I should be okay talking about it, but this means opening myself up to pity, scrutiny, blame, shame, and more all over again. Joe is my soft underbelly, and I pretend I don't care what people think, but I do.

"Think about it," Brad says. "It's a big decision, and I want you to be completely comfortable with it."

"Okay. I will. Thank you."

"I think you can influence this campaign and our organization in great ways. I've watched you with the kids, and they really relate to you. Adults will, too."

"I want to make a difference more than anything."

Brad smiles and leans forward on the table. "I know you do. Can I offer some advice?"

"Sure."

"Step out of your shoes and look at what happened. More often than not, the way we see ourselves is not how others see us."

"I can try and do that. Thanks."

"And if this doesn't work out, maybe we can find another way for you to be a part of MASF."

The thought of sharing my story is worse than thinking about losing a limb. But another part of me is grateful Brad thinks I'm worth the effort if I can muster the courage to speak out. God, making adult decisions sucks.

"When do you need an answer?" I ask.

"Soon." Once again he squeezes my arm. "I want you to feel you've had enough time to give me—and yourself—the best one, but the board does want to move forward."

Of course he's going to be sympathetic and kind and

fatherly about this. My stomach is in a terrible knot at his consideration. I hate the idea of letting him down. Of letting myself down.

"Okay. Thanks." I stand up. "If you don't mind, I'm going to go."

Understanding shines in his eyes as he stands to walk me out. "Thanks for coming in this morning. I look forward to hearing from you soon."

"Oh, wait." I stop and force myself to look him in the eyes. "I almost forgot. There's something I need to tell you."

"Shoot."

"I may have skinny-dipped in public with Levi and gotten caught by your brother-in-law, Tim."

Brad raises his eyebrows. "May have?"

"I did."

"I already know. Tim told Hadley the second he got home, and Hadley immediately called Amelia and she told me. Nothing is kept secret with those women."

"You already knew and still offered me the ambassadorship?" I slide my hand down my skirt to dry the perspiration on my palm.

"I imagine it's something you won't let happen again."

"I won't. I'm sorry."

"For what? Having some fun? I probably shouldn't have mentioned Levi that day at the pool. My brother-in-law seems happier than he's been in a long time, and I think I have you to thank for that."

His comment makes my heart pound, but I'll think about it later, when I've had time to process it. "So, we're good?"

"We're good."

Relieved, I say good-bye and hurry to my car. Once inside the safety of the two doors, my entire body deflates. I sit for a long time, staring off into the distance while I try to reconcile my past with my present, my hopes with my fears.

I get nothing but a headache.

I'm startled out of my fog when my phone buzzes with a text. It's my cousin. She reminds me we're getting manis and pedis tomorrow afternoon. I type a quick text back all in emojis. I'm not feeling the words at the moment. It's a good thing I took the entire week off from swim lessons. Between the wedding and MASF, I'm stressed out.

As soon as I put my phone down, another text comes in. Colleen is probably confused by my emoji selection. I pick my cell back up, but it's not her, it's Levi.

Hi Ham, my shoot was postponed, and I was wondering if you were free. I need to go clothes shopping for a wedding this weekend.

I stare at the text, unsure how to respond. It's the first time I've heard from him since Sunday night. I was half hoping he'd forget about the wedding. And me. The other half hoped he'd get in touch before now. Not that I blame him. My tears and snot were all over his chest as I dumped my past on him.

My forehead hits the steering wheel. I don't know what I'm doing anymore. Not in my personal life, and not in my professional one. I like Levi. I think he likes me. For a normal person, this would be winning the dating lottery. Levi is a catch. He's all kinds of hot and amazing, but I'm terrified of letting him all the way in.

I'm good at being on my own. I'm not good at navigating a relationship. Not that Levi and I are in a relationship. We're not. Not at all. We're just two friends enjoying some benefits. The novelty will wear off after Colleen's wedding. He'll go back to his normal routine, and I'll go back to mine.

Only I don't have one anymore.

I lift my head and text Levi back. Bottom line, we have fun together, and for the rest of the week I'll focus on that. Colleen deserves a cheerful bridesmaid. Levi does more than put me in a good mood.

I'm free. Meet at Barneys on Wilshire in forty-five?

Great. See you there.

Shopping therapy is exactly what I need right now. I get to the high-end clothing store in twenty so I can look in the women's section first. I find a cute white off-the-shoulder Rag & Bone sweater that will go great with the asymmetric cream-colored lace skirt I bought last week. It's the perfect outfit for the rehearsal dinner. After a few more minutes of perusing, I make my single purchase and hoof it back to the first floor to wait for Levi.

"A guy walks into a store and sees this backside and wishes the girl's clothes would spontaneously fall off," he whispers in my ear like he's narrating a show on the mating habits of men.

I grip the shoe shelf I was wasting time with. His breath is hot on my nape. His hand wraps around my waist. I drop my chin to hide the smile his greeting instigates. Not that he can see my face with my back to his front.

"I've missed you, Ham," he adds before I can turn to give him a proper hello.

Once I do twist around, I'm unexpectedly...thrilled. My heart gives an uncharacteristic flutter. I've missed him, too. All of him, but especially his shimmering light-brown eyes, which are always so absorbed in *me*, a girl who never imagined having strong feelings for a guy ever again.

I take a step to the side so I can function a little easier. "Hi."

"Hi," he says around a smile that could slay every paranormal creature in existence. You know, if vampires and such were a real thing. "Thanks for meeting me."

"Thanks for asking me to meet you." I mean that sincerely, which is freaking me out. It's not as weird as I thought, seeing Levi after I confessed my deepest shame.

He palms the back of my head and brings my lips to his in a kiss searing enough to send tingles to my toes. I'm off-balance when he pulls back.

"So, wedding attire." He rubs a hand over the stubble on his jaw. "I thought you'd like to pick out what you want me to wear. I live in jeans and T-shirts, so I'm highly underequipped for important events."

I take in said light-blue jeans and plain, V-neck black tee, openly surveying down his body and back up—long legs, trim waist, flat stomach, well-defined chest, neck I want to bite. My body temp goes up a notch. Casual is his jam, and looking around our surroundings, I'm not the only female to think so.

"Let's do this." I spin on my heel to lead him upstairs to the men's department. He falls in step beside me. "The wedding is in my aunt's backyard. Did I tell you that?"

"No."

"Preparations have already started." My mom invited me back home so I wouldn't have to deal with all the construction and arrangements, but after the mini panic attack I had at brunch, I can't go there right now. "And because it's a backyard wedding, the invite calls for casual dressy."

"Which means?"

"A suit and tie, but I'm thinking we can get away with a sport coat and dress pants since it's still summer and we'll be outside."

"I'm yours to dress…and undress," he says.

"Do not flirt with me while we're shopping."

"Or what?" he teases.

"Or I may end up in the dressing room with you." Just thinking about wrapping my legs around Levi's waist while he fucks me against the dressing room mirror makes me throb between my legs.

"Fine by me."

"Of course it is."

He leans sideways so his mouth brushes my ear. "I'd like to push up your skirt and bury myself inside you right this minute."

I shiver. "Maybe later."

"Definitely later."

Our sideways glances collide, then just as quickly run away. It's reassuring to know I'm not the only one affected here. Unsettling, too. I'm beyond scared about feeling too much.

A well-dressed man greets us when we arrive in the land of suits. Since I helped my brother with a suit a few weeks ago in this very place, I'm good to dress Levi without assistance. I thank the sales guy and tell him I'll give a shout if we need help.

I grab a few pairs of pants and matching coats, along with a white button-down, and hand them to Levi. "Give these a try."

"Sure." He takes the items, sweeping his thumb across my knuckles on the handoff. On the way to the dressing room, he holds the clothes up and tells the sales guy he's trying them on.

"I need a fashion show!" I call after him. Because even though I'm not big on guys in suits, I am big on Levi. I palm my overheated cheeks. This Levi-is-the-bomb mentality has got to stop.

But it doesn't. Not at all. I know this because when he steps out of the dressing room in an ill-fitting suit, he still looks hotter than any guy I've ever seen. I shake my head. He agrees.

Neither of us is sold on the follow-up outfits he models for me, either, so I grab a couple more. Levi haphazardly dumps the clothes he's already tried on in my arms with a sheepish look. He places the empty hangers on top. God, he's cute.

"I'm trying these on," he announces to the sales guy once

again. What is up with that?

I re-hang his discards then run my hand over the silk ties while I wait. I think Levi will look sexier with an open collar, but a tie could be fun for other things.

"What do you think?" he asks.

I raise my head. I think he's gorgeous to the millionth power. The charcoal linen sport coat and gray slacks fit him perfectly, but I need to play it cool. "I like it, but maybe try it with a light blue shirt?" I hurry over to the shirts to pick one up in his size.

My breath hitches when I sense him right behind me. He brushes my hair over my shoulder and ever so softly kisses my neck. His lips are warm. They rouse every nerve ending in my body. "Want to help me try it on?" he whispers.

"*Yes.* No." I turn around. Look up into his eyes. "Yes."

He dips his head to nuzzle my nose with his. "Let's go." He takes the shirt out of my hands. I follow behind like a puppy after a bone, and I don't care.

"Trying this on," he says, lifting the shirt above his shoulders to show the salesman that I'm vaguely aware of in my periphery.

Salesman. The guy who's checked me out no fewer than five times while Levi's been inside the dressing room. "Stop," I say, halting my steps. "We can't. Also? What is the deal with you announcing everything you're trying on to the sales guy?"

"Umm…" A blush blooms across his cheeks. "No deal. Just…"

I veer us behind a manikin, out of direct sight of Sales Guy, who thankfully becomes busy with another shopper. "Tell me." It's not a plea, more like inquiring-minds-want-to-know.

He threads his fingers through his excellently tousled hair, making it look even more sexed-up. I want to throw a baseball cap on his head so no one else but me gets to see him like this.

"I have to do it," he says with a touch of embarrassment.

"Do what exactly?"

"Long story short, when I was eight, my sister, Stephanie, got caught shoplifting some clothes, and I was there with her and my mom, and it left an impression. So now whenever I go shopping, I have to tell the salesperson what I'm bringing into the dressing room so they don't think I'm trying to steal it."

I glance at the black shirt folded neatly atop a display case to my right and extend my hand toward it. "So, if I were to try and slip this shirt inside my bag, you'd flip out?" I've never stolen a thing in my life—except a candy bar I thought my mom saw me take that one time, so it shouldn't count—and am only messing with Levi. Now that I know the reason behind his dressing room announcements, they're kind of adorable.

"Nice try, Ham," he says calmly, but he grabs my wrist nonetheless.

"Come on," I argue, easily pulling my hand back. "Let's take something. Maybe it will cure you."

"Or get us arrested." He's only half teasing me in return, his stony-faced expression one I imagine he picked up when he was eight and hasn't let go of since.

"You're right. I'm sorry." I take a step back, then another, angry with myself for ruining the mood. "Bad joke. I'll wait for you over here."

"No need to apologize. I knew you were messing with me, but you're the first person I've told that to, so I guess I felt a little self-conscious."

"No one's ever noticed you do that?"

"I do most of my shopping online, otherwise I shop by myself." He lifts the light blue shirt. "Be right out."

My head swims with "first person." After Joe died, I

didn't care about firsts anymore. I gave my virginity to my brother's college roommate when he brought him home for Christmas break my junior year of high school. We had silent sex in my room with one repeat and then I never saw him again.

I got my first job lifeguarding because Teague pushed me into it.

My first "date" after losing Joe was during my second week at UO, when some grad student mistook me for his blind date and I got the feeling his actual date was a no-show, so I felt bad for him. We had dinner. It was nice and taught me I could hang out with a member of the opposite sex without falling apart. Afterward, he hugged me good night and asked if he could have my number. I nicely said no.

Being Levi's first anything stirs a myriad of emotions inside me, not the least of which is how he's my first for a lot of things, too.

He steps out of the dressing area in the new shirt. The light blue wins over the white, adding a bit of color that does crazy things to his already good looks. "That's it," I tell him.

"Great. Want to help me undress?"

I can't help but smile, happy we're back to flirting. But Sales Guy chooses that moment to offer his positive opinion on Levi's attire, so there goes the sexy thought of seeing him without clothes on.

"Later" he mouths before he disappears to change.

One little word and I'm counting the seconds until he reappears, because naked or clothed, I like looking at him, talking to him, and being in the same airspace as him.

Fifty-one, fifty-two…

"Ready?" he says, picking up my hand on the way to the cash register. He engages in small talk with the sales guy as he pays, his friendly disposition claiming another layer of my affection.

A cloudless blue sky, pencil thin palm trees, and small city din greet us when we exit the store onto Wilshire Boulevard. "Can I keep you the rest of the day?" Levi asks.

"That all depends. What did you have in mind?"

"Lunch, sex, the Santa Monica pier, a walk along the beach, kissing, dinner, more sex."

I laugh. But on the inside, something is unfolding, blooming, breathing new life into my ruined heart. I'm not sure I like it. "You've given this some thought."

With his arm around my waist, he positions us against the side of the building, away from foot traffic. "I need to tell you…" He trails off and searches my face. "While in the dressing room, yeah. You game?"

What was he really about to say? I chew on my bottom lip, a move calculated to draw his eyes to my mouth and give me a moment to think. Does it matter what he wanted to say before changing his mind? The second he said he wanted to keep me, he had me.

For today.

Because I won't fall any more than I already have. I can't. After Colleen's wedding, I'm going to tell him I can't be with him anymore. We'll see each other because of Teague and Mateo, but not like this.

"I'm game."

"Great." We resume walking side-by-side, but he doesn't take my hand. "How does The Farm sound?"

"It's one of my favorite places to eat lunch."

We stop in the parking lot to deposit our bags in our cars. While I wait for Levi, I lean against mine to slip off my shoe and rub my foot. I'm wearing my most uncomfortable heels, thinking I'd meet with Brad and return straight home.

"Your feet hurt?" Levi asks as he rounds the hood. "We can drive if you want." He takes my foot into his hands, easily covering my size seven. After a brief inspection, he massages top and bottom.

I melt against the car. "No. The fresh air is nice. I'm just not used to these shoes."

"I meant to ask earlier what had you dressed up."

My chin drops. Levi's hands are skilled. I'm ready to sit on the hood and kick off my other heel. "I had a meeting with Brad this morning."

"What about?"

"The ambassadorship."

Levi stills. He carefully slips my shoe back into place and lowers my foot to the ground. *He knows.*

Without making eye contact, he steps around me to fill the spot by my side, connecting us from hip to thigh. "He told you what he hopes to get from you."

"How do you know that?"

"He mentioned it the other day. He didn't tell me about Joe. I didn't know about him until you told me, but he asked if you shared anything about your past with anyone while we were on our shoots. He said he hoped to get you to open up. That he needed you to, if you were to be the kind of ambassador they want."

I wrap my arms around myself, a chill suddenly racing through me. I'm two seconds away from getting in my car and deep-sixing the rest of the day with Levi, when he leans over and kisses me.

Lips soft yet solid glide over mine with unmistakable care. He takes his time making my mouth feel adored, cherished. He kisses the left corner, then the right. He kisses above my lip line and below. The kiss is one of the most tender he's ever given me. I'm not sure what he's trying to tell me, but when I open my eyes and find his already on mine, once again I'm lost to him. He slowly pulls back.

"I don't talk about it," I say softly.

"You talked to me."

"That's different."

"Why?" He nudges my knee. "Because I've been inside you?"

Because of so much more than that. "Yes. You're not a stranger, and wrapped in your arms, I felt gutsy enough to tell you."

"You're not weak, Harper. Far from it."

"Can we not talk about it anymore?" I need time to think about it on my own, without discussion or interference.

"Talk about what?" he returns lightly, helping to right my world.

At the same time, I fear it's crumbling.

Chapter Seventeen

Harper hasn't noticed me yet, idling inside the entrance of the restaurant, so taken with her that all I can do is stare. She's standing across the semi-crowded room talking to her cousin and a few other people. Her lustrous brown hair is in a high ponytail. Her white off-the-shoulder sweater stretches across her chest and hugs her small frame. A lacy skirt shows off her calves.

She is stunning. Sexy as all get-out.

"I'm sorry. The restaurant is closed for a private party."

I turn my attention to the person on my right just as Harper's eye catches mine. "Hi," I say to the attractive middle-aged woman. If I hadn't run into Harper's mom a few weeks ago, I'd think this woman might be her. "I know. I'm late." Really late. Why didn't I just forget coming? I extend my hand. "I'm Levi Pierce. Harper invited me."

"You're Levi," the woman says, like she's heard all about me. "It's nice to meet you. I'm Betsy, mother of the bride and

Harper's aunt."

"Nice to meet you, too. And congratulations."

"Hey," Harper says, coming up beside me. "I thought I told you—"

"I'll leave you two alone," Betsy says. "Levi, please be sure to grab a drink and some food if there's any left."

"Thank you. I will."

"I thought I told you not to come," Harper says with annoyance.

She did tell me that, when I texted her I was stuck at work for a few more hours and I'd meet up with her as soon as I could. I'm probably breaking some rule of etiquette showing up late like this.

"I missed you," I say. It's the 100 percent truth. After a long day on set for a new television show, I wanted to see her. It's not my smartest move. I'm getting in way over my head with her now, but I can't seem to stop.

"That is not an okay reason to do something I asked you not to."

I take her hand and play with her fingers. "Are you annoyed I'm here or because I'm here now?" She fiddles with my fingers in return. "Because whichever it is, you're beautiful when you're in a bad mood."

"Stop complimenting me."

"Never."

"God, you're annoying," she says with very little agitation behind it now. She's trying to push me away, but not really. I get it. I'm feeling like I want to push, too, before she breaks my heart.

"That's not what you said the other day when I had you in my bed and—"

"Zip it." She pinches my lips together.

We had a fantastic day after shopping at Barney's. The highlights of which were sex on her kitchen table when we stopped at her place so she could change her clothes, riding the rollercoaster again and again at the pier, showing off my sandcastle skills, sex on my couch, sex in my shower, and sex in my bed.

What can I say? I'm a Sex God.

A thought I immediately toss out of my head when a man who looks like he could be in the mafia approaches us. His stern stare is much more intense now than it was when we were kids.

"Hi, Dad, having a good time?"

"I am," he says, not taking his eyes off me.

"Levi, you probably don't remember him, but this is my dad, William. Dad, this is my date for the wedding, Levi Pierce. We were friends as kids."

I give him a firm handshake. "I do remember. Hello, sir."

"Hello. I trust you won't be late to the wedding." His tone is difficult to decipher, but I think I hear a warning.

"No, I won't. I'm not on-set this weekend so no worries there."

"Levi is a cameraman," Harper supplies.

William's brows arch up. He's about to say something when Harper's mom joins us.

"Levi! Hello." She wraps me in a motherly hug, meaning she hangs on for a minute, like she might not get another chance before I'm out the door. "I'm so happy to see you."

"It's nice to see you, too."

"Don't they make an adorable couple, Bill?" Harper's mom is all smiles as she tilts her head to study Harper and me.

I smile back because I was taught to be respectful of my elders. Harper, however, tenses next to me. I don't think her parents notice, since she's doing her best to act calm so her love life isn't under scrutiny this weekend, but I can feel her nerves like pinpricks on the skin of my arms. I'm not sure how I feel about it.

"Harper!" someone calls from across the restaurant. "You ready?"

She holds up her pointer finger rather than yell back.

"We'll let you guys go," Harper's mom says as she wraps her arm around her husband's to tug him away. "Levi, we'll see you at the wedding. Harp, I'll talk to you tomorrow."

"Bye." Harper gives a little wave to her parents before she turns to me. "That's my ride."

"Your ride?"

"A few of Colleen's second cousins or first cousins twice removed or something like that, are staying at the guesthouse and they want to continue the party there. They got in this morning from New York, and we drove here together."

"You don't sound very happy about it."

Her shoulders slump. "I'm not, which is why I owe you an apology. I took out my annoyance with them on you, and I'm sorry about that."

I run my finger down her bare shoulder. That's why she was grumpy when I got here. "How about I drive you home?"

Her face brightens. "I don't see why not. Be right back." There are still quite a few people enjoying themselves around the restaurant, including Colleen and George and their friends. Harper grabs her purse off the back of a chair and speaks with a small group of girls. They nod and then say hello as they pass me on their way out. Harper weaves around the rest of the room to give her good-byes.

My phone buzzes with a text. I pull it out of my pocket. Fuck. It's Kayla. She's been texting me every day since she showed up at my house. She wants to see me.

"Okay, I'm ready."

I startle at Harper's return and almost drop the phone.

"Is something wrong?" she asks.

"No. Let's go." I put my phone, and thoughts of my ex,

away.

We hit the sidewalk and a warm SoCal evening breeze greets us. This part of town is lit with streetlights, car lights, and iron lanterns on the side of the building. The valet sees me and gives a little salute to let me know he'll grab my car key.

"Have your valet ticket?" Harper asks.

"Didn't need one."

"Here you go," the valet says. He hands me the key fob. I hand him a ten.

Harper looks up and down the street. "Where's your jeep?"

"I lent it to one of the producers on the show I'm working on. He was meeting his girlfriend's young daughter for the first time and taking them both on a date tonight, and he wanted to pick them up in something a little more family oriented than his regular ride."

Harper turns her head toward the curb. There's only one car sitting just beyond the valet sign. "No fucking way!"

"Way."

She bounds over to the silver convertible Aston Martin. I follow close behind as the valet opens the passenger side door for her. "This is an Aston Martin," she announces all breathy, like she ran ten miles, not took ten steps, to get here.

"I didn't know you liked cars." I walk around to my side and climb in.

"I like *fast* cars." She runs her hands over the leather, admires the interior lines, the detail. "This is James Bond's car," she adds, her eyes meeting mine over the center console.

I lean over, cup the back of her neck, and kiss her with lips, tongue, and teeth. She kisses me back with equal enthusiasm before settling into her seat and reaching for her seat belt. I needed that. Needed to remind myself the girl sitting next to me is not a crazy person who likes to make me miserable.

"Sure is, Bond Girl."

"Take the long way," she says, looking out the windshield as I rev the engine.

"What?"

"Take the long way to get me home."

"How long are we talking?"

She pulls her phone out of her purse and texts someone before saying, "As long as you want."

My heart pounds. Not only do I have a kick-ass sports car at my fingertips, I've got an amazing girl in my passenger seat. I probably shouldn't do what I'm about to, but fuck it. "Hang on."

With the wind in our faces and the smell of the ocean teasing our noses, we drive in comfortable silence. When the road allows it, I exceed the posted speed limit. More than once we glance at each other at the same time. When it happens again, Harper reaches over and runs her fingers through my hair.

"I thought when I first saw you at the restaurant your hair looked sexier than normal. Now I know why."

"You think my hair is sexy?"

She nods and hums an agreement at the same time. "I love touching it."

Aaand my dick twitches. By the innuendo in her voice, she means more than my hair. I want to put my hand on her thigh and tiptoe my fingers under her skirt and into her panties so fucking bad, but Harper's safety is more important, so I've got to keep both hands on the steering wheel as I navigate the canyon road to our destination.

"This is the longest way to my house ever," she says, dropping her hand to my lap.

The car gives a sudden jerk when I startle. "Harper," I warn. If we were in my car, I'd be all for a hand or blow job while I drive. But I'm used to my jeep. I know the exact way it handles and runs. The machine we're in now is a whole other very expensive story. And she doesn't belong to me.

"*What?*" Harper responds innocently while she rubs her hand over the growing bulge in my pants.

I slow the car and carefully lift her arm away from my body. "We're almost there."

"Spoilsport."

"When I'm carrying precious cargo, yeah."

She thinks she hides her smile by turning her head, but I catch the happy curve at the corner of her mouth. As tough as she likes to pretend she is, there's softness at her core.

I turn right off Sunset, make a couple more turns down residential streets, and we arrive at the empty lot at the end of a cul-de-sac. I drive slowly onto the dirt parcel until the unobstructed view of the ocean drops in front of us.

"Wow." Harper unclicks her seat belt. "It's beautiful." She stares out at the sea then tilts her head back to gaze at the stars. Away from commercial lights and traffic, the stars shine brighter than normal.

"Recline your seat back," I suggest.

"Good idea."

We stretch out, hold hands, sneak peeks at each other. "This is much better than hanging out with Colleen's cousins. Thank you."

"They're staying with you until Sunday?"

"Yeah. Two are crashing in Teague's room since she's out of town, and one is sleeping on the couch. It's not that they aren't nice; they're just a little too nosy for my comfort level. And they talk nonstop." She rolls her head to the side so we're face-to-face. "My ears are literally going to fall off."

I reach over with my free hand to gently rub my finger along the rim of her ear. "That would be terrible. I like these ears."

"They're good ears," she asserts.

"You could come stay with me." The invitation is out of my mouth with zero thought, but now that the words are there, I really want her to say "yes."

"Stay with you?" She double blinks in confusion.

"At my place. Mateo is out of town with Teague, and Elliot is leaving tomorrow morning for a work thing in Chicago for the weekend. I've got the house all to myself."

Her eyes dart back and forth between mine, like she's trying to figure out my true intentions. "Are you serious?"

"Yeah. *Mi casa es su casa* if you want it. No strings attached. You can even stay in one of the guys' rooms. Wherever you're most comfortable." Okay, that's a lie, because she is staying in my bed even if I have to carry her over my shoulder to get her there.

"Umm..."

"Think about it. It's not a big deal." It's a fucking big deal if she agrees. This isn't smart, but apparently I excel at being stupid when I'm around her. "But you would have your own bathroom. And peace and quiet, if you want it. And have I told you that I make an excellent pre- and post-wedding breakfast?"

She wiggles her mouth back and forth in indecision.

"I'm also very good at delivering orgasms any time of day."

"So is my vibrator."

"Excellent. Bring him over, and we'll work together." Now I'm competing with myself and want her to agree for no other reason than my pride.

That's a lie. I want to be skin to skin with her again, to hear her say my name when I make her come.

She licks her lips and toys with the ends of her ponytail. "You've got yourself...a maybe!" She sits upright and climbs out the passenger door.

I laugh to myself. She is so coming to stay with me. I join

her at the front of the car where we stand in silence to look over the bluff. After a few minutes, she leans on the hood and scoots back so her feet are off the ground. The ocean is a sea of inky blackness, but it still commands attention.

"C'mere," I say, joining her on the hood while tucking her under my arm, our backs against the windshield.

"How did you know about this spot?" she asks.

"Found it when I was driving around looking for a hiking trail a friend recommended."

"One day there will be a house here."

"Probably. Which makes every time I visit special." I lightly rub my hand over her shoulder.

"Exactly how many girls have you brought to this spot?"

"One."

I love when I render her speechless. I continue to tickle my fingers over her bare skin, dipping lower and lower until I reach the elastic topline of her sweater. She sucks in a breath but arches her back the smallest measure to let me know I'm good to keep going.

"You look amazing tonight," I whisper in her ear. "When I walked into the restaurant you literally stopped me in my tracks and all I could do was stare." I slide my hand over her sweater and palm her breast, cup it, rub my thumb across it. "I swear you get prettier every time I see you." I smooth my hand down her stomach to the apex of her thighs. She squirms, kicks off her shoes. Her legs come up and she drops her knees to the side so the soles of her feet touch.

I lift the hem of her skirt so I can make contact with her underwear. The second I touch the silky material, she lifts her hips. Every little move she gives makes my dick twitch and satisfaction swell inside my chest. I'll never get enough of touching her.

I stroke her the way I know she likes, coaxing inarticulate murmurs and little sighs of pleasure. I'm about to sink two fingers inside her when she twists out of my hold. She faces me on her knees, her eyes sparkling with arousal.

Without a word and without breaking eye contact, she lifts her skirt and positions her pussy over my face. She pulls her panties aside with one hand, exposing her swollen flesh, and braces her other hand on the windshield.

It's sexy as hell when she takes what she wants from me. Confidence glitters in her eyes now, too.

I palm her ass to keep her steady. She watches as I dart my tongue out to lick her. One swipe compels her eyes to close. The hand on her panties moves to the back of my head. She brings me tighter, rocks against my face, unrestrained, needy. Beautiful.

I love doing this, making her feel good. Burying my nose and mouth in her most intimate spot. Feeling her legs squeeze around me, her sex grow wetter. She vibrates under my hands and grips my head more firmly, like she's hanging on for more than balance. She can ride my face for stability anytime.

"Oh my God. That feels…" She trails off, her breath quickening.

She's almost there, and if we weren't in a public spot, I'd back off to make this last longer. Instead, I slide a finger inside her, suck on her clit.

"Leeee Viiieee." She hugs my face to her center and lets go. Unrestrained. Loud. Her orgasm lingers, so I keep going, savoring her sweet taste.

When she stops shaking, I free my mouth but don't release my grip on her backside. She's limp and I don't want her to slip off the car. I slide her underwear back into place and kiss the inside of one thigh, then the other.

Her hold on my head softens further. She runs her fingers through my hair. The scrape of her nails on my scalp sends heat down my spine.

I lift my chin. Her eyes are heavy-lidded, but I get a peek

at their rich, brown-green brilliance. "You are insanely good at that," she says.

"You taste insanely good," I say in return.

"Now it's my turn." She drops down between my legs. "I want to suck you off and taste every drop."

Jesus, with the way she's looking at me, and the sexy sounding dirty talk, she's about to get her wish in no time.

She unzips my pants and reaches inside my boxer briefs. My cock springs up, ready for her full lips and wet tongue.

I'm a goner the second she takes me inside her mouth.

Chapter Eighteen

HARPER

"Stop! What are you doing?"

I freeze at the sound of terror in Levi's voice. "I'm cleaning the dishes."

He reaches around me and flicks off the garbage disposal. He made us a delicious breakfast of bacon, eggs, and toast, so the least I can do is the cleanup.

PS. He cooked shirtless. Ate shirtless. Is still shirtless. *Sigh.*

"Are you trying to lose a finger?" he asks. His brows are furrowed, his face a little pale.

I lift my arms out of the sink and grab a paper towel to dry my hands. "Don't be silly. I always push food down into the drain like this."

"*With your hands?*" A shiver visibly racks his body.

"Usually." The groove between his eyebrows deepens. I'm not sure if he's trying to look appalled or worried, but both are cute. Then it hits me. "Are you...are you afraid of the garbage disposal?"

"No," he answers quickly. Too quickly.

He is! I cross my arms over my chest.

"Maybe," he amends. "Okay, yes."

I twist around. "I'll just put the rest of this down while the disposal is off then."

"No!" He grabs my arm. "Please don't." He picks up a wooden spatula. "Use this to do that." He is totally freaked out over this.

"You know it can't suddenly turn on by itself, right?"

"It could." He is dead serious. And I realize he's terrified of even the idea of the disposal hurting me.

"You don't ever use the garbage disposal?"

"Sometimes I do, but usually I dump everything into the trash can. I know it's ridiculous."

I put my hand on his chest. His heart pounds underneath my palm. "It's not, and I'm sorry if I scared you." This strong, capable, confident man has fears just like the rest of us. It makes him even more endearing. He's human, just like me.

"I can think of a way for you to make it up to me." He traps me against the counter. Gone is his anxiety, and in its place is playfulness.

I duck under his arm and make a run for it. We've been naked together for almost twenty-four hours, and do I want to rub my body against his again? Hell, yes. He's wildly addictive. But... "Can't! I need to get dressed and head out."

He gives chase. "Five minutes."

"Ha! You know that won't be long enough." I run around the couch, giggling.

We eye each other over the leather sofa. "I'm going to catch you, Ham."

"No, you're not." I take a little step to my left.

"Want to bet?" He takes a little step to his right.

"Sure. What do you want to lose?" We circle the couch,

both of us grinning like fools. His faded jeans hang low on his waist, and he's not wearing any underwear. It's very distracting.

He laughs. "Funny thing. With you, I never lose."

"What does that mean?" I edge closer to the hallway. One more step and I'll make my escape.

But Mr. Pants Charming is also Mr. Athletic. He springs over the couch and captures me around the waist before I can bolt. "Gotcha!"

I try and squirm out of his hold. "You cheated!"

"How do you figure?" He brings me flush against his chest so the more I wiggle, the more I feel all that hard, sexy muscle through my thin tee. My heart beats faster. I don't hate that he makes my heart race. I like it, which is so much worse. I know what to do with hate. I don't know what to do with feelings of want. Desire. Need so strong I want to beg him to touch me.

Which is why all I manage to say is, "Huh?"

He grins and walks me back against the wall like we're one four-legged person, connected in all the right places. "You smell really good," he says, nuzzling my neck as his hands move down to cup my butt. All I'm wearing with my tee is a thong.

"Levi." I scrape my nails over his back, gaining some composure. "I really don't have time for this. If I'm late, my cousin, aunt, and mom will all kill me. Then I'll be triple dead, and there is no coming back from that."

"All right." He backs off, leaving me immediately in want of his body on mine again. He's like a second skin, warm and protective.

"Thank you." I give him a quick kiss on the lips. He gives me a little spank on the ass when I turn to go get dressed.

It's a good thing he doesn't follow me into his bedroom, because I would probably cave and pull down his pants. I lean against his bed to change my shirt, pulling deodorant out of my toiletry bag to swipe more under my arms first.

My phone dings with a text, but while I hear it, I don't see it. I look through the small pile of clothes I brought with me without luck. A second text sounds, drawing my eye to my pillow. The phone sticks out from underneath it. My mom had texted early this morning reminding me not to be late to my aunt's house, and I'd read it while still curled up beside Levi.

It's probably her again, asking if I'm on my way, or worse, wanting to know how Levi is. The one flaw—actually there are a couple of flaws—in staying with Levi this weekend is that everyone in my family knows I'm here. Kind of hard to keep it a secret when I'm not in the guesthouse only a few feet away from wedding central.

I stretch across the bed to pick up the phone. It's not my mom.

Your ass is spectacular.

My cheeks flame around my grin. I've received compliments from guys over the years, but none have ever gotten a reaction from me like Levi's continue to do.

I want to bite it.

Levi Pierce is ruining me. *It's yours whenever you want it*, I quickly type then hold my finger down on the backspace key to delete it. I try again. *Stop. I need to get dressed.* That's better. I hit send and notice the little dots are already at work on his end.

How am I going to get through the day now, when all I'll be able to think about is you bending over my bed like that.

I spin around. Levi is leaning against the doorframe, one leg casually crossed over the other, an entirely too-attractive look of appreciation on his face. I pin him with an annoyed glare.

"Do not step foot in here," I say. If he gets within touching distance, I will lose what little self-control I have left.

His gaze rakes over my body, threatening said control in a big way. I never imagined feeling this way again, like I'd do anything to have this one person keep looking at me like I'm everything he's ever wanted.

"I won't. Just admiring the view. You don't mind if I watch you dress, do you?"

Gah. He makes me feel powerful and helpless at the same time. I clumsily put on my bra, followed by my shirt and shorts, then slide my feet into flip-flops.

"Is it safe, now?" Levi asks, pushing away from the doorframe.

"No," I answer truthfully. Levi isn't safe. Not in the slightest.

He saunters into the room anyway, wrapping me in a hug and kissing the side of my forehead in that cherished way of his. "Have fun getting ready today."

"Thanks."

"Oh, hey. I got you something. Meant to give it to you yesterday." He steps over to his dresser and picks up a small drawstring gift bag sitting atop it. "A little girl down the street had a booth set up on the corner and was selling these to raise money for cancer research."

I take the gift with an uncomfortable ache in the middle of my chest, so of course I say something insensitive. "What happened to good old-fashioned lemonade stands?"

"I still see those sometimes, too," he says, seemingly unaware of my nervousness.

He takes my elbow and we sit side by side on the edge of his bed. I hold the lightweight bag in my lap, not at all sure I want to see what's inside. It's not only that Levi is the first guy to buy me a gift since Joe. It's that a gift tied to charity, and the kindheartedness of a child, makes it something special whether I want it to be or not. After all, my own heart is wrapped up in philanthropy.

"Is it one of her parents?" I ask.

"Her brother, actually," he says with compassion.

I close my eyes for a moment to say a silent prayer. My world was forever changed in one day. What happens when you have to live with the possibility of horrific change day after day after day? "I hope she sold out of these."

"I'm pretty sure she did." He gently bumps my arm. "Open it. When I saw what she was selling, I immediately thought of you."

Inside the bag is a piece of jewelry made out of thin black nylon cord and a silver charm.

"It's an anklet," Levi says as I pull it out. "She made them herself. The charm is a Tabono, an ancient African symbol that represents strength and perseverance. At least, that's what she said."

Emotions I don't want clog the back of my throat. There's no way Levi could know that those two traits matter more to me than almost anything else. I hold the charm between my fingers. The simple metal is shaped like a four-petal flower, the kind I used to doodle in my notebooks at school.

Because I'm well aware of what the Tabono symbol means.

"Let's put it on you." Levi kneels down and gently slips the anklet over my foot. The nylon is stretchy so he's able to adjust the tightness by pulling on the two short strings that meet where the knot is. "Perfect," he says, his fingertips lightly grazing my skin once he's done.

He's mapped my entire body with his hands and mouth, but something about this moment seems more intimate than the others before it.

All of a sudden, it's difficult to remain in the same room as him. I love this gift. More than I've loved any others. I dig my fingers into the comforter so I don't flee. Levi deserves more from me than that.

"What do you think?" he asks, sitting beside me.

I nod. "I like it. Thank you." I'm never going to take it off.

"You're welcome. You okay? I'm thinking my timing could have been better here."

"Your timing does kind of suck."

"Because you want to make out with me now?"

"Yes, that's exactly why." I get to my feet, grateful for his sense of humor at the perfect time. "And I do need to go."

Levi stands. "I'll see you on the aisle. Five o'clock, right?"

"Right." I put my hands on his shoulders, then stretch up on my tiptoes to kiss one eyelid, then the other, followed by light kisses to his cheek and the corner of his mouth. It's the most tender I've been with him, and long overdue. I might be planning to break things off with him tomorrow, but I've cherished our time together, too.

Soft caramel eyes look down at me. "What was that for?"

"Being really good to me." I quickly grab my bag. "I'll see you later. Don't be late!" I add over my shoulder. I'm out the bedroom door and in my car a minute later.

It's happy chaos when I get to my aunt's house. The wedding coordinator is directing the florist, caterers, and rental company people with a small bullhorn. Yes, a bullhorn. The house is really big, as is the backyard. I hurry upstairs to Colleen's room.

"Hi!" Colleen waves to me from across her old bedroom, transformed into a bridal suite for today. She's sitting in a chair wearing a short satin robe, eating an apple with her feet propped up. Her wedding dress is hanging beside her.

"Happy wedding day," I say. (In case you were wondering, I'm five minutes ahead of my assigned arrival time.)

"Harper," my mom says with delight, sweeping me into the room to join the party. There's a table set up with food, champagne, and bottled water. Bridesmaids' dress bags hang on a portable garment rack with our names written on the outside. Fresh flowers are everywhere.

I greet my aunt and Colleen's maid of honor. Within minutes, Colleen's other bridesmaids arrive. There's a ton of excitement in the air, and for the rest of the afternoon we eat, talk, laugh, take pictures, and get prepped for the wedding.

Once my hair and makeup are done, I slip into my dress. Standing in front of the full-length mirror to look at myself, my first thought is, *I wonder what Levi will think.*

"You look beautiful, sweetheart."

"Thanks, Mom."

She hands me my shoes. I lift the hem of the strapless, emerald green dress, and with the attention on my feet now, my mom notices the anklet Levi gave me. "What's that?" she asks.

"An anklet."

"I know that. I've never seen you wear it before."

I slide my foot into the strappy heel dyed to match the color of the dress. "It's new." I'm not being a very nice daughter. I know this. But my mom will make a really big deal out of it, and I don't want to encourage her to be any more interested than she already is.

Mom, the queen of McKnowing Everything, crosses her arms over her very pretty pale-yellow dress and commands me without saying a word to spill the whole truth. It's her superpower, goddammit.

"Levi gave it to me."

"He did?" With her enthusiasm, it's hard to tell if it's a question or announcement. Thankfully, everyone else in the room is busy, or all eyes would be on us.

"Yes." I go on to tell her about the charm and what it means.

She pats the corner of her eye. "Follow me, please."

"*Mom.*" I follow her into the hallway where she wraps me in a hug. "Mom, please don't make this a big deal."

"I'm not. But I have a question for you."

"Okay."

"Have you told him about Joe?"

I let out a breath. "Yes."

She brushes a tendril of hair off my neck. "I'm glad. That's a big step for you."

"Please don't get your hopes up here."

"Too late. But they're not up for the reasons you think."

I've no idea what to make of my mother right now. She's acting more confusing than normal.

"Now really isn't the time to talk about it," she says, "but for reasons I'll share with you later, I've been seeing a therapist."

"Is everything all right?" My legs shake. My mom isn't big on delving too deep into feelings, so I'm afraid something is wrong.

"Yes. Everything is fine." She squeezes my wrist. "What I quickly want to say to you is I'm optimistic about you not settling for things the way they are. I hate that you've let the past hold you hostage, and letting Levi in tells me maybe you're ready to let go."

"It's not like that."

"I think it is. And I hope you realize the person holding you back is yourself. Not Joe. First loves are hard to get over, and he will always hold a special place in your heart, but clinging to him isn't living your life."

I grip the iron banister, rocking back on my heels. "I'm not clinging to him. He's dead." My words are cold, clipped, like a slap to the face, and my mom flinches. "Sorry," I say more softly.

"You have no reason to be sorry." Several beats of silence pass. I really don't want to talk about this, but I can tell my mom wants to say more. "It's not that you can't love again. It's that you've chosen not to." She puts her arm around my shoulders.

"You're still young, and still figuring out who you are, and I'm sorry if I push a little too hard on the relationship front."

"A little?"

"Or a lot. But it's because I believe in you. You have more love in your heart than anyone else I know, and it would be a shame not to give it to someone who wants to love you back."

The whispers in the back of my mind telling me I don't need anyone grow louder. My mom is right. This is my choice. Because it would kill me to lose someone I loved again. "Can we finish this conversation another time?"

"I hope we do."

I put my happy face in place when we walk back into the room. Watching my mom with my aunt and cousin, I think it's the high of today and the love in the air that prompted her openness. Maybe it's the passage of time, too. I craved her perspective when I was sixteen, but she didn't—or couldn't—share it with me back then.

She smiles at me from across the room. I smile back. When we separate for the ceremony, she tells me she loves me.

As I walk down the aisle on the arm of a groomsman, my gaze immediately finds Levi's. His eyes, already on me, tell me he very much likes what he sees. For the entire service, I feel his gaze, and it makes me lightheaded. Smiley.

A little while after the ceremony, his strong arms firmly envelop me from behind, and a feeling of trust and utter protection seeps into my bones. "Hi, beautiful," he says. He nuzzles my neck and nibbles on my ear. "You look unbelievable."

My head falls back on his shoulder. "Thank you. You're not so bad yourself."

His lips graze my jaw, then the corner of my mouth, then I'm turning in his arms and we're kissing, right there for anyone to see.

And I don't care.

Chapter Nineteen

If the douchebag moves his hands any lower on Harper's back, I'm going to lose my shit and march onto the dance floor to physically remove them from her body. This is fucking torture, watching her dance with him. Screw first dances and bridal party requirements.

"Here," a guy says, thrusting a bottle of beer in front of me.

I take the drink and note the giver. It's Harper's brother, Carson. "Thanks."

"You looked like you needed one."

"That obvious, huh?"

"Yeah, but don't sweat it. We've all been there."

"Wanting to break a guy's nose?"

Carson laughs. "More than once, my friend. More than once."

I down a large gulp of the ale. We're standing in the backyard under a large umbrella. There are umbrellas all over, blocking most of the sun, but spaced to allow for some beams to filter through, too. The dance floor is transparent and spans the swimming pool. A bar, cocktail tables, and flower arrangements fill the rest of the area. Food servers weave through the guests. In another part of the yard I didn't even realize existed, dinner will be served.

The song ends, thank fuck, but rather than come to me like I hope, Harper stays put to dance with the other bridesmaids and her cousin. The song is "P.Y.T." by Michael Jackson.

Her eyes briefly catch mine when she glances over her shoulder. One little look and my pulse picks up. Good to know she's as aware of me as I am of her.

"Funny how you and my sister met up again," Carson says. "I vaguely remember being pissed at you because she wanted to play with you instead of me."

"Really?" Carson is a couple of years older than Harper, and yeah, I recall him not liking me very much.

"Yeah. She also told me in that bossy tone of hers she was going to marry you."

"Who's being bossy?" Harper's dad asks. He's got a glass filled with amber liquid on the rocks in his hand. His free hand, he extends to me. "Nice to see you again, Levi."

We shake. "You, too."

"Harper can be bossy," Carson says.

"When you grow up with two older brothers who let you get away with everything, that's what happens."

Carson shrugs. My attention drifts over to the dance floor. Harper is shaking her hips and swinging her arms, and if her father weren't standing next to me, my dick would have a strong reaction to her skills.

"Harper mentioned you're a cameraman," William says.

"Yes."

"Did she tell you about the job I want her for?" He takes

a sip of his drink, like he casually tosses out that question all the time, but I get the feeling he doesn't.

"No. I thought she wanted the ambassador job with MASF."

A twenty-something girl bounces up to Carson, says they need to boogie, and tugs him toward the dance floor. He doesn't look too pleased by the invitation, but stumbles along behind her anyway.

"She does," William says. "But I always pictured all three of my children working for me. I admire her philanthropic aspirations, but they're a hobby, not a job."

"What is it you do?" I think it's something to do with the media.

He explains he owns numerous companies around the world involved in mass media enterprises. He also invests in films, and he wants Harper to work on an upcoming film as a swim consultant. Normally, I'm all about talking movies, but I don't want to get in the middle of anything between Harper and her dad. Thankfully, I'm saved from further discussion when my phone rings. It's not often I get an actual call, so I quickly check it.

"Sorry, but I need to answer this." I reach over to put my beer down on the closest cocktail table. William nods then turns his attention to another guest.

"Hello?" I say to Elliot, pressing my cell to my ear and walking toward a quieter area of the backyard. I press a finger to my other ear so I can hear better.

"Hey, where are you?" Elliot asks. We've seen each other for all of ten minutes over the past week, what with our busy work schedules.

"I'm at a wedding."

"You are? Whose is it?"

"Harper's cousin." I hadn't mentioned it. And I haven't mentioned Harper to him, either. Technically, I won the bet, but I forgot about our stupid wager a while ago and plan to give him the money. I don't want what I did with Harper tied to my competition with him. "Aren't you in Chicago? Is everything okay?"

"I quit."

"Your job?" I knew it stressed him out, but I thought he liked it.

"Yeah. They piled one too many ridiculous demands on me, and I walked out of a meeting and caught the first flight home."

I lean against a giant tree on the periphery of the reception. I've still got Harper in my sights, but barely.

"I was fucking tired of all the bullshit," he adds. "I've busted my ass for the past two years, and I'm done."

"I'm sorry, man."

"I need to get shitfaced."

And he needs a friend to do it with. Since Mateo is out of town, that leaves me. "Want to crash a wedding?" By the looks of it, there's enough alcohol here for three weddings, and this way I don't have to ditch Harper.

"Brilliant idea. I can drink and hook up with someone." I hear some rustling, like he's changing his clothes. "Speaking of hooking up. Where do we stand on our bet? Did you sleep with Harper again?"

Right on cue, the woman in question comes into clearer view. I don't want to have this conversation in front of her. "Yeah, but not because of the—"

"Well, shit. I owe you a Ben, then."

"Hey," Harper says floating over to me. Her strapless green dress brushes the ground, and the way she moves gives the illusion she's drifting. She is incredibly beautiful, graceful, and by the look on her face, curious about what I'm doing over here and who I'm talking to.

"You don't. Gotta go. I'll text you the address." I

disconnect the call.

"Is everything all right?" she asks.

"That was Elliot. He quit his job."

"Mr. Suit-and-Tie quit? That seems very out of character for him."

"Yeah. I don't think it's sunk in yet, but he needs some company and alcohol. Do you think anyone would mind if he came here?"

She glances over her shoulder at the crowd of people eating, drinking, dancing and talking. "I think it's fine." She gives me the address, and I text it.

"So," I gather her into my arms. "This is much better."

She wraps me closer. "Yeah? Why is that? Because you're trying to cop a feel of my ass, or because you're angling to look down my dress?"

I grab her ass and glance down at her chest. "Both."

"All the single girls are drooling over you, by the way. Some of the married ones, too. I'm being bombarded with questions about us."

"What are you telling them?"

"That I hired you for the weekend." She gives me an exaggerated grin. "And that you're very expensive but, so far, well worth it."

"That explains the invitation I got to go to Hawaii," I tease back.

"How fun. When are you leaving?"

"Okay, you two, get a room," Colleen says, brushing by us. "But not until after I throw the bouquet!"

Harper gives me a serious look. "I don't do the bouquet thing."

"That's good. Neither do I."

"I might be up for the room thing, though. Want to sneak into the guesthouse?"

"Lead the way." She's had me turned on since the second

I saw her. A quickie is exactly what I need to tide me over until we're back at my place later.

"Come on." Taking my hand, she leads me around cocktail tables and the dance floor, where the photographer intercepts to ask us for a picture. That ten-second delay costs us.

Good friends of Harper's parents stop to chat with us next. Then it's friends who've known Harper since she was a little girl.

When Elliot arrives, we abandon any hope of sneaking away, but that's okay. It's a great evening, and when we get back to my house around midnight, I show her just how well worth it I am.

. . .

"I turned it off," Harper says matter-of-factly.

"Really?"

"Yep."

"Let's see." We're on the couch, her feet are in my lap, and apparently she's "turned off" her ticklishness. She's got several ticklish spots—under her arms, on her right side, on her stomach near her hipbone. And the bottoms of her feet. I lightly trace my finger along the sole of one foot.

Sure enough, she stays still.

I keep going. She flinches a tiny bit when my finger tickles the soft center, but I can tell she's concentrating on keeping her body under control.

"See?" she says. "Not ticklish."

I could get used to mornings like this. Harper lying beside me, wearing one of my shirts and a tiny pair of underwear and nothing else. Her hair a wild, sexy mess around her shoulders. Her smell on my skin. The television tuned to ESPN, the volume low.

"What about if I move here?" I slowly drag the tips of my fingers to the inside of her ankle, over the anklet I gave her, and continue up her calf.

"Nope," she forces out. It's getting more difficult for her to keep still. Because there's one more place she's ticklish, and the anticipation is sometimes worse than the actual tickling.

"What about here? Have you turned it off here?" I trace one finger behind her knee.

"Okay! Stop!" She giggles and kicks her feet.

I roam my hands all over her body as I climb on top of her. She tries tickling me back, but I'm not ticklish anywhere. Her shirt rides up her thighs. Her legs open so I can better situate myself. Then we're kissing. She slides a hand inside my boxer briefs and grabs a fistful of my tee with the other.

She tastes like coffee and feels like cashmere, and I want this girl for more Sunday mornings.

The timer on the oven beeps. I ignore it, but Harper squirms and says, "the cinnamon rolls." For breakfast, she wanted the refrigerated rolls you buy at the store and just put in the oven, so that's what she's getting.

I lift up on to my elbows. "Do you want to put the icing on?"

"That's okay, you can do it. I'll just lounge here on the couch waiting to be served," she says playfully. One thing Harper is not is a pampered princess, which makes doing things for her that much more enjoyable.

"I hear it's best to eat cinnamon rolls shirtless." I get to my feet and give her a hand sitting up.

"Great idea. You should take yours off."

"I will if you will."

She swats my butt. "Go. I don't like my cinnamon rolls too well done."

"Be right back." I stride across the hardwood floor and around the corner into the kitchen with a ridiculous grin on my face. I'm stoked she seems in no rush to leave this morning. Elliot went home with a friend of Colleen's last night, so we've got the house to ourselves. "They look good," I call as I pull the pan out of the oven.

"Great!" she calls back.

I'm plating our breakfast when the doorbell rings.

"Want me to get that?" Harper asks loudly.

It's probably my next-door neighbor, Zoe. She's the cutest kid and usually makes an appearance on the weekends to see what the guys and I are up to. She's especially close to Mateo and most likely checking to see if he's home from his trip. "Sure."

"Hi. Can I help you?" Harper says.

"Who are you?" The familiar female voice floats to my ears, and my body immediately goes rigid, every muscle in my body flexing.

A second later, I'm at Harper's side, looking at Kayla on my doorstep. Her eyes slide to mine. The hairs on the back of my neck stand up. "Hi. Can we talk?" she says sweetly.

Beside me, Harper tenses.

"I'm busy, Kayla, and I thought you weren't coming back here again." This is what I get for not texting her back.

Harper darts a look at me out of the corner of her eye. Her face is blank, so I've no idea what she's thinking.

"I needed to see you. There's something you should know."

"You have nothing to say that concerns me anymore."

"Levi." She reaches out to touch my arm, but Harper blocks her hand.

"Don't touch him," Harper says in a possessive tone.

"Excuse me, but who are you?" Kayla bites out.

"I'm his girlfriend, and I know all about you, so please turn around and leave us alone."

My girlfriend? I fucking love the save.

Kayla doesn't. Her eyes turn into slits. "This is none of your business."

"It kind of is."

"Levi, can I please have a word with you alone?" She puts a hand on her stomach, no doubt to draw attention there, and the part of me that does wish her well rises to the surface.

"Whatever you have to say, you can say in front of both of us," Harper says.

Fuck. While I want that to be true, I'm worried about what Kayla might say. She's not here to play nice. She's here because she wants something.

"I don't think so, slut. And if you think I'm wrong, ask him."

"What did you just call me?"

"Kayla, that's enough. You can say whatever you want to me, but don't talk to her like that." I'm trying to keep my cool and be careful not to say the name "Harper." I don't want to give Kayla any more ammunition to use against me later.

"I'm sorry," she says to me, not Harper. "My emotions are all over the map with the baby and all."

Oh hell no. If she brings up the baby and me in the same sentence in front of Harper, I'll lose it. I don't know what her end game is, or what she hopes to accomplish by standing at my front door, but I don't want Harper involved any more than she already is.

"Understandable, but I have nothing to say to you. I told you the other week, you need to talk to—"

"I just need you to listen for five minutes," she says in a way that's both desperate and pleading.

Harper cringes. I'm not sure in reaction to who, but it's enough that I want Kayla gone.

"No. I'm sorry." I start to shut the door.

Kayla slaps the wood, making a loud *thud* to halt my progression. "You have to listen to me! You have to help me!"

"Whoa," Harper says, putting a hand up. "It's okay."

A look crosses Kayla face. One I've seen countless times. It's her Academy-Award–winning, smug, got-you-where-I-want-you face. I don't buy it anymore, not for a second. My temper flares. I'm reminded that this girl is toxic and doesn't care about anyone but herself.

"Get the hell away from me," I say, reining in my escalating anger—and my fear. That Kayla didn't heed Elliot's warning, that she's about to get worked up again, concerns me.

"Levi," Harper says quietly.

"She's crazy," I say.

"I'm not," Kayla argues. "I'm still in love with you, Levi, and want us to raise this baby together."

Harper stumbles back like Kayla punched her in the stomach.

My pulse flies out of control. If Kayla thinks for one second that we'll ever get back together, she's delusional. I clench my fists and take a deep breath. "Leave right now, Kayla, and don't ever come back, or I swear to God—"

"It's a boy," Kayla announces. "Another boy for us to—"

Harper gasps.

"Stop fucking talking and leave before I call the police." I close the door on her protests and lock it. She knocks and screams my name. I hate that she's forced me to act like this, but there's no reasoning with her when she sets her mind on something.

The neighbor up the street is a police officer. I call him and tell him the situation, that my ex is mentally unstable and pregnant—*not* with my child—and on my porch. He agrees to run over and escort her off the property, making sure she's okay to drive. I thank him and hang up.

When I look around for Harper, she's not in the room. My stomach sinks.

I find her in my bedroom getting her things together to

leave. Seeing her visibly upset hurts worse than anything Kayla could have said.

"Hey." I put my phone on the nightstand and hug her from behind, the feel of her body against mine instantly helping to ease my anxiety.

"Your heart is pounding," she says.

"Yeah."

She gently moves out of my arms and sits on the bed. "So is mine. That was kind of intense."

"It was. I'm sorry."

"This isn't the first time Kayla's been here recently," she says to the floor.

I kneel before her, hands on top of her knees. I'm grateful when she meets my eyes. "She showed up here out of the blue a week and a half ago. I hadn't seen her in months before that."

"What did she want?"

"To upset me. Tell me lies so I'm miserable like her."

"It sounds to me like she wants you back and the baby is yours."

I straighten my back and tilt Harp's chin up between my thumb and finger so I can look her right the eyes. "The baby is not mine, and it doesn't matter how she feels about me. I don't want anything to do with her ever again."

"Are you sure?"

Fuck, it hurts for her to even ask that question after everything that's happened between us.

"I'm sure I can't be around her, and I'm sure she's lying about the baby. She's married to the guy who knocked her up."

"The guy she cheated on you with?"

"Yeah, but supposedly he's leaving her. That's the only reason she came looking for me. She's good at preying on my sympathy."

Harper takes my wrist and laces our fingers together atop her leg. "You've been good at saving her. You said so yourself."

"Not anymore. Honestly, she makes me sick to my stomach when I see her. She's manipulative and selfish, and I don't know what's going to come out of her mouth next."

My phone rings on the nightstand. I glance over, as does Harper. We both see the caller ID: Kayla. Unbelievable.

"She still calls you?"

"Rarely. She, uh, usually texts."

Harper stands. "I need to go."

I get to my feet. "Yeah, okay." Fuck, it hurts to say that. But this situation is messed up, and maybe we both need a minute to ourselves. Harper isn't Kayla, I know that. But the thing is, in some ways, Harper scares me more than Kayla ever did.

"You know you can block her number?" She finds a pair of shorts in her pile of clothes and pulls them on.

"I'll do it now if you want."

"It's not a matter of what I want," she says hastily. She changes out of my shirt and into one of hers, not bothering with a bra. "It's what you want."

Without a second thought, I grab her around the waist so we're face-to-face. "I want *you.*" It's staggering how much I suddenly want that. My head may have doubts, but my heart is telling me to hold on to this amazing girl and never let go.

She puts her hands on my shoulders. If she tells me she doesn't want me, I'm calling bullshit. I see it and feel it whenever we're together.

The silence hangs heavy between us.

I speak first. "I can't promise you anything right now, Ham, but I don't want to let you go, either."

"I don't know," she murmurs, the words a life preserver. If she needs help and guidance to keep hanging out with me,

I'm happy to give it.

"You want this, too. If you didn't, you wouldn't have stood up for me like you did." She scrunches her nose. I kiss the tip.

"I said that to protect to you."

"Because you like me."

"I like having sex with you," she fires back.

"Perfect. I feel the same, so let's keep doing what we're doing." If she's not ready to deal with the emotions that connect us, too, then we can keep it casual. I'm willing to do things her way until she feels differently. I can't give up the calm she brings me. Can't quit her like this, cold turkey. If she hadn't been here this morning when Kayla showed up, I'd probably be on my third beer by now.

She breaks free of my hold to pace around the room.

I watch her. When we're in the same room, I can't take my eyes off her. "There's just one thing…"

"What?"

"It has to stay exclusive. I want your body all to myself, Ham."

Conflict plays in the depths of brown staring back at me. "So, I see you when I see you, and we only have sex with each other."

"Yes."

Seconds tick by. "Okay."

I grin and pull her close for one more kiss to seal the deal.

But when she leaves a few minutes later with a "see you later" I wonder if I've made a huge mistake.

5 Reasons Why I Deserve a High Five Right Now

1. I was a great bridesmaid and Colleen had a stress-free wedding.

2. I found my most-loved pair of flip-flops when I cleaned my closet and got rid of a bunch of clothes to give to charity.

3. Josh drew me a picture of the two of us in the pool with Spider-Man and put it in a frame to give to me at his last swim lesson. It's the most precious gift I've received from a student. It made me feel like a great teacher. Not to mention he swims across the pool like a champ now and loved the gold medal I gave him.

4. I put on my big girl pants and realized what this thing with Levi is. He doesn't want my heart, just my body, so I'm in no jeopardy. On the contrary, I'm the lucky girl who gets to see him naked and have orgasms and leave it at that.

5. Last night I had a good dream about Joe rather than my usual nightmare. Does this mean I'm ready to move on? I think maybe it does. Baby steps.

Chapter Twenty

"I'm not sure what to do."

"I wish I could tell you, but this has to be your decision," Teague says.

"Can't it be yours?"

She bumps my hip in a good-natured show of support. "Sorry, Charlie. However, I can decide what our next drink should be."

We're currently enjoying a sunset cocktail cruise in the Marina Del Rey harbor. It's research for Teague. Her job as a honeymoon planner has really taken off. She works exclusively with Gabrielle Gallagher, the biggest wedding consultant on the west coast—and Mateo's mom. They call it concierge honeymoon planning because Teague personally experiences every trip and activity they suggest. About once a week when Teague's in town, she picks a romantic activity in the L.A. area to write about for her travel blog and to add to her list of best spots for honeymooners in SoCal. She's a tough critic and unless the experience is exceptional, she won't recommend it. She also usually brings Mateo on these outings, but he had another commitment tonight.

I take a sip of my Madras. "What if telling my story blows up in my face? What if people think I'm a horrible person for what happened to Joe?"

Teague stops mid-sip on her strawberry cosmo. "No one will think that."

"How do you know?"

"Because a teenage boy you *loved* drowned. A mom and dad lost their only son. It was an *accident*."

"I shouldn't have—"

"Do not start with that again or I will kick your butt."

"What if I have a panic attack talking about it? What if people pity me? What if my story causes backlash from conservative families who frown on teenage drinking?" I grip the rail with my free hand. The harbor is busy tonight with sailboats, paddle boarders, and other yachts floating under the setting sun.

"What if you *don't* have a panic attack? What if people applaud you? What if you raise awareness on teen drinking, too, because the fact is most teenagers drink, and it's often the ones from strict families who like to rebel the most.

"*What if…*" She pauses until I turn my head to look at her. "What if this is the first step to finally letting go of the past? Are you afraid to do that? Worried that if you do move on you'll have to face your feelings for a certain hot cameraman?"

"I hate *what if*." And I have no feelings for Pants Charming. No deep feelings.

Right. Keep thinking that and your new nickname will be Pants on Fire.

She laughs. "I think we all do a little bit. The unknown is scary. But if anyone can handle it, it's you."

"I just make everyone think I can," I admit. "I'm good at hiding my insecurities and making people believe everything is okay."

"When you walk into a room, Harp, people notice. You don't just turn men's heads, but women's, too."

"What does that have to do with anything?"

"Appetizer?" a server interrupts. She holds up a tray of stuffed mushrooms. Since Teague is here to scrutinize everything, she says "thank you" even though mushrooms aren't her favorite food. To help her out, I take one, too.

"What do you think?" she asks after taking a small bite.

"I think it's really good," I say while chewing. I tossed the whole damn thing in my mouth. When finished, I go back to our conversation. "So what does my walking into a room have to do with anything?"

"You think on some level you're fake with people, but you're not. The only way someone commands attention like you is if they're genuine. You may have secrets and things you don't like to talk about, but you're sincere in everything you say and do. Even with the guys you go out with, you've only always been truthful."

She's right. I've never doubted myself this much before. But that's because I've never had this much at stake. To further complicate my decision, my dad has decided I need more time to think about the film offer before I give him a definitive "no." I'm not changing my mind, but I agreed so I could get him off my back. My worry is if he doesn't chill, and I stick to my guns, what will that do to our relationship? Will I cave to make him happy? It's possible I can work on the film, teach the few swim lessons I have in the fall and winter, *and* be the ambassador for MASF?

I spin around and lean my back against the railing. Teague does the same. We sip our drinks. There are about a dozen other couples on board with us. Across the deck, a man gets down on one knee. He pulls a velvet box out of his pocket.

"Oh my gosh," Teague says excitedly.

The woman's hands fly to her mouth, covering a smile evident in the crinkle around her eyes. I can't hear what the guy says, but whatever it is, it's good because the woman starts to cry and visibly shake. The man pulls a ring out of the box. It sparkles from all the way over here. The woman nods like crazy and puts her hand out so he can slide the ring onto her finger. She falls to her knees and they embrace.

"That was so romantic," Teague says.

I put my arm around my believer-in-happily-ever-after best friend. I have to admit, it kind of was. I've never witnessed a proposal before, and this one was simple and, okay, romantic, given the setting. I, for one, would prefer to be alone when I get engaged, but...

When you get engaged? Since when is that ever going to happen?

I eye the contents of my drink. They must put something in their cocktails to cause crazy, starry-eyed thoughts.

"How long have you two been together?" a woman asks beside Teague and me.

I turn my head in surprise. The woman is with a man I assume is her husband, and they're looking at my BFF and me like we're adorable. Teague glances at me in confusion. *Don't worry, sweetness, I've got this.*

"Five and a half years," I say honestly, squeezing her tighter and kissing her cheek. It's been that long since we met our first day at UO and fell into mad friendship-love.

"I could tell it had been a while," the woman says with a smile.

"College sweethearts," I say, feeling the situation register with Teague when her shoulders shake with amusement.

"Yes. We started as roommates, and then it became

more," she adds. Another truth. She's the sister I never had.

"Would you like us to take a picture of the two of you?"

"That would be great, thanks." I hand over my cell. The woman takes the photo then hands the phone back. She and her husband tell us to have a good night and they head toward the main cabin. Once they're out of sight, Teague and I look at each other and crack up.

"If you ever get tired of Mateo," I say through a giggle, "I'm your girl."

"If you ever get tired of Levi, I'm yours."

"I'm not his," I say.

Teague gives me the you-are-lying-to-yourself look.

I had the best intentions of letting him go after Colleen's wedding, but I couldn't do it. I'm straddling some invisible line I don't even know how to name. The thought of being with him scares the shit out of me. The thought of being without him scares the shit out of me. The latter won out on Sunday morning when he made it clear he wasn't emotionally invested in me. *I want your body all to myself, Ham.* That's what I wanted from the start, right? So, I can keep things light between us because it *does* hurt to think about him with anyone else but me.

Seeing Kayla at his doorstep cut through my bones. I ached all over while trying to stay calm and unaffected. Her declarations, true or not, weren't something I ever wanted to hear. On top of that, seeing her pregnant was hard to swallow. I wondered about her first pregnancy. Wondered if Levi wondered. I believe him when he says he wants nothing to do with her anymore. But I also *know* Levi. He isn't the kind of guy to turn his back on someone who needs help, even if that someone's stabbed him.

Maybe he needs my help to deal with Kayla, just like I need his to help me deal with Joe.

Snapping fingers under my nose rouse me from my

thoughts. "Hello? Did you hear what I said?" Teague asks.

"Sorry. No. I zoned out for a minute."

"Are you okay?"

"Honestly, having to make a decision about MASF and thinking about Levi at the same time is stressing me out." I swap my cocktail for a new one when a server brings us fresh drinks.

"Do you want to talk about him more?"

"It's nothing." I wave away her concern. I'd given her the quick and dirty version of what happened between us, and I'm being ridiculous right now. The proposal thing just got me a little worked up, I think.

"It's not nothing, Harp. Whatever is on your mind you need to get it off your chest."

I blow out a sigh. She's right, of course. "I'm afraid to trust myself, I guess. And I'm maybe a little worried I won't be able to keep it casual. I feel…I feel a pull to him I've never felt with anyone else before. Not even…"

"Not even Joe," Teague finishes for me.

I nod, my heart pounding. I'm an idiot. I feel so much more than friendship toward Levi. He might not want my heart, but I want his.

"Don't be ashamed for feeling that way. You're not the same person you were at sixteen. Joe was your first love, but maybe Levi is your last love." Teague gives me a thoughtful look. "Don't give up on him. I've seen how he looks at you."

For the rest of the cruise we talk about Teague's upcoming trip to Hawaii for her sister's destination wedding.

As the sun sinks below the horizon, the yacht pulls into the dock. On the way to the parking lot, Teague gets a text from Mateo. He's home and wants her to come over. "Levi is home, too," she says. "And a couple of other guys are there. Want to stop by?"

I haven't seen or talked to Levi since Sunday morning.

I texted him once, to thank him for being my wedding date since I'd been remiss about voicing it while we were together. He texted back it was his pleasure. Other than that, I've gotten exactly what I'd wanted: space.

"Yeah, I do."

It takes forty-five minutes to get to their house. I'm a Nervous Nelly the whole way. Not the shy or timid kind of nervous, but the excited, can't-wait-to-see-you kind. Which, for the record, is way worse.

We don't bother knocking on the front door, just go right inside and shout "hello." "Back here," Mateo returns, meaning the backyard. He jumps up from his chair when we step outside.

Their yard is smallish but inviting, with a stone patio, grassy area, and cushioned furniture situated around an outdoor fireplace. Trees and ivy-covered fencing give privacy. Elliot is standing at the grill barbecuing something that smells delicious. He waves a pair of tongs as a greeting. He's got a beer in his other hand. Levi and the guys' friends Sullivan and Puck are sitting in chairs, also drinking beers.

Levi is on his feet a second after Mateo.

We exchange hellos with everyone, and then Mateo is kissing Teague so hard he lifts her feet off the ground. Levi stands in front of me and says, "I want to kiss you so badly, but I wasn't sure if that was—"

I wrap my arms around his neck and answer him with an openmouthed kiss. His arms go around my waist, bringing my hips to his and reminding me that this right here, this closeness, feels more right than anything I've ever felt before.

"It's okay," I whisper against his lips before pulling back.

"I know it's only been four days, but it feels like forever since I saw you," he says. "Would it be rude if I picked you up, carried you to my bedroom, and kept you naked for the rest of the night?"

I swallow the humiliation of having just thought how special it was to be close to him. This is all physical for him. *Walls up, Harper.* "Yes, that would be rude. Plus, I'm hungry. My date earlier only fed me appetizers."

His face drops. "You had a date earlier?"

"With my girlfriend, Teague." I slap Teague's butt as Mateo stops accosting her mouth. "I went with her to check out a sunset cruise."

"Oh, okay. Come sit down. The sooner I feed you the sooner we can get naked, right?"

Armor on, too. I lean into his side and breathe in his yummy, one-of-a-kind scent. I'm good at sex. Great at it. I can do this. "Right."

"Burgers are ready," Elliot announces.

"I'll grab you some food." Levi steers me to a cushioned bench seat. "Save the spot next to you."

"How's it going, Van?" I say to Sullivan when he sits across from me with two burgers on his plate. He looks exactly like Zac Efron, and from what the guys say, he's used that to his advantage. Yep, he's pretended to be the movie star to get laid. According to him he never actually *tells* a girl he's Zac, she just assumes.

"Excellent. You?"

"I'm good."

"Just good? Levi is doing something wrong if you're only good." He winks at me.

"That's why I'm here."

His forehead wrinkles in confusion as he takes a bite of his burger.

"I'm good right now, but later I'll be outstanding." I wink back. My shoulders relax. This is me, how I've operated for the past seven years.

He smiles while he chews. Once he's swallowed he says, "Nice comeback."

"What's nice?" Levi asks, handing me a cheeseburger then sitting beside me. "Are you flirting with my girl, Van?"

I'm under no delusion he meant "my" in any way other than making sure Van doesn't piss in the same place he does.

"I can't help my natural state," Van says with a grin.

"Of smelling bad?" Puck interjects as he joins us.

"That's not what your sister said last night," Van fire backs.

Puck glares at his friend. It's always like this with the guys. Banter with no real menace behind it, because they're all the best of friends and truly respect each other. "Fuck you. You better not even think about my sister like that."

Van gets a teasing glint in his eye. "She said you'd say that."

Puck throws a pickle at him. Van catches it and pops it in his mouth.

Teague, Mateo, and Elliot join us with their plates, and we eat and talk about work, football, baseball teams heading into the playoffs, and the mile-high club.

"She was the hottest flight attendant I've ever seen," Elliot says, "and it's weird that she was on my flight to *and* from San Francisco, right?"

"Not really," I say. "I think they have regular routes, so it's not entirely unthinkable."

"If I get asked back up there for a second interview and she's on the flight, I'm getting up her skirt."

Puck shakes his head. "Bro, she won't let you near her skirt, let alone what's under it."

"Not while she's working anyway," Levi adds.

"A hundred bucks says I get her in the lavatory."

Levi's back straightens. He shakes his head.

"Come on dude, you're two up on me now. I need a win."

"I can't believe you keep track of your bets," Puck says. "Nerd much?"

"How many bets have you guys made?" Teague asks.

"It's not important," Levi says, staring straight at Elliot.

"We've been at it since our freshman year in high school when I bet him I could run the mile faster than he could."

"Did you?" I ask.

"No. And that's probably why we still make them. If I'd won, Levi probably would have dropped it, but I had to get back at him."

"What's the last bet you guys made?" I put my plate down on the ground, finished inhaling my burger. I really was hungry.

Levi and Elliot look at each other and some weird vibe passes between them. I'm not the only one who notices.

"Aww, did one of you get your feelings hurt this time?" Puck asks.

Neither of them answers. "Anyone hungry for dessert?" Teague asks, popping to her feet with her trademark winsome smile.

"Yes." Mateo stands and lifts her over his shoulders. "Ice cream's in the freezer," he shares with the group before he carries my best friend away. "Mateo!" she squeals, but doesn't even try to wiggle out of his hold.

"I'll go get it." I gather up some plates on my way to the kitchen.

"Seriously, what's wrong with you two?" I hear Van ask from over my shoulder.

"Hey." Levi brushes up beside me a moment later.

"You making sure I don't put my hand near the garbage disposal?" I tease because suddenly things seem too serious.

Levi takes the plates out of my hand and puts them in the sink. "No, I need to tell you about our last bet." He laces his fingers with mine, the touch always welcome, and leads me to the couch.

We sit facing each other. Regret is carved in his handsome

features, making him no less attractive, only heartbreakingly honest. "You bet about me," I surmise. I've seen these guys be competitive and since the first time I met Elliot—which happened to be the first time Teague met Mateo—I knew he was interested in me.

"Yes. It wasn't my idea, but I went along with it."

I scoot back until my butt hits the arm of the couch. I don't want to be within reach anymore. The only reason I don't get up and leave is because I won't give him the satisfaction of knowing how much it hurts to think I meant even less than I thought.

"Ham." He reaches for me, but I lean away.

"Don't touch me."

"Fuck," he mutters under his breath. "It's not what you think. I did agree at the start, but that was only because I wanted to be near you. I couldn't understand why you disliked me so much after our night together, and I wanted to get to the bottom of it."

"So you bet him you could what? Fuck me again? Make me fall for you?"

"It wasn't like that."

"No? Instead your pride was ruined so you decided to use me for what, a hundred bucks reward?"

"Jesus, no." He jams his hand through his hair. "He didn't know about us when he made the bet, and I didn't tell him. I couldn't stop thinking about you. I *can't* stop thinking about you, and I agreed because I didn't want him or any other guy having you. None of what happened between us was because of a stupid bet. And I told Elliot I wanted out, but he wouldn't listen."

"So that makes it okay?"

"No. I should have told you right from the start, but honestly, I forgot about it."

I study him. His eyes, his mouth, the rise and fall of

his chest. Everything I've learned about him over the past several weeks points to a kind, upstanding person who might not want a relationship but has always treated me well. Complimented me. Been there for me. If I was just a bet, he could have one-and-done me.

Still. "You're an ass."

"Who is really sorry." He scoots closer. "I swear to you, I'm with you because I can't help myself."

A double knot lodges itself in the back of my throat. What the hell kind of declaration is that? Whether he realizes it or not, he just insinuated he's been using me. To help him get over Kayla? To forget whatever demons sit on his shoulders weighing him down?

A deep breath whooshes out of me. I get that. Totally 100 percent understand it. Because until Levi, it's what I did.

"Then take me," I say, crawling into his lap. I fuse my mouth to his. The kiss is hard, angry, volatile. And so is the sex we have up against the door in his room because it's the last time he gets to use me.

SEPTEMBER 8TH

Dear Harper,

I fucked up.

And I'm sorry.

For saying the wrong thing. Doing the wrong thing. And any other wrongs you want to pin on me. (Although, sex with you when you're pissed is hot as hell.) I've been up all night, angry with myself for letting you walk away without talking more. I should have asked you to stay.

I should have done the entire night differently, starting by saying how you've taken everything I thought I knew about liking someone and changed it. You make me wonder if I've ever really known what it's like to feel attraction. Because close to you isn't close enough. Crazy about you isn't crazy enough.

That's right. I'm crazy about you. Every kiss with you is better than the last. Every time I'm inside you is better than I imagined. And I don't know what to do about it.

I do know I don't want to go without it.

That makes me selfish, I know, but I'm greedy when it comes to you.

It's not just the sex, either. I like talking with you, watching TV with you, eating In-N-Out with you, being in the water with you. I like your laugh and the smile you don't easily share. I like your loyalty to your friends. I like your passion for swim safety and philanthropy. I like how much you love dogs. I like how adventurous you are, and how uninhibited. I like that you're ticklish.

I adore everything about you, Ham.

Sincerely,

Levi

Chapter Twenty-One

LEVI

I remember the first time I told Kayla I loved her. I said it first, and her answer was, "You do?" like she couldn't believe someone could love her. When I nodded, she flung her arms around my neck and told me she loved me, too. But over the past week, I've done a lot of soul searching, and you know what? The love we shared wasn't the forever kind. It was young love. Learning love. Love with struggles. It came with highs and incredible lows, but it helped shape me into the person I am today.

You're thinking, *How thoughtful of you, Levi*, aren't you? Well, I had some help. When your four older sisters kidnap you and take you to Catalina for the day (trapping me on a boat, then on an island), it's inevitable your *feelings* are dissected and analyzed. To quote my oldest sister, "The past is the past; now get on with today." "Be fearless," my youngest sister added. "Because fear is good for only one thing." I'd asked what. She said, "Making something out of nothing."

So here I am, ready to put my past behind me once and for all.

"Hi." At the sound of Kayla's voice, I raise my head from my coffee cup. "Thanks for agreeing to meet me here," she says.

We're at a coffee shop in Beverly Hills. I got here early to snag a table in the center of the small eatery. I wanted to be in as public a spot as possible with her, not tucked away in a corner. "Sure," I say, getting to my feet to pull out her chair.

"Thank you," she says.

"I wasn't sure if you could drink coffee so I didn't get you anything," I say. "Would you like something?"

"An iced tea would be great."

"Okay. Be right back." I buy her drink and return to the table.

"Are those for me?" she asks, accepting the tea while she eyes the flowers I left sitting atop our square table.

"No," I say, leaving it at that. In hindsight, I should have stopped at the flower shop after meeting Kayla, but every morning I wake up, my mind is on only one person.

"Are they for the girl I saw at your house?"

"Yes." Whether or not Harper accepts them is a different story. We haven't talked or texted since she left my house almost a week ago.

Kayla takes a sip of her drink. "So," she says.

I'm all ears, ready to hash out whatever we need to in order for us both to move on. Independently. After agreeing to meet her here, I erased her text messages and blocked her number.

"I've been wanting to talk to you about Anson. He wants us to move to Atlanta." She fiddles with her straw. "His family is there, and his father has offered him a job."

This is what she meant by him leaving her? This is great

fucking news. "Congratulations."

"I don't want to go."

That is bad fucking news. The skin on the back of my neck prickles. "Kayla."

"I still love you."

"No, you don't."

"I do." Her lying eyes dart to the floor then back to mine.

"You don't, because if you did, you wouldn't have cheated on me. But that doesn't even matter anymore because I don't love you."

"You love *her*?" She makes a face like she's repulsed by the idea.

"My life is none of your business anymore. I agreed to see you today to say good-bye for good. I wish you the best, but please don't contact me ever again."

"You don't mean that."

"Kayla." Her features relax at the quieter way I say her name. "You need to make it work with your husband. Georgia sounds like a great idea. It's a fresh start and a second chance for a happy life with this baby and his dad." I glance down at her stomach.

She rubs her hand over her round belly. "I wish—"

"Don't. The fact is, we were never meant to be, and the sooner you realize that, the better off you'll be."

"Why are you being so mean to me?"

"I'm just being honest."

Her fist comes down on the table, startling the people sitting on both sides of us. "Then tell me you want me."

I remain calm, hoping it carries across the table. "I don't."

She stretches across the table to take my hand. I let her because I don't want any more displays of anger. "Please, Levi."

The front door of the coffee shop opens. It's not the first time its opened since I've been sitting here, but for some reason, I turn my head. Harper steps inside and holds the door open for an elderly couple. Her eyes find mine. Lock. Until they sweep down to the flowers and Kayla's hand on mine. Her face pales, and then she's gone, back out the door before I have a chance to say anything. *Fuck.*

"Oops," Kayla says, her tone smug.

I yank my hand free. "If you really care about me like you say you do, then you'll move to Georgia and leave me alone." I pick up the flowers and stand.

"Wait." For the first time in I don't know how long, something close to care and understanding registers in her eyes. She swallows thickly.

"Good-bye, Kayla. Have a good life." I don't wait to hear anything more from her. I hurry out the door to find Harper.

She's nowhere in sight. I have no idea where she's gone, but eventually she'll go home, so that's where I drive.

Her car isn't in front of her aunt's house. I check out the guesthouse anyway, getting no answer. It's a cool September morning with cloud cover blocking the sun, so I decide to sit in my car and wait for her. The few hours of sleep I got last night catch up to me and I close my eyes.

When I wake up, it's almost three o'clock. I'm sweaty, and the flowers are wilted. Shit. The good news? I see Harper's car.

I knock on her front door louder than I intended, but I really need to see her. Teague and Mateo left yesterday for Teague's sister's wedding so I know she's home alone.

"Who is it?"

"Levi."

The longest seconds of my life tick by before she finally opens the door. My body immediately reacts when I see her. She obviously just took a nap, too. "Hi," I say to her nipples. I can't help it. They're poking through her thin blue tank top.

"Hello," she says curtly, then, surely to torture me, she

stretches against the door with her arms raised above her head. Her top rises, exposing the piercing in her navel that drives me wild. My gaze continues lower. She's wearing underwear, or rather a scrap of material hanging off her hips by strings. Her legs are tan and shapely. The anklet I gave her is still there. My eyes bounce back up to her fresh face and mussed hair. She's the most incredible thing I've ever seen.

"These are for you." I extend the drooping bouquet.

She doesn't take them, so I quickly add, "I bought them for you before I met Kayla. If you'll let me, I'd like to explain what you saw earlier."

Once again, agonizing seconds of quiet pass while I wait for her decision. She had to see me sleeping in my car. That's got to earn me some points.

"Thank you." She takes the flowers and sniffs the petals. "They're beautiful, even if a little wilted." She rests her bright, assessing eyes on me again. "Do you want to come in?"

"So badly, you have no idea."

She frowns.

Shit. Now is not the time for any innuendo. Can I stop thinking about sex with her for one goddamn minute? I brace myself for the door to slam in my face, but she surprises me by backing up to allow me entry.

"I'm going to put these in water."

I step inside, reaching my arm back to close the door because my eyes are glued to her. There is nothing but a tiny strip of lace between her ass cheeks. How the hell am I going to talk to her when she's dressed like this? *You're going to do it because she means more to you than a piece of ass. A lot more.*

I sit at the kitchen table, figuring it's the least comfortable and therefore safest place to talk without getting sidetracked by her body. "Do you think you could put on a robe or something?"

She sets a glass vase with the flowers near the window above the sink. "Why would I want to do that?" She sashays toward me, clearly on a mission to make me sorry for how we left things. I deserve the torture.

"It's hard for me to concentrate when you're barely dressed." I'm here to reestablish closeness that has nothing to do with getting her naked. *She* deserves that.

She considers what I've said and then, without a word, walks down the hallway. She returns wearing the sweatshirt I gave her to cover up after we got caught skinny-dipping. It hangs to the middle of her thighs, blocking my view of her soft skin and curves.

"Okay. Talk," she commands, sitting across from me and taking a tone and stance I haven't seen from her since the night at the bar when I clumsily spilled her drink on her.

I launch right into my sisters kidnapping me, work being insane—not that that's a good excuse for not getting in touch before now—and my conversation with Kayla.

Harper pulls her knees up, feet flat on the edge of the chair, and covers her legs with the sweatshirt. Since it's mine, there's more than enough material. She listens intently, puts her chin on her knees.

"Do you really think she'll leave you alone?"

"I'd like to think so."

"I'm happy for you."

"Thanks. Listen, about last week. The bet and—"

"Old news," she says, waving a hand to dismiss the topic. Dismissing me.

She drops her legs to the floor, gathers her hair and ties it in a knot behind her head. A few loose tendrils fall around her face. She's so gorgeous, and even with tension between us at the moment, the chemistry far outweighs it. The air practically crackles with electricity. If we lit a match, the area around us would sizzle like a hundred hand-held sparklers.

I rub the scruff on my chin. No way is she getting rid of me that easily. "I'm free the rest of the day. Want to hang out?"

"I'm not having sex with you."

It's impossible not to smile at that. She's thinking about sex. With me.

"Okay. How about dinner? A movie?"

"I'm also not dating you."

"Our agreement is null and void now?" My muscles clench. I won't let her go without a fight. I'm finally free of my past and...and I don't know exactly what the future holds, but I want to live right now with her.

She blows a wisp of hair out of her face. "I don't know."

"How about this? Since I ruined your breakfast this morning, let me make you a late lunch/early dinner."

Her dark lashes sweep down then up. I take that as a "yes." Walking around the table, I lean over, brush my lips on her earlobe. "Thank you," I whisper.

"It's hard to say no to you," she whispers back.

"I promise not to give you a reason to." I can't remember the last time I made a promise.

The food selection in her fridge is minimal. Same goes for her pantry, but she's got eggs, cheese, tortillas, and a tomato.

"What's on the menu?" She lifts herself up onto the kitchen counter. I'm temporarily frozen as I stare at her smooth, tanned skin, one leg crossed over the other.

"How does a breakfast burrito sound?"

"I could eat that."

I want to eat her. Bury my face between her legs and taste her until she comes all over my mouth. I get busy cracking the eggs. "Have you decided what you're going to do about MASF?" I ask.

"Not yet," she says with a sigh. "Brad has been really patient with me, though, so I need to give him an answer soon."

"Should we talk pros and cons?" I find a frying pan, put it on the stove.

My suggestion puts a slight quirk in her soft, full lips. "No, that's okay. I'd rather just watch you cook."

I remember what she said to me when I made her cinnamon rolls. I pour the eggs into the frying pan then turn to face her. I reach over my shoulder, grab the collar of my shirt, and pull it over my head. Her jaw drops.

Excellent.

She's about to say something when her phone rings from across the room. She hops off the counter. "I'm waiting on my dad to return my call."

"Everything okay?"

"It will be, but maybe…" She picks the phone up off the couch. "Hey, Dad."

I turn back around to scramble the eggs and give her some privacy, but to my surprise she's put the call on speaker.

"Hi, sweetheart. What's up?" her dad says.

"Since you've apparently hired yourself as my manager, I'm firing you."

"Excuse me?"

I glance over my shoulder. Harper is sitting on the arm of the couch, facing me with the phone palm up in her hand.

"I can't believe you resorted to having some agent call me about being a stunt double on the film! He said my *business manager* got in touch with him. I can't believe you would do something like this behind my back."

"You know I only have your best interests at heart."

"No, Dad. You have *your* best interests."

"Can you fault a father for trying?"

The sound of papers rustling comes over the phone line. I turn off the burner and move the frying pan away from the heat. Harper watches me pull out the tortillas and open the shredded cheese.

"No more trying, Dad. I told you I thought about it some more, and my decision was final. Please respect my wishes, and please don't interfere in my life anymore."

"You call it interfering; I call it guidance."

"Guidance is when you give advice or direction, not try and steamroll your daughter into working for you."

"I'm afraid I won't be happy until you do."

"What about my happiness?"

Silence fills the room. I stop slicing the tomato.

"I'm sure"—her dad breaks off and lets out a breath— "you're right," he finally says. "I'll back off. But there's always a job for you in the company whenever you want it."

"Don't hold it for me," Harper says. "Please don't let a job loom over my head. Or yours. I don't see it happening, Dad. Not now and not months or years from now. We'd end up hating each other if we worked together, and I love you too much for that. I'm sorry if this hurts your feelings, but it's past time I was one hundred percent honest with you. And myself."

"Since when do you put your father in his place?"

"Since he pushed too hard, I guess."

"I'm sorry about that." There's a beat of quiet. "I'll do my best to leave you alone from here on out."

"I have a witness to that. Levi's here." Her eyes glitter from across the room. "You heard all that, right?"

"I did," I say.

"Did you just one-up me?" her father asks.

Catching Harper's unguarded smile as she straightens from the couch takes my breath away. "I think I did."

"I know you're more than capable in your pursuits, sweetheart, and if I haven't told you lately, I am proud of you. It's hard for me to let go of the reins after twenty-three plus years is all."

"I know."

"Will you do me a favor?"

"Sure."

"Go up to the house in Big Bear this weekend. Take a few days to relax and enjoy the fresh mountain air. Your mom and I were going to go, but a business meeting I can't miss has come up. The place is being stocked and readied as we speak, so you won't have to worry about a thing."

"Thanks, Dad. A quick getaway sounds great."

"Good. Enjoy yourself."

"I will."

"Levi?" her dad says.

"Yes, sir?" I stop mid burrito making.

"Be sure my daughter gets off safely."

"Okay." I fight a smile. I know her father didn't mean that to sound dirty, but it's where my mind went.

Harper and her dad talk for a minute more before she practically floats over to the kitchen table to join me. Seeing her visibly cheerful tugs on my chest.

"This smells yummy." She lifts her burrito. "I love eating breakfast for dinner."

"Nice job with your dad. You continue to impress me, Ham."

She eyes me, her gaze dipping to my bare chest before biting into her food. "Thanks. It helped that you were here."

"Yeah? I should probably join you in Big Bear, then. I have the weekend free, and I could keep you safe and get you off."

"You think so?"

"I've been told on more than one occasion I'm very smart."

"Only one? I'm not sure how smart that makes you." She busies herself with eating. She's hilarious.

"That's okay. I know it's not my brain you're after." I flex my biceps as I lift my burrito to my mouth.

For a split second, she doesn't look amused. "Tell you what, bring me my heart's desire and you can meet me up there."

Her heart's desire? How did we go from my body to that? I sit back in my chair to study her. This is a test of some sort. To get back at me for the bet?

"What if I bring the wrong thing? You gonna send me home?"

"Yes."

"You're serious."

"Take it or leave it." Her tone allows for zero compromise.

"I'll take it." And hope like hell I bring what she desires.

Chapter Twenty-Two

The lakefront house in Big Bear is my favorite getaway. It's bright and airy with a spectacular sunset view courtesy of vaulted ceilings and an entire wall devoted to windows. I slept like a baby last night upstairs in my room overlooking the lake. I left the window open so a cool breeze and the subtle sounds of nature could lull me to sleep. This morning the sky is blue for miles, the lake smooth like glass. I'm cozy in a pair of loose sleep pants and a ribbed long-sleeved shirt.

My plan for today is to watch Buffy reruns, shop Etsy for sunscreen lotions (I bought a coconut raspberry-seed lotion last time that I need to buy again for sure), and if the water isn't too freezing, take a swim in the lake.

When the doorbell rings, all my plans go up in smoke.

He came.

I'd given Levi the address yesterday after we finished eating and I told him I wanted to pack and drive up here before it got dark. He'd kissed me on the cheek and said,

"Later gator," so I let my hope go. I hadn't made it exactly easy for him to join me, and that makes me someone I'm not proud of, but I'm scared. He gives me a sense of hope that is beautiful and terrifying at the same time. I want to be upfront with him, tell him how my emotions are freaking me out, yet I've kept my feelings close to my chest for so long, it's easier to push people away.

I pad across the hardwood floor to the front door in my bare feet. What will I do if he's brought me something I don't like? Worse, what will I do if he's brought me something I love?

Worse, worse, *he* is my heart's desire, so it doesn't matter what he brought. His showing up is all I really want.

Maybe I'm overthinking all of this, and it's Gail from next door.

I open the door and am completely unprepared for the vision in front of me. It's not our friendly neighbor, but Levi, looking incredibly hot in aviator sunglasses, jeans, and a fitted gray V-neck T-shirt casually tucked-in at his belt buckle. Sitting beside him is the cutest fawn-and-white-colored bulldog I've ever seen.

"Hi," Levi says, sliding his sunglasses to the top of his head. His eyes eat me up in a way that makes my body tingle.

"Uhh..."

He tilts his head a little to the left—and I swear the dog does, too—and stares at me with an aren't-you-forgetting-something expression.

"Hi," I say. That one tiny greeting earns me one great big smile. My knees wobble at the impact. "What...how..." I'm so delighted to see him, his smile, and his friend, that I can't form a proper sentence now.

"The 'what' is we're here to be with you. This is Hank. He's just turned one, is potty trained, likes to take walks along lakes, and thinks you're beautiful. He's on loan from a couple that lends out their dogs." Levi bends to pet Hank's head. "True story. They let dog lovers who don't want or can't have a full-time pet borrow their dogs in exchange for a donation to the shelter. The couple screens each borrower carefully so they know their dogs are in good hands. I'm certain he's in good hands with you, and I'm thinking I nailed the heart's desire."

It's a miracle I don't melt right there on the doorstep. I do, however, kneel down and say hello to Hank. "Hi, Hank. It's very nice to meet you." I rub the top of his head and scratch behind his ears. Hank gives me a sweet, laid-back look, which obviously means he adores me as much as I already adore him.

I rise to acknowledge the other adorable male. "I don't know what to say."

"Say we can stay."

"You can stay."

Levi drops the leash, cups my face in his hands, and kisses me. All I can think is *we get to do this all weekend long,* and nothing makes me happier.

"Come inside," I murmur against his lips.

"I plan to, multiple times." He sucks on my bottom lip before letting me go.

Oh lordy.

"Did you find the house okay?" I ask as they follow me toward the family room. The bottom floor is one spacious room divided into sections so I detour into the kitchen to get a bowl of water for Hank.

"Yeah." Suddenly, Hank's leash clinks on the floor and Levi is right behind me. He puts his hands on my hips and slides them down my thighs while he kisses the side of my neck. "I've been thinking about my hands on you the entire drive here."

I turn and take his wrists before we're naked and on the

kitchen island in ten seconds. "Let's not rush," I say, and walk backward to lead him to the couch. I'm still getting used to the amazing fact that he drove all this way to see me.

The view catches his eye. "Wow. We may never leave here, Ham."

There's something very appealing in those words. So many things he says to me hold weight inside my head and heart. I don't know what to do with all of it, so I shove it away.

Hank follows us, plopping down on the area rug before we sit. "Did you bring stuff for him?" I ask.

"Yeah." He glances at Hank. "I should probably get him situated before we…" He trails off.

"Good idea. I'll undo his leash while you go to the car."

"Okay." He gives me a quick kiss.

I flub getting Hank's leash off three times because I'm watching Levi's broad shoulders. This is too much. Crazy-ass thoughts run through my head. Like, *I want to have his babies.* What the ever-loving fuck is that about? I have never had a thought like that in my life. I need to get my hormones under control immediately.

And avoid the naked thing until I do.

Levi strides back inside with his arms full. His biceps bulge underneath his shirtsleeves in a sexy, effortless way that does nothing to curb my affection.

I put Hank's leash back on him and pop to my feet. "How about a walk? You guys have been in the car for a while and should probably stretch your legs."

"Sounds good." He puts down a dog bed, a canvas bag with "Hank" written on the outside, and a duffel bag I assume is his.

"Let me put my Uggs on and we'll go." I slip my feet into the fur-lined boots I left next to the sliding French door, tucking my pants legs in, and snag the house key off the coffee table.

Fresh, cool, late-morning air fills my lungs. We're the only ones out for a stroll along the lakefront, since the uncultivated ground dissuades most people on this stretch of quiet beauty.

I hold Hank's leash. Levi holds my hand. We walk in comfortable silence.

For the first couple of years after Joe died, I went from one day to the next silently punishing myself. I shut down my emotions. I quit friends. Quit swimming. Not because I stopped loving it, but because I couldn't bear to be in a pool. My magic was contained in that water. Out of it, I was nothing special, which was how I wanted it. But the pool was also the place where I always found myself. Giving it up meant I lost a huge piece of who I was.

Instead of persevering, I crumbled. And I was glad for it. Now? That's not the case.

The wound Joe's death left will never be gone, but it doesn't torment me like it used to. The reason for that is the incredible person beside me. I feel *everything* again when I'm with Levi, most significantly happiness. Joy. Love.

I throw the uninvited thought out of my mind. I want that as much as a bull wants a cattle prod up the ass.

Lying to yourself isn't going to make the feeling go away.

"What are your thoughts on anal?" I blurt into the silence. Jesus fucking Christ. I can't believe I said that. It's because I was reading Cosmo last night in bed. Not because I want Levi *there*. Although, he is the first guy I would entertain doing it with. Oh my God! Stop, Harper.

Levi chokes. "Umm…is there a right answer?"

"No answer. There is no answer. I can't believe I asked you that. I was reading Cosmo, and you know that Confessions section? Wait. You probably don't because you're a guy and the magazine is for women. Mostly. I think." I'm babbling like a weirdo, and I cannot stop. And Jesus, I just thought that to the tune of "I Like Big Butts and I Cannot Lie."

I'm going crazy.

Love does that to you.

"I mean, if you read it, that's cool. It wouldn't bother me. I'm sure there are lots of guys who read it with their girlfriends. There are some great articles on sex I bet couples would be interested in together. Not just articles on anal sex, by the way, but all kinds of sex. So, yeah, I'm going to stop talking now."

Levi is quiet so I turn my head to look at him. I've mentioned his smiles a gazillion times, I know, but the ear-to-ear grin he's giving me now is new. I don't know how to describe it, except to say it makes me fall for him even more.

He's not laughing at me. He's accepting me.

"One more thing," I say, because seeing that look on his face makes me nervous so I drop my defenses entirely. "I've never done it." I lift one shoulder like it's no biggie. "But with the right person, I'm open to anything. I think you know how much I enjoy sex." *With you.*

His eyes shine like liquid gold. "You're saying I'm the right person? Because there is nothing I don't want to do to you." He brings us to a stop and guides my hand to his crotch. He's most definitely enjoying our topic of discussion.

I palm him over his jeans. "The thought of anal turns you on?"

"The thought of *you* turns me on."

Hank snorts. Levi and I chuckle at the timing and look down at our four-legged friend before we resume walking. We've got plenty of time for sex. The house is stocked with lots of food so we don't have to go anywhere until it's time to leave.

"So, I heard from Cane," Levi says after we've taken several steps.

"He's the kiteboarder, right?"

"Right." He brushes something off his shirt. "He wants

me to join him in Australia. I told him I was in. Movies are filmed in L.A. all the time, but I might not get another opportunity to go to the Sunshine Coast."

"Congratulations!" I hope I sound excited. My heart is in my throat. Levi will be an ocean away rather than a few city miles. "How long is the shoot for?"

He squeezes my hand. "Thanks. I'll be there for two months."

Sixty days. That's a long time. Anything could happen. He could forget about me. Meet some cute Aussie and marry her.

"Until then"—he steers us around so we're headed back toward the house—"I think we should read Cosmo together."

I beam at him. Fucking beam.

• • •

Levi toys with my anklet. I'm lying on my stomach on top of the bed, naked. My arms are bent, elbows out, with my hands tucked under my cheek. The sheets are warm, tangled, smell like *us*. We've been here most of the day. Hank is sleeping in his bed in the corner of the room, snoring.

Levi kisses my heel.

Kisses the tiny mole shaped like a heart above the bone on my ankle.

His lips graze up my calf, leaving a lightweight touch that rumbles all over my body. He likes to take his time with me. I watch the glow of the candles on the bedside table. He likes to be romantic, too.

He passes over the ticklish spot behind my knee, and moves to my other leg, kissing the back of my thigh. I love the texture of his stubble, sharp at times, yet soothing at others. His fingers traipse along my skin, edging closer to my center.

"I love every inch of you," he murmurs.

I close my eyes to let those words wash over me. He spends time alternating kisses and massages on the backs of both legs.

"The way you feel. The way you smell. And the way you taste." He licks and nibbles and sucks up to the curve of my butt. His hands gently press my legs open. I suck in a breath. Squeeze my pillow.

He hooks his arms underneath my legs and lifts my hips, just enough to expose me to the air and his perusal. The bed shifts underneath his weight. He lies on his stomach, his face between my legs. I throb in anticipation of him touching me where I'm swollen and pulsing. Finally, his tongue flicks against my most sensitive spot. From this angle, the contact is exquisite.

I spread my legs wider and shamelessly grind against his face as he licks me from behind.

Fastens his lips around my folds.

Applies perfect pressure to my clit.

Over and over and over again.

When he slides a finger inside me, my eyes roll to the back of my head. I hold on for as long as I can, pressing back, throbbing, not wanting this incredible sensation to end. God, what Levi does to me. I know I'll feel the effects of his stubble tomorrow and want to repeat everything multiple times.

"Oh God," I pant. His mouth and fingers are too much. I can't keep my orgasm from barreling down on me. I give in, moaning loudly. Flying high. Emotion slams into my chest and crowds my heart as I float back down to Earth.

Levi slowly breaks his mind-blowing suction as he lowers my hips to the bed. He kisses my butt cheek. "You." He kisses my lower back. "Are." He presses his lips to my spine. "Beyond." He brushes my hair off my neck. "Compare." He kisses the curve of my shoulder then lays his naked body on top of mine, slightly to the side. He wraps an arm around my middle and drapes his leg over my lower half so his hard, thick cock can slide inside me.

The first moment he stretches me always borders on the pleasurable side of pain. I'm small. He's big. But the rest of the moments are all pleasure. He rocks against me in unhurried, steady thrusts, setting our tempo to a wicked-good rhythm. I'd never had sex without a condom before today, but I'm on the pill and clean. He's clean. And since we reestablished that we've got this exclusive thing going on, it seemed right.

Having him bare is amazing. Special. I like him in my mouth, the weight, texture, and firmness. But I love him uncovered and buried inside me.

He moves deeper, hitting a place inside me I thought was untouchable. His lips graze the back of my ear. Our mingled breaths, strained with passion, fill the room. This. This is everything I imagined when I was sixteen, and *so* much more.

"Fuck, you feel good," he says. "I'm not going to last much longer."

"Me, either." I don't need to chase orgasms with Levi. They come after me. Especially when he slows the tempo to an agonizing slide like he's doing right now. I scream his name when I come. He rocks once. Twice. And follows right behind.

Then he holds me in his arms as I fall to blissful sleep.

Blissful until I dream about him underwater, unable to reach the surface. He can't breathe. He struggles, kicks and flails, but it's no use. The pool, the ocean, I'm not sure which, is swallowing him. There's no one to help him. He's drowning.

I jerk awake. My hairline is slick with sweat. It takes a moment for my eyes to focus and for my mind to clear. I'm in bed. Levi has his arms wrapped around me. He's right here. Sound asleep. Safe. Warm.

He's okay, and I'm anything but.

Chapter Twenty-Three

LEVI

I look out the window at the back of Harper's head, the love bite I left on her neck, the curve of one shoulder left exposed by the oversize neckline of her blue sweater. She's curled up on a chair on the deck, looking out at the lake, and I am so enamored with her there are no words to describe it.

Which is okay, because I'm not going to tell her how hard I'm falling. Not today. After a phenomenal Friday spent mostly in bed, something was off when we woke up yesterday morning. She says she's okay, but I know her. The few smiles she's given me haven't included her tongue darting between her lips. She's looked preoccupied then tried to cover it up, lacking her usual wit. And she's distracted me with sex whenever I've asked one too many questions.

She's got an internal struggle going on, and I hope to get to the bottom of it this morning before we head home.

Hank is passed out on the couch, snoring loudly. He can take or leave the view outside, preferring the ragged plush toy at his side. He's made himself comfortable the past couple of days, drooling and slobbering over everything—including Harp and me. She doesn't care in the least. Loves it, really, which is one more reason I fall harder for her.

"Here you go," I say, stepping outside to hand her a cup of coffee.

"Thank you." She wraps her small hands around the mug and lets the steam float up to her face. "I love the smell of your special coffee."

I've brewed my signature cup of java for her. My sister taught me to add a couple drops of hazelnut extract to make it slightly sweet.

I sit next to her with my own cup. "It sucks that today is Sunday."

"Said no one ever." She takes a sip of her drink. "But I have to agree."

It's like a postcard in front of us—azure sky, one large marshmallow cloud and a mountain range in the distance, a placid steel blue lake. "That makes two of us, then."

"Do you ever think about moving somewhere like this? No traffic, fewer people?"

"I haven't, but now that I've experienced it, I get the temptation." I put my coffee down on the wooden end table. "What about you? Could you live here?"

"No. I'd get bored. But it's my favorite place to visit for a weekend."

I focus on her profile as I consider my next words. She's beautiful from every angle, and I forget myself for a minute. When she turns her head to meet my open gaze, I ask about what I think has been on her mind.

"Have you decided about the ambassadorship?"

"No," she says, relaxing her head against the chair. "Every time I think I have it figured out, something happens to set me back."

Alarm runs down my spine. "What happened?"

She looks away. "Nothing really. I'll work it out. I told Brad I'd have an answer for him this week, so…"

She's keeping a secret, and I fucking hate it. I've proven myself trustworthy, made myself available to her. What more can I do to get her to confide in me again?

"What happened, Ham?" I repeat. My muscles tense while I wait for her answer. No matter how hard I try, she may never let me all the way in, and I'm not sure I can handle that. I want to be the one she shares everything with, without having to beg for it.

"I had a bad dream," she says, eyes back on me. "But I'd rather not talk about it, okay?" If not for the misery coloring her voice, I'd press for more. Not to be a jerk, but to hold her in my arms and be supportive.

"You know you could start your own foundation," I say, relenting with her but not avoiding what's been on *my* mind.

She tips her chin up and focuses on me with surprised interest.

"You've got the money. The smarts. Know some influential people. You could be your own boss and hire a good staff to work for *you*. People who want to help others as passionately as you do. MASF is about swim safety and teaching kids to swim, and, yes, Brad is passionate about that. But what about the people like you who have suffered because someone they loved drowned? Your foundation could also be about helping those left behind, the victims of loss, so to speak, back on their feet."

I've just flicked on a lightbulb. I can see it in the flecks of gold in her eyes.

"You'd still have to tell your story, but you could do it on your terms. You'd be in charge of what and how and when your personal life is shared. And if you get others to share their stories of loss, then the focus wouldn't be entirely on you."

Her chest rises and falls.

"What was Joe's last name?"

"Myles," she whispers.

"You could start the JM Foundation."

She squeezes her eyes shut for a moment and gives a small shake of her head. "His middle name was Anson."

Joe Anson Myles. JAM.

"It could be called the JAM Foundation," she says.

"I think that would be awesome, Ham." I cup her cheek. "And I think you've just figured out how to reconcile your past with your future."

She swallows thickly. "I think you might be right." She climbs out of her chair to straddle me. Her arms take their usual spot around my neck. The tip of her nose touches mine.

Then she kisses me.

It's unlike anything I've felt before.

• • •

I've known since I was sixteen that I wanted to work behind a camera. Sophomore year, I took a photography class to fill the arts requirement for high school graduation and quickly found myself shooting everything, everywhere. I loved capturing something unique in ordinary things. It didn't take long to move to video, and shoots with my buddies doing whatever dumbass trick we could think of when our parents weren't around. Then I saw The Lord of the Rings films some ridiculous amount of times, and that led me to become a huge fan of Australian cinematographer Andrew Lesnie. Eventually, I want to be a Director of Photography and win an Academy Award like he did.

Which brings me to today and the ocean at my feet. For the past three days, I've been shooting with a friend in Malibu to prepare myself for Australia. Cane's got a guy who's sick with a drone, so I'm the kitecam guy. This shoot is different from anything I've ever done, with a huge learning curve, so I'm trying out different options with the camera.

I toss my towel to the side for one more practice run before we call it done. Since getting back from Big Bear a week and a half ago, I've been insanely busy with work, and Harper and I have spent all of one night together. That changes tonight, when I pick her up for a romantic dinner and sleepover. I want to talk to her about my trip. Tell her two months will fly by. And make her officially my girlfriend so there are no doubts during our separation. I'm taking the next four weeks off from any jobs and hope to spend as much time with her as she'll let me.

I also plan to tell her I love her.

"Bro, you ready to do the handheld?" Flynn asks. He's been nice enough to kiteboard for me the past few days while I figure out the best way to use the camera. The guy is an epic kiteboarder and surfer, which means I don't have to worry about him in the slightest.

"That's the plan," I say, looking over my camera. "Give me one more minute." I've tried mounting the camera to my kite, mounting it to a helmet, and mounting it to my kite lines. All three techniques have left me with little to no control over the camera, and thus the footage is jumpy and abrupt, the image quality poorer than I'd like.

I think the pros outweigh the cons if I hold the camera. Holding it means I have control over the camera angles, can shoot close-ups, and the hand strap will allow me to shoot the board, kite, *and* Flynn. The downside is I might drop the camera and lose it, or get distracted from kiting while I focus on the camera and its direction instead of my ride. I'm a decent kiteboarder, but I've taken my share of spills.

I do one last check of my camera settings. It's near

impossible to make adjustments out on the water, so I need to have the camera 100 percent dialed before I hit the water. Flynn and I will spend a few more days out here over the next month so I can put in more time with the camera, but ultimately, I'd like this run to go well. With one more look at the lens to check for moisture, I'm good to go.

Flynn and I check our lines and kite before launching. The winds have picked up, making for gusty conditions, but we can handle it.

The first twenty minutes are golden. We keep our backs to the wind, the kites right in front of us at twelve o'clock, and fly. My hands keep steady on the handlebar, controlling the direction and power of the kite with relative ease while I film.

Flynn sets a brisk pace, and I keep up with him. We move our kites in and out of standard positions, dragging our boards through the surf. The pull of the kite lifts me out of the water. I lean back, keeping the board's edge submerged, and move with Flynn.

I'm having a blast, as both a cameraman and kite surfer.

Until I'm not.

Maybe it's because the kite and lines have taken some abuse the past three days. Or maybe it's human error—my error because I'm fatigued from more kiteboarding than I'm used to. I'll never know for sure. All I know is that one minute I'm soaring with the saltwater splashing my face, and the next I've lost control of my kite. And because I'm focused on my camera, I'm unable to trigger my emergency quick release before I'm yanked into the water.

Then under the water.

As I struggle for air, I think this can't be happening. I cannot fucking drown.

Chapter Twenty-Four

Harper

I can't keep still. Today is one of the best days ever. For sure the best hump day of my life. I can't wait to tell Levi about it when he picks me up in half an hour. It's because of him that I feel invincible again, after all. He planted the seed in my mind, helped me water it, but most of all, he believed in me when I didn't. When I once again let fear rule me.

I'm done with that *F* word. Drop a tarantula in my lap, and fear will dig her claws into me, but everything else gets no say. I'm in control now. It took me a long time to get back here, and now that I am, I want to stay.

The papers on my desk confirm as much. I've spent the past ten days putting my business degree to good use and making the JAM Foundation a reality. A girl always needs good counsel to start, and I'm lucky my oldest brother, Landon, loves to hold his law degree over his little sister's head. Lan helped me with the 501(c)3 filing and creation of bylaws based on plans I wrote up. With Joe as my inspiration, it took no time to take the vision in my head and develop the foundation's mission.

I'm nervous. But it's the excited kind of nervous. The kind I hope inspires, heals, and educates.

Filling my advisory board has been more challenging, mostly because I told my dad I only had room for one parent. My mom is thrilled I chose her, and my dad will get over it eventually. What's made today in particular so great, is one of the biggest influencers in social media has agreed to sit on the board. Her Instagram reach alone is over three million. She has amazing ideas for creating a sustainable fundraising plan, and I can't wait to introduce her to the rest of the team.

Have I mentioned my board is made up entirely of women?

It is.

Teague shyly agreed to help me. She doubted her offerings until I reminded her she basically started her own business and works with her boss now, not for. Plus, she's my BFF and I couldn't do this without her.

Brad's wife (and Levi's sister), Amelia, is also on the board. Honored when I asked her, she brings personal insight because of Brad, and additional networking opportunities given her part-time work as an educator.

Brad was disappointed when I told him I was passing on the ambassador job. We talked for a long time, or rather I talked. He listened as I shared some of my most painful feelings. It was important to me that he understood how hard this decision was and how much creating JAMF helped me feel whole again. Strangely, when I finished, he didn't look at me with pity or displeasure, but pride. He said he'd support my foundation however he could. I told him I would always help MASF.

Before I left his office, we watched the PSAs. They packed a profound punch that left my heart full. My thoughts had turned to Levi after each one. If not for working together, we might not be where we are today. I owe Brad big time for that.

I flit around my bedroom some more, picking up a pair of mismatched flip-flops peeking out from under my bed and tossing them into my closet. After our dinner date, Levi is staying the night. Levi is also going to hear the words *I love you*.

He hasn't said those three precious words to me, but I've felt them. I'm fairly certain he's felt them from me, too, and is waiting for me to say them first. It doesn't matter if he says them, though. I don't want to wait another day to tell him what's in my heart.

Slipping my feet into a pair of red pumps, I smooth down my little black dress. Then I pick up my phone and text Levi a quick, *can't wait to see you! xoxo* because I really can't. He's spent the past three days at the beach learning his kitecam. My mouth waters picturing him with a deeper tan, windblown hair lightened by the sun, and arm muscles that flex when he moves.

"Hey, guys," I say to Teague and Mateo as I walk into the kitchen. They're sitting on the couch with Teague's laptop, poring over all the pictures from their trip to Hawaii.

"Hey," they both respond, still engrossed in the process they started an hour ago. Teague's sister, Erin, sent them hundreds of photos to look at from her wedding.

I put my purse down on the counter and join them. My roommate and her boyfriend are the most beautiful couple I know, so I imagine there isn't one bad photo. "How's it going?"

"Slow. There's so many good ones," Teague says modestly. See?

"I like this one best," Mateo says, pointing to a pic of the two of them on the beach at sunset.

Teague's already picked several posed and candid shots

with her family that she wants to keep, so now it's just a matter of a few with Mateo. Teague's mom is putting together an album for each of her children.

"Me, too," she says, grinning at him.

I glance at the decorative clock on the wall in the kitchen. Six o'clock. Levi should be here any minute.

The three of us talk and look at more pictures. At six-thirty, I start to worry, which is very unlike me. I'm not a worrier. But Levi is usually early, not late. I grab my phone. No texts or voicemails. It's rare for him not to respond to my messages.

I bet he lost his phone at the beach. Or dropped it in the ocean. Something silly like that. And there's probably a lot of after work traffic.

Teague says something to me, but I don't hear her. Suddenly, I've got a bad feeling in the middle of my chest. With every tick of the second hand on the wall clock, my concern grows. What if it isn't his phone?

I'm so startled when my cell rings that it almost slips through my fingers. *Thank God.* Only the name on the screen isn't Levi. It's Elliot.

"Hello?"

"Hey, Harper. I don't want you to panic, but Levi's been in an accident."

Elliot sounds calm, but it doesn't matter. I'm hit with a wave of fear. My dress feels too tight. I can't catch a breath. "What happened?" I manage to ask. I barely recognize my voice.

"He lost control of his kiteboard."

My eyes flash to Teague, and she must see the absolute terror in them because she's got her arms around me a split second later. Mateo is on my other side.

The phone shakes in my hand. I can't talk. Levi almost drowned. Elliot doesn't have to say it. That's what happened.

Teague takes the phone and puts it on speaker. "Hey, Elliot. It's Teague. I've got you on speakerphone. Mateo is here, too. What's happened?"

"Levi took a bad spill off his kiteboard. An ambulance brought him to the hospital, but he's going to be fine. Harper?"

"Yes?" I squeak out.

"I just saw him, and he asked me to call you right away. He said to tell you he's sorry he screwed up your date tonight, but that he'll make it up to you, no worries."

I cover my face with my hands. No worries? No worries! I feel like my skin is being ripped off my bones. If Levi is at the hospital, it means he was injured bad enough for someone to call 9-1-1.

"How hurt is he?" Mateo asks. I'm grateful for the question I'm too afraid to voice.

"He hit his head on the board and has a concussion. He actually can't remember what happened. The doctor said that's not uncommon, and he might or might not get the memory back."

Teague gently pulls my hands down. "He's okay," she says for my ears only.

"I've had a concussion," Mateo says. "It knocked some sense into me."

I know Mateo is trying to make light of the situation, but I cringe at his teasing. It could have knocked Levi dead.

"Oh hey, the hot nurse is walking back into his room, so I've got to go. We're waiting for his discharge instructions, and then I'll bring him home. Harper, can I tell him he'll see you there? He's going to need someone to watch him overnight, and he's already nominated you."

I nod before remembering Elliot can't see me. "Yes," I say.

"Excellent. See you guys soon." He hangs up before we have a chance to say good-bye.

Mateo gives my arm a squeeze. "Seriously, Harper. He's going to be fine." He stands up from the couch and looks at Teague. Some secret communication takes place between them. "I'm going to go and pick up dinner for all of us. I'll see you guys back at my house."

Teague kisses him good-bye then returns to my side. I'm numb everywhere. I want to vomit. I want to close my eyes and go back to this morning when Levi called to tell me to have a good day. And this time I want to tell him to blow off the beach and meet me earlier.

"You're freaking out," Teague says. Her voice is sweet, quiet, pacifying. "And that's okay because someone you care about is hurt. But he's fine. He didn't..."

Drown.

She almost said drown.

"Accidents happen, Harp. We don't want them to, but they do."

"I know. I'm okay." I'm not. "Let me change clothes, and then let's go. I want to have his bed all ready for him when he gets home." I'm unsteady when I stand, but to my relief, Teague doesn't notice. I don't *have* to hide my emotions from her, yet it's all I have in me to do.

In the privacy of my room, I collapse onto my bed and cry. I cry out of grief and fear and heartache. I'm sixteen all over again. It's not the same thing—Levi is okay. But it is the same thing. It's the same gut-wrenching feeling of losing the person I love more than anyone else in the world. It's the same sense of dread, of my body trembling so hard I can't get it to stop. Levi is leaving for Australia in a few weeks to be in the ocean day in and day out for two months.

I wrap my arms around myself. I'm shaking. I'm crying. I'm confused and scared and I want it all to stop.

Teague knocks on the door. "You ready?"

"Just a minute." I sit up and wipe the tears from my eyes.

After a quick change and face wash, we're in the car. I've collected myself, put up my shields, and while Teague keeps throwing me worried glances and asking if I need to talk, I slide back into the old me. I still know her best. And I'll need her strength to get through tonight.

We pull up to Levi's house at the same time as Mateo. He and Teague set out food on the kitchen table while I pick clothes up off Levi's bedroom floor, open his window for some fresh air, and make his bed, fluffing his pillows. I've found it's always nicer to climb into a made bed than an unmade one.

"Hey."

I spin around. Levi is leaning in the doorway. He's wearing board shorts, a T-shirt, and a crooked smile. His complexion is a little pale. His eyes are turned down at the corners a little more than usual. He's tired and not feeling well and still the most gorgeous human being I have ever seen. I rush to him, wrap my arms tightly around his middle, and goddammit, cry.

"It's okay. I'm okay," he says, stroking my back, burying his nose in my hair. "I'm sorry if I worried you." His voice is raspy, like it's been rubbed raw. I don't want to imagine why that is.

"Come on, let's get you in bed." I wipe away the stupid tears *again* and help him undress. "How are you?"

"My head aches, and I'm a little nauseous."

I pull the covers back. He slides between the sheets and looks up at me. "You have too many clothes on."

"You have a concussion."

"That means you can't get naked?"

"That's exactly what that means." And we need to talk. *I'm breaking things off with you, and it's going to be hard enough as is.*

His eyelids droop. "Okay."

"Are you hungry?"

He shakes his head.

"I'll be right back," I say to his sleepy face. I'm not hungry, either, but I find Elliot and ask him about the discharge instructions. He tells me I need to wake Levi every few hours, and if he vomits, we need to call the doctor.

I close the door when I get back to his room. He's asleep. I haven't pulled an all-nighter since college, but I'm sure tonight won't be a problem. I love the man lying in that bed, so I'll make sure he's okay. Then I'll say good-bye.

It's not like I have a choice. This feeling chewing a hole in my chest is only going to get worse the longer I think about what could have happened to Levi today. I climb onto the bed beside him and gently comb the hair off his face. I am so terrified of losing him that I'll cut my losses now.

His eyes blink open. "That feels nice."

I keep doing it. "Is there a bump I need to watch out for?"

"If you go lower there is."

"Levi."

"I love all the ways you say my name."

"I'm here to watch you tonight, that's it."

"And talk," he murmurs.

"*What?*" Did I say we needed to talk out loud and not realize it? My thoughts are definitely a tangled mess, so it's possible.

"You want to talk. I saw it in your eyes. I scared you today and…" He sinks deeper into the bed.

I stop rubbing his head. "And what?" He doesn't answer. "Levi?" I give him a little shake. "And what?"

His gaze is fleeting when he says, "And you want to run away from me."

My heart caves in.

"But don't," he whispers. "Don't do that." His eyes are closed, his breathing peaceful. He's almost asleep. "Stay."

Tears roll down my cheeks. He knows me so well. But

does that make these emotions inside me okay? Can I live with this fear just because he understands it?

No. I don't think so. I prop my head in my hand and watch him sleep. He deserves someone who isn't afraid, someone who will love him with wild surrender and her whole heart.

I keep a watchful eye on him throughout the night, waking him three times to give him sips of water and make sure he feels okay. When the sun rises, so do I. I kiss Levi's forehead and take the coward's way out. I'm not proud of it, but I can't imagine an actual conversation with him where I don't fall apart. I leave a note for him on his bedside table.

I'm sorry.

Two words that signify my heart is breaking for a second time.

Dear Harper,

The only thing I remember from my kiteboarding accident is you. I know that sounds insane, since you weren't there. But you were. Right before I was yanked underwater, I saw your beautiful face. Your soft, pillowy lips were puckered in a kiss, and your warm hazel eyes were sparkling with love. It wasn't a good-bye kiss. It was hello. And it's the reason I didn't drown.

No way in hell was I missing out on kissing you.

They tell me the first word I said when I woke up was hamburger. I'm pretty sure I meant Ham and they misunderstood. Who asks for ham after an accident? But a hamburger? Maybe.

When I found you in my room when I got home from the hospital, I told you I loved you. The back of my throat was raw, though, and the words scraped out in a whisper. Also, your back was to me. I wanted to say it again, but I was so tired, and you looked like I might break you, so I made a joke instead.

The rest is a little hazy.

Did I tell you I loved you while we were sleeping? Is that why you took off? Because I can take it back if it means being with you. We can do this your way. I know you're scared.

I am, too. But I'd rather be scared with you than without you.

Give us a chance, Ham. Be the bold, outspoken, caring person I know you are, and I promise I won't let you down.

Love,

Levi

Chapter Twenty-Five

LEVI

I throw my phone at the wall, only for it to be caught one-handed by Elliot when he enters the room. "Aw, still no text or call back?" he says in a tenderhearted tone that pisses me the fuck off. It's his new strategy to get me over Harper. He knows I hate the baby talk.

"No," I grumble from the couch.

He takes a seat across from me and tosses the phone. I let it land in my lap. Fucking piece of technology. What good is it if the girl I love won't communicate with me?

It's Saturday morning. She's ignored me for the past three weeks. I take that back. She sent me one text after I practically begged her to meet me: *I can't.*

I know why she can't. Because she's a chickenshit. A beautiful, gorgeous, smart, funny, amazing chickenshit. She thinks because I had an accident in the water she can't be with me. I get that she's afraid. I do. But is drowning in loneliness and fear any way to live a life?

"We're going out tonight," Elliot says.

"I don't want to."

"Too bad. We're meeting some people at Boardners." He picks up the remote for the TV and flips the channel from Animal Planet to a college football game.

"Some people?"

"Mateo, Teague, Madison…"

The way he says Madison's name raises my suspicion. "Madison? Why?" She's tight with Mateo, so we've known her for years, but she doesn't usually do the bar scene with us.

"She likes you."

I choke. "Sorry?"

"You heard me. I'm making it happen."

"Nothing is happening with Madison and me." She's nice. Pretty. But I'm not giving up on Harper.

Elliot rubs his chin. "I didn't want to tell you this, but I saw Harper with some other guy."

My stomach sinks. "What? Where?"

"Last weekend at Donahue's. They looked pretty cozy sitting in a booth."

Donahue's is the restaurant where Colleen's rehearsal dinner was held, and I think there's a family connection there. "What did he look like?"

"I don't know. Dark hair, business suit. I heard the bartender call him Landon when he grabbed a couple of beers to take back to the table."

I laugh, and my stomach resumes its normal position. "That's her brother, you ass."

"Really?" He pulls a face.

"Yeah. He's helping her with her foundation. He's an attorney." A foundation I sent a donation to with congratulatory flowers and from which I received a very nice thank-you letter in return. Yeah, it was a standard reply, but Harper signed it.

"It's still a good idea for you to see Madison."

I study my best friend. He's full of shit. Madison is friendly with Harper, and a nice person. She might like me, but there's a girl code I don't see her breaking, unless Harper threw me at her. I rub the back of my neck. Shit. Is Harper in on this, too? Is this her way of saying she's not good enough, but Madison is?

No. I refuse to believe it.

"Why?" I say. "Even if I were over Harper, Madison is a friend, nothing else. She's also friends with Harper, you know."

"Oh yeah. Shit. There went that idea. Well, there will be other girls there, too."

I scratch the side of my head. The mere thought of going to a bar to meet girls makes me uncomfortable.

"Look, you've been holed up in the house for weeks. You're leaving next week for Australia. Don't make me get sappy and tell you how much I'm going to miss your ugly face in order to get you to come out tonight."

He's got a point. We haven't hung out except for at home, and I've been shit for company 99 percent of that time. "Fine."

"Good."

He reaches for the PS4 controller. "Call of Duty?"

"Sure."

We play for a couple of hours, but it doesn't take a genius to guess where my mind is. Am I an idiot for sulking around, waiting for Harper to…to what? Continue to keep me guessing about our relationship?

I'm out of my goddamn mind if I keep pining away for her. I don't need drama like this. I had enough of it with Kayla. There are plenty of other girls out there, and Harper's silence makes it clear she's done with me, so it's time I move on.

Only I can't. I can't get her out of my head. Or my heart. If I can get over my past, she can get over hers. We need to talk like two mature adults and work this out together. If she needs outside help, we'll get it. *We.* I'm ready to be all-in.

I tell Elliot I've got an errand to run and drive straight to Harper's.

Confession. This is the third time I've driven to her house since I had my concussion. The first time she wasn't home. The second time, I swear she stood on the inside of her door and held her breath until I left. I pictured her palm on the other side of the wood, lined up perfectly with mine. I talked through the inches separating us, telling her I missed her. I asked her to please call me. She didn't.

I park my car, then let myself into the backyard through the side gate. The yard is quiet, but there's a wrinkled towel on one of the lounge chairs by the pool and an open magazine on the wood-slatted table beside it. I can't help myself. I detour to take a peek. It's Cosmo. We read it cover to cover together in Big Bear. Laughed. Kissed. Tried some crazy position. (No anal, in case you were wondering.) Made love. I'm smiling for the first time in a while when I knock on her door.

She doesn't answer. I knock again. This time when I get no response, I glance down at the doorknob. It's worth a try. I turn the handle. The door opens.

"Hello? Harper?" In deference to her silent treatment, I've only got one foot inside the door. The house is quiet. She isn't here.

My body deflates.

When I get back to my car, I shoot off a text. *Stopped by to see you. I'd really like to talk. If that doesn't sound good, how about I buy you a drink? I'll be at Boardners tonight. Meet me there. 9PM. I'll be the guy with eyes only for you.*

I tell myself not to get my hopes up.

On the drive home, it occurs to me that I caught sight of something in my periphery when I rounded the pool to leave. I didn't think anything of it, but the flash of red came from the direction of the large windows of the main house. Harper *had* been home. Well, in her aunt's home. Had she seen me?

Fuck. I squeeze the steering wheel so tight my knuckles turn white. That's it. This is her last chance. I've got my pride, too, and if she doesn't meet me tonight, then I'm done trying. I'm off to Australia in six days, anyway.

Chapter Twenty-Six

HARPER

"...I was broken for a long time, and thought I deserved to stay that way. I'm still not entirely whole. It's hard for me to get close to someone. But recently someone did knock down my walls, and he made me realize how lonely I was. He saw through my self-loathing and helped me remember who I've always been. And that's a person who is willing to share her deepest secret and shame in order to help others. I hope my story gives you the courage to share yours. Thank you."

Applause rings out from the group of high school students seated around me in the library. I never imagined being back at my alma mater to talk about Joe. But when I decided to open myself up, I knew this was the place to start. It's where I met Joe, where we spent a lot of our time together. And it's where I struggled to get through the days after he drowned. Being back here today, I feel like I've lifted a dark cloud from over my head.

"Thank you," a girl says as she passes me on her way out.

"Thank you for having the courage to share your story," another girl says.

"Thank you."

"Thanks."

"Thank you."

I'm hit with several more acknowledgments, not one of them said with pity.

"Miss McKinney?"

"Hi," I say to a girl standing before me and chewing her bottom lip.

"I just wanted to say hearing you talk made me feel better about some things. My boyfriend drowned last year."

My stomach lurches. I didn't think I'd hear something like that my first time speaking. "I'm so sorry…" I trail off, hoping she fills in her name.

"Kaitlyn."

"It's nice to meet you, Kaitlyn. Do you want to sit down and talk about it?" I gesture toward a table and chairs nearby.

"No, thank you. I just thought you'd like to know you're not alone."

The back of my throat burns with appreciation and admiration for this young person who is way more together than I was at her age. Maybe more than I am now. The thought is sobering.

"Right back at you," I say.

She nods and files out with the rest of the students.

"That was a wonderful speech. How are you holding up?" Mrs. Harris asks.

"I'm okay," I tell my high school counselor. Mrs. H. helped keep me on track after Joe died. She'd insisted I check in with her often and let me hang out in the counseling office when I needed a place to be alone.

"For the first few minutes, I thought I might throw up, but then my stomach settled down when I noticed no one was looking at me like I'd done something wrong. It was more like they could relate." In the back of my mind I also heard Levi's encouraging voice, whispering I had this. Even though we're not together, he's still with me every day, giving me strength.

"Your sincerity and friendly disposition make you very relatable, Harper. I see good things in your future."

"That's nice of you to say. Thanks."

"Have you spoken to Joe's parents?"

I hang my purse over my shoulder, ready to walk out. "I haven't. But I sent them a letter and told them all about JAMF. We've emailed since then, and I hope next year when we do our first big fundraiser that they attend. Joe's sister is here, though, and"—I pause for a moment to gather myself—"she's agreed to be on my board of advisors."

Mrs. H. opens the library door for me. We face each other outside under the awning. "That's great. I'm really proud of you," she says, and gives me a hug. "Can I get you to come back sometime?"

"For sure."

I'm so sure that on the drive home I stop and pick up cupcakes to celebrate this small victory with Teague. My first talk went well. Better than well. I didn't hyperventilate. I'm not freaking out over anything I said. My heart is beating a steady rhythm. I haven't perspired through my shirt. And best of all, I have no regrets.

"Hey Tea," I call out when I walk through the door.

Teague spins around on the couch. "Hi! How'd it go?"

"Fantastic. I brought us cupcakes to celebrate." I put the Sprinkles boxes on the kitchen counter. "It's the least I could do after the pep talk you gave me." Slipping off my shoes, I walk over to my best friend.

"Congratulations! But you shouldn't have. I knew you'd do great." She settles back into the couch with her head down over her phone.

"What the hell?" flies out of my mouth the second I see what she's looking at.

She spares a glance over her shoulder. "Problem?" she asks sweetly.

"What is that?" I say, pointing to the picture of Levi and Madison looking way too chummy. I loom. Loom over my roommate because all sorts of unfriendly emotions are suddenly rioting inside me.

"Levi and Maddy?" Her innocent tone is infuriating.

I round the couch and angrily sit down. "Yes, I can see that. What are they doing?"

"You didn't think he'd pine away for you forever, did you?"

"No, but…" I wanted to think he would. I sag against the cushion, the weight of what I've done sinking into my muscles.

Saturday night, everyone went out to have a good time with Levi before he leaves for Australia. Everyone except me. I was invited, of course, but I couldn't bring myself to go. I still miss him too much.

"Here's another good one." She turns the phone so I can see a picture of Madison and a girl I don't know with their arms around him. He's smiling.

I'm too upset to say anything. I want to claw those girls' eyes out—and Madison is a friend! My stomach churns. *Now* I think I may be sick.

"We missed having you there," Teague says. "I wish you would have come. Oh! Look at this one." She flips the phone again. This time it's Levi and Elliot with Madison in the middle. I look a little closer. Is that Elliot's hand on Madison's boob?

Teague watches for my reaction. Why is my best friend torturing me like this? She knows I'm still in love with Levi. She makes me talk about shit I don't want to talk about on a weekly basis.

"Oh, and there was this girl there visiting from Australia! She was super nice and super cute. I think I have a picture... here it is." Once again she flashes me a picture I don't want to see. "She said Levi's name with the best accent."

"Stop!"

Teague flinches in surprise and tucks her phone away. She's not ashamed, though, or mad that I yelled. No. She's smug.

"You wanted me to see those pictures on purpose."

"Of course I did! You're being a butthead."

I want to go to my room and curl into a ball on my bed. I know I am. I know I've screwed up the very best thing to ever happen to me. But I don't know how to fix it. I've ignored all of Levi's attempts to get in touch over the past month, thinking we were both better off.

"I know," I mutter.

"Then do something about it."

I want to. I want to so badly. The thought of never being with Levi again kills me. But I can't get my brain to coordinate with my body. It's like I need to step over hot coals to get to him. All I have to do is take that first step, and then I can run across the rest and fall into his arms. If only I could gather the courage to do it, and know he'd still be there to catch me.

"He misses you, Harp."

"It's too late."

"It's not."

"Even if it isn't, he's leaving. And leaving to be in the ocean day in and day out. I don't want to think about that."

You will anyway.

"I've got to get ready." I jump to my feet, done talking about it. "I'm meeting Chad in an hour."

"You're really going on a date with him?"

"No. I'm meeting him for drinks."

"That's your version of a date."

I pause before walking down the hall to change clothes. "It's my version of getting my mom off my back." She thinks meeting her best friend's son is a great way to get me out of my funk. And maybe she's right. Chad may be just the guy to get my mind off my troubles. I'm willing to give him a shot.

Because no matter what, I'm a better person than I used to be, and whatever funk I'm in isn't permanent. It comes down to *me* letting it go.

"Fine. But Harp?"

"Yeah?"

"Your heart is your friend, not your enemy. Listen to it."

I spin around before she can see how deeply I feel those words and wish it were that simple.

My room is a mess, clothes everywhere, the bed unmade. I've managed to keep my closet semi-clean, though, and pull out my favorite little black dress. I remind myself what a successful afternoon I had. Tonight, I'm going to celebrate it.

Chad is waiting for me at a high cocktail table when I walk into the upscale bar on Sunset. It's been at least a year since we've run into each other, and the months have been good to him.

"Hi," he says, standing to kiss my cheek and pull out my barstool "It's great to see you. Thanks for meeting me."

"I think we owed it to our scheming moms." I wiggle into a comfortable position and put my small purse down on the table.

"I'll be sending them both a thank-you tomorrow. You look beautiful."

"Thank you."

He lifts a finger to snag the attention of a waitress. It's Monday, so there aren't a lot of customers, and she quickly reaches us. I order a Madras. He orders a beer.

"I'm trying to remember when we last saw each other," he says.

"Someone's party, right?"

He snaps his fingers. "That's it. Down in Malibu."

I nod. "You were with a girl with really big…"

"Teeth," we say at the same time, then crack up. She also had really big boobs, and he knows I remember that, too. It was impossible not to notice them in her ill-fitting top.

"I hear you've started a foundation," he says.

"Yes." I go on to tell him about it. He listens attentively. Asks questions. Tells me he's impressed.

This is not the Chad I remember. He's changed from an arrogant ass to a charming flirt. We order a couple of appetizers. He fills me in on the tech firm he works for. They supply editing software for film companies.

My mind immediately goes to Levi.

"Dollar for your thoughts," Chad says. Shit. Could he tell I wasn't really listening?

"Not a penny?"

"Nah. I think your thoughts are worth a lot more."

Cheesy, but complimentary nonetheless. This guy deserves my full attention.

We talk about mutual friends, our families, and why Hollywood seems to be remaking the same movies over and over again. I liked *The Mummy*. He didn't. I also liked *Baywatch*. He looks like he wants to throw up in his mouth when I say that. Um, hello? Swimming is my jam, and there were shirtless hotties. Finally, around ten, we're ready to call it a night.

He puts his hand on the small of my back as he opens the bar's front door for me. The cool night air puts goose bumps on my legs.

"Thanks for a nice night." I pull my car key out of my purse.

"I had a great time catching up and getting to know you better," he says sincerely. He brushes the hair off my bare shoulder, his fingers gently grazing my skin. It's different than his palm on the back of my dress. Without thinking, I take an abrupt step back. Normally a gesture like that from a guy I spent a few pleasant hours with wouldn't bother me, but the thought of anyone touching me who isn't Levi sparks a devastating ache down to my core.

"Sorry, I didn't mean—"

"It's okay."

His friendly eyes study me. "I'd love to see you again."

My heart pounds. My ears ring. Car traffic blares around us. Light from streetlamps, storefronts, and flashing billboards swirls around my head.

"No rush," he adds when I don't immediately answer. "And no pressure. How about I get in touch this weekend?"

"Okay."

"Great." He smiles. It's a nice smile, but it's not— "Can I walk you to your car?"

I nod. He makes no further moves, just sees me safely off then walks away. I'm parking at home when a text sounds on my phone. It's my mom. *Well?*

Well.

Chad is great. He's smart, good-looking, funny, and no longer takes himself too seriously. He laughed when I told him I hated him in seventh grade for not liking bulldogs.

But.

I'm not attracted to him whatsoever. Not even the tiniest bit. I know what my mom will say. She'll say give it a chance. Sometimes it takes time for attraction to bloom. I'm pretty sure Chad's ready to pollinate me right now if his peeks at my legs and cleavage are any indication. Once upon a time, I would have let him.

I unlock the guesthouse. There's a note from Teague on the kitchen counter.

Sorry! I couldn't wait to share cupcakes. They were calling

*my name! I left you half of each one. I'm spending the night at
Mateo's. Text me if you need me. Love you! PS You're a good,
kind person Harper McKinney, and you deserve happy things
that start with an L. Don't forget that.*

Levi.

Love.

Love and Levi.

My best friend sure knows how to postscript.

A stupid tear rolls down my cheek. I may have been out
with Chad tonight, but there wasn't a second that my heart
wasn't with Levi.

When I was a little human, my happy place looked like swimming pools and puppies and mint chocolate chip ice cream and medals and my bed with all my stuffed animals. It was friends and family and getting to camp out in the family room to watch TV past my bedtime.

Now that I'm a big human, my happy place still includes swimming pools and puppies and MCC ice cream and friends and family and camping out on the couch to watch TV. But I realize now that all those things add *to my happiness.*

My happy place in on the inside. It's mind over matter. It's bravery over fear. It's trouncing would've, could've, should've, and never giving in to "didn't." It's in my heart. It's up to me.

I'm in charge, and right now my own personal brand of happiness
    tastes like Levi
    looks like Levi
    smells like Levi
    sounds like Levi
    feels like Levi

It took me long enough, but I'm done putting limitations on a happy life.

Chapter Twenty-Seven

HARPER

Thinking about doing something and actually doing it is like texting your mother you're not going out with her best friend's son again—much harder than it should be. Granted, when I finally did respond to my mom's message three days later, her reply was, *Okey dokey.* I think I caught her at the wine hour.

Or else she's being weirdly agreeable again.

That was yesterday.

I push thoughts of my mom out of my head and focus on driving to Levi's house without getting a ticket. I'm in kind of a hurry. According to Teague, he's taking the red-eye. Mateo is driving him to the airport—I glance at the clock on the dashboard—in a little over an hour.

Yes, I suck for waiting until the last minute. You don't have to tell me. My best friend already did. But the important thing is, I've finally arrived at this place. This place in my head where I tell fear to suck it and go after what I want. I pray I'm not too late.

My heart races the entire car ride. I've never been this nervous in my life. Not even the talk I gave at school had me this anxious. That tells me this is the most important thing I've ever done, and I can't screw it up. Levi has every reason to turn me away. I haven't said a word to him in weeks.

I've treated him terribly, but I'll do whatever I have to do to make it up to him.

Starting right now.

My legs shake like crazy as I walk up to his front door. The porch light is on and there's a glow from the windows. Emotions buzz through me. Fear is there, just under my skin. But more than that is excitement. Possibility. Hope.

Love.

All those songs about love being all you need can't be wrong.

His love will set you free.

I think that's a song, too. My song. I knock on Levi's door then slap my hand on the side of my thigh to stop my leg from bouncing.

When Levi appears around the wood frame, my insides light up like nothing else I've ever experienced. I haven't stared directly into his eyes in twenty-eight days and eleven hours, so I'm going to stay in them for a minute.

Thankfully, he seems content to stay in mine.

Until he isn't. "What are you doing here?"

My heart sinks. It's the first time he's ever greeted me without a hello. *He's treating you how you treated him.*

He's hurt, upset with me, and has every right to be.

"Hi," I say. Then I give a little tilt of my head.

His beautiful mouth gives me a small twitch back. My heart recovers a tiny bit. "Hi, Harper."

"Hi," I say again because I'm painfully out of my element here.

He waits for me to say something else. He's not going to

make this easy. He's not going to sweep me into his arms, kiss me until I'm breathless, and tell me he loves me without me having to work for it.

"Was that so hard?" I tease, tossing his words from months ago back at him.

"A little."

It kills me that he said that. "Can we talk?"

"Hey," a stunning girl says, coming up behind him. My heart crumbles into a million tiny pieces, turns to dust right there on his doorstep. He's moved on without me.

Levi turns, and the two of them hug.

I can't swallow. Can't move. Why can't I move? I don't want to see this!

The girl kisses him on the cheek. "I'll miss you."

"I'll miss you, too," he says.

She glances at me then gives Levi a look I can't decipher. Probably because I'm numb all over. He shrugs.

It's the shrug of death. I'm dying. And it's my own fault.

"Hi," she says to me.

"Hi," I manage to croak back.

She looks at Levi again, her pretty eyebrows raised. "It's okay," he tells her.

Oh my God. I'm the evil ex. I'm the girl who hurt him, and this beautiful bitch is the girl who gets to eat his cinnamon rolls. My legs are about to give out when Levi catches me. "Whoa. You all right?"

No, I am not fucking all right. I keep telling my feet to run away, but they won't listen.

"You sure you got this?" she says.

"I'm sure. Thanks, Had."

"Don't forget to Facetime." She steps off the porch.

"I won't."

"Love you!"

"Love you, too."

He loves her.

I try to wiggle away. I have to get the hell out of here before he sees how destroyed I am. How incredibly stupid of me to think this was a good idea.

"Harper."

Something about the soft way he says my name calms my boiling over nerves. I stop squirming. He releases my elbow. "I need to go."

"I thought you came here to talk."

"That was before."

"Before what?"

"Before I saw you have a new girlfriend!" I spin around to go. I will not be humiliated any further.

He chuckles. Fucking chuckles. Okay, maybe I'll stay for a minute to tell him what a dick move that is. And bloody hell. This means I won't be able to hang out with Teague and Mateo anymore. Not if he's with *Had*. I get right in his face.

"You are a total—"

"She's not my girlfriend."

"What?" I stumble back.

"She's my sister Hadley. She stopped by to say good-bye, since she missed dinner at my parents' house last night."

"Oh."

"Oh," he mimics.

For what feels like forever, but is probably only a few seconds, we stare at each other. His warm brown eyes are all it takes to mend my decaying heart. There is definitely something between us still. "Do you have a minute to talk, then?"

He lets out a deep breath, like he's not sure, but finally says, "Okay." He closes the door behind him and sits on the porch step. The moon shines through the leaves of the trees around us.

I take the spot next to him, close enough that our arms

touch. Every time we come in contact, I'm hit with a powerful sensation. This time, though, the current that swims through me is more than electric, it's *home*.

Please don't let me be too late.

"First off, I'm sorry."

"For what?" Yep, he's not going to make this easy.

"Would you accept it if I said 'everything'?"

"If I knew what 'everything' was, possibly."

"I'm sorry I've given you the cold shoulder this past month. It wasn't very nice of me."

"Agreed."

"I'm sorry I freaked out after your accident and shut you out instead of"—my voice wobbles—"talking to you about it."

He finds my hand and laces our fingers together but stays quiet. The small but mighty gesture helps me continue.

"I'm sorry I haven't been here for you, and that I waited until now to tell you how I feel."

"How do you feel?"

Whether or not he tells me what I want to hear, it's time to woman up. No regrets.

"I love you. I love you so much it terrifies me. So I pushed you away and acted horribly, thinking that would fix me, and I'd be able to live without you. But you know what? I don't need to be fixed. I need to be loved, and I want that love from only one person. I know I screwed up, and if you don't want to be with a girl who's got flaws that often get in her own way, then I understand. But if I'm not too late, I want to love you so hard. You're worth—"

He halts the rest of my sentence with his mouth. He takes me in his arms, lays me back, and kisses me. His tongue is warm and wet, his lips unyielding. I run my fingers through his hair. His thigh slides between my legs. He makes love to my mouth, and it's everything, so right that it's scary.

Scary good.

When he eventually lifts his head, I stare up at him, positive that this is where I'm supposed to be. "I love you," I say. I'm never going to stop saying it.

He looks deep into my eyes. "I love you, too."

In the history of my smiles, there has never been a bigger one than the grin splitting my face in two right now. "Does that mean you forgive me?"

"Not entirely."

"*What?*" I ask in a panic.

"I'm really pissed at you for wasting this last month that we could have been together. I'm leaving for the airport in an hour. Your timing, while perfect, also sucks."

"I'm really sorry."

"What took you so long?"

"Two things."

"Tell me."

I gaze up into his face, gripping his shoulders. If we're going to hold on to each other, I need to share my fears and concerns. "I'm worried about you being in the ocean for two months. I know you're a good swimmer, but I'm not sure I'll ever get over my fear of someone I love drowning."

He runs his fingers along my hairline. "That's understandable, and I promise I will take every precaution every minute of every day."

"I know you will. But I wasn't sure I could live with that fear. That I could carry it around with me and not let it interfere with my happiness."

"You're sure now?" he asks with apprehension.

I thread my fingers through his hair. "Yes. Mostly. I can't guarantee I won't have my moments, but I want you to go to Australia knowing I'll be waiting for you to come home."

"You have no idea how much I love hearing that."

"Which brings me to the second thing."

"Okay."

"I didn't know where you stood. I knew you enjoyed my body and hanging out. I figured you liked me, but I had no idea if you wanted my heart as part of the package."

He squeezes his eyes shut as if in pain.

"It became more than our deal to me, and I didn't want to be the one to break our agreement if you didn't feel the same way."

"Fuck," he mutters under his breath. When he opens his eyes, he rubs the pad of his thumb across my bottom lip. "I'm so sorry I put you through that."

"It's okay."

"It's not." He blinks a few times. "Honestly?"

I nod. "Always."

"I didn't at the start. I thought if I kept my emotions out of it then I wouldn't get hurt again. I was afraid to trust you, but Ham, that didn't last long. You made me feel things I've never felt before. I've loved you for a while but had trouble accepting it, and like you, I wasn't sure that's what you wanted to hear. More than anything, I wanted you to be happy."

"Should we make things crystal clear now?"

"Me first," he says. "I love you with all my heart, Harper Annabelle McKinney. Everything you say. Everything you do. Everything you are."

"I love you back, Levi— Oh my God, I can't believe I don't know your middle name."

He laughs. I push him in the chest.

"Anderson," he says.

LAP. I actually feel my eyes soften. "I love you with all my heart, Levi Anderson Pierce. Everything you say. Everything you do. Everything you are. You make me the happiest girl in the world."

He glances at his wristwatch. "We've got about thirty minutes to seal this new deal."

"What are you waiting for?"

He jumps to his feet, lifts me up, and tosses me over his shoulder.

"Hey! Put me down!"

"In a minute," he says, carrying me into the house. Elliot and Mateo are sitting on the couch, grinning, no doubt amused by this caveman display. "We're busy for the next half hour," Levi tells his roommates.

I laugh. Like they don't know why we're going to his bedroom. We've got a month to make up for, not to mention the two upcoming months. My boyfriend is so fucking cute.

Levi kicks the door closed behind us and lays me down on the bed. Papers rustle underneath me, so I reach back. "What's all this?"

"I forgot those were there," he says. "Lift up for me."

I raise my butt, and he pulls out several sheets of white paper. I catch a glimpse of one. It looks like a letter. "Are you writing to someone?"

"You."

"Me?"

He gathers up the papers and puts them on his desk. "I was about to write you one more when my sister showed up."

"How many have you written? Can I read them? Why didn't you send them to me?"

"Six. Yes, you can read them. And I was planning to mail them to you from the airport."

I bounce up onto my knees. "Are they love letters?" I ask excitedly.

"I guess, in a way." He eyes me like there's so much he wants to do to me, he doesn't know where to start. "Now, no more talking."

We can't get our clothes off quick enough.

Then he's on me. His mouth is everywhere. His hands, too. Minutes later after I've come on his fingers, he buries himself deep inside me. "Drive me to the airport?" he asks as he slowly slides in and out.

"Yes." I want every second I can get with him.

"We'll make a plan for while I'm gone."

"Yes." It's going to be torture being away from him.

"The time difference might be a challenge, but I promise I'll be thinking about you every day, all day. I'm going to miss you so damn much."

"Me, too." Oh God. His slow drag is a delicious ache I will never get enough of. My lids grow heavy with pleasure.

"Harper?"

I open my eyes.

"I love you."

"I love you more," I say, keeping our eyes locked until we both find release.

Chapter Twenty-Eight

2 MONTHS LATER...

"Thanks, bro," I say to Mateo as he lets me inside Harper's place. I texted him yesterday to tell him I was coming home early so he could be here this morning to help me surprise my girl.

We hug, slapping each other on the back. "Glad to have you home. We'll catch up later."

"Yeah."

He ambles back down the hall toward Teague's room like he's half asleep. It's a little early for a Sunday. I owe him one.

I roll my luggage out of the way before grabbing a glass of water. I'm incredibly stoked to be home. The shoot in Australia went phenomenally well, but damn, I missed Harper. I missed the feel of her soft body against mine and the way she shivers when I kiss behind her ear. I missed the sweet smell of her hair and the coconut-raspberry scent of her skin. I missed her taste, sometimes minty, sometimes tangy, always mouthwatering good.

The distance sucked.

But hearing her happy, enthusiastic voice on phone calls, and doing some sexy skyping, kept us connected on days when I really needed a fix. I loved receiving her selfies, too. Her lush lips smiling, or pouty, or blowing me a kiss. Each one stopped my heart in the best possible way, and I've fallen even more in love with her while gone.

I was busy as hell every day of the trip, all of them good. And each day I'd text, call, or write to Harper. I didn't want her to worry about me, not for one second. I shared everything with her, sent pictures, and when Leo Gaines showed up to have Thanksgiving dinner with the entire crew, I think she was more excited for me than I was. (I've got Leo's number saved in my phone. He told me to get in touch.)

Ham filled me in on all the details of her busy schedule, too. I'm so proud of her and everything she's accomplished with her foundation in such a short time.

I put the water glass down on the counter. I'm finally home, and knowing Harper is under the same roof sends an electric current sizzling through me. It's time to wake her, then spend the rest of the day in bed loving her.

• • •

HARPER

Heart-whipped. Cock-whipped. Mind-whipped. I'm all of those things, and I don't care. I had no idea I'd fall even more in love with Levi while he was gone. Absence has made my heart grow infinitely fonder. I reread his text and bicycle-kick my sheets. His sweet, sexy words never fail to put butterflies in my stomach. I'm like a schoolgirl with her first crush. Waking up every morning to a message from him is the best, and the only thing better will be having him home in two days.

We've talked, X-rated skyped, and texted over the past two months, learning more about each other, laughing, teasing, and sharing things no one else knows. He's mailed me several more handwritten letters to add to my collection, too, filled with more love than I ever imagined, and gorgeous pictures from the sunshine coast with captions about wishing I were there with him. I'm so proud of him. He's working really hard, and physically exhausted, but the joy in his voice when we talk is tangible.

I've kept busy, too, learning how to operate a non-profit. It's energizing and fulfilling and sometimes stressful, being that I'm in charge, but I wouldn't change it for the world. I'm learning to trust my instincts and not linger on my mistakes.

I put my phone down beside me on the bed, noticing the time. It's a little after eight a.m. on New Year's Eve. Teague and Mateo are in her room and will probably be asleep for a while longer, so I think I'll surprise them with pancakes. They've been awesome, keeping me company when they're in town, never allowing me to feel like a third wheel.

As I push up, there's some rustling out in the hallway.

My door opens.

And standing there dressed in jeans and a T-shirt, his hair a fourteen-hour plane ride mess, is Levi. "Omigod! You're home early." I scramble out of bed and run to him.

He catches me with an *oomph*. "Hi, beautiful."

My legs go around his waist, my arms around his shoulders. I bury my face in his neck, breathe him in, and tell myself not to cry. "Hi."

He walks into my room, kicking the door shut behind him. "You feel incredible," he says.

I lift my head. Time stands still as we soak each other in, looking our fill until I lower my feet to the floor. He's here!

"God, I missed you." He cups my face and looks at me

with such reverence my knees go weak.

I touch his face in return, the pads of my fingers getting reacquainted with his sexy stubble. "I missed you more."

He smiles. "Doubtful." He rubs his thumb over my bottom lip. This is it. Once he kisses me, we won't stop. "Have plans today?"

"I do now."

"Tomorrow?"

"Same as today."

"Happy New Year, Ham." He lowers his mouth to mine.

I have a feeling it's going to be my best year yet.

Acknowledgments

I'm so grateful to the following people:

My editor, Stacy Abrams, for being awesome and always making my stories better. (I think I say this every time, but it's true every time!)

The team at Entangled—Candy, Holly, Riki, Curtis, Heather R., Rosemary, Melanie, Liz, and Katie, for everything you do behind the scenes.

My best friends for the past thirty years, Karen and Robin, for listening to me talk on and on about writing and for reading my books. Love you both!

Samanthe, Charlene, Hayson, Roxanne, Paula, Marilyn, Maggie, and Jax, for being amazing writers, teachers, supporters, and romance rockstars. I learn from you, admire you, and am blessed to know you.

My Facebook friends (most notably Robin Reul) who helped me name the bulldog in this story, "Hank."

The bloggers who help spread the word about my books. I know your time is valuable and I so appreciate you sharing some of it with me.

My readers! For your amazing support and enthusiasm. I'm beyond thankful that you spend time with my characters. MWAH!

My mom, for being the best ever.

And finally to my hubby and sons, for your love, patience, understanding, and humor—you guys make me laugh at the perfect times! xoxoxo

About the Author

When not attached to her laptop, *USA Today* Bestselling Author Robin Bielman can almost always be found with her nose in a book. A California girl, the beach is her favorite place for fun and inspiration. Her fondness for swoon-worthy heroes who flirt and stumble upon the girl they can't live without jumpstarts most of her story ideas.

She loves to frequent coffee shops, take hikes with her hubby, and play sock tug of war with her cute, but sometimes naughty, dog Harry. She dreams of traveling to faraway places and loves to connect with readers. To keep in touch sign up for her newsletter on her website at http://robinbielman.com.

NOVA

a *Renegades* novel by Rebecca Yarros

He's Landon Rhodes, four-time X Games medalist and full-time heartbreaker. This tatted-up adrenaline junkie has earned his nickname Casanova, going through girls in an attempt to forget the one who got away. But now she's back and determined not to let him destroy her again. The problem is, he will stop at nothing to prove to her that they are meant to be together.

THE RULE MAKER

a *Rule Breakers* novel by Jennifer Blackwood

Ten Steps to Surviving a New Job:

1. Don't sleep with the client. It'll get you fired. (Sounds easy enough.) 2. Don't blink when new client turns out to be former one-night stand. 3. Don't call same client a jerk for never texting you back. 6. Ignore accelerated heartbeat every time sexy client walks into room. 8. Don't let client's charm wear you down. Be strong. 9. Whatever you do, don't fall for the client. You'll lose more than your job—maybe even your heart.

7996